MIDWINTER BREAK

By the same author

MIDWINTER BREAK

Bernard MacLaverty

JONATHAN CAPE
LONDON

5 7 9 10 8 6

Jonathan Cape, an imprint of Vintage,
20 Vauxhall Bridge Road,
London SW1V 2SA

Jonathan Cape is part of the Penguin Random House group of companies whose
addresses can be found at global.penguinrandomhouse.com

 Penguin
Random House
UK

First published by Jonathan Cape in 2017

penguin.co.uk/vintage

A CIP catalogue record for this book is available from the British Library

ISBN 9781911214212 (Hardback edition)
ISBN 9781787330214 (Trade paperback edition)

Typeset in India by Thomson Digital Pvt Ltd, Noida, Delhi

Printed and bound in Great Britain by Clays Ltd, St Ives plc

Penguin Random House is committed to a sustainable future for
our business, our readers and our planet. This book is made from
Forest Stewardship Council® certified paper.

for all the grandchildren

MIDWINTER BREAK

In the bathroom Stella was getting ready for bed. Gerry had left the shaving mirror at the magnifying face and she was examining her eyebrows. She licked the tip of her index finger and smoothed both of them. Then turned to her eyelids. She was sick of it all – the circles of cotton wool, the boiled and sterilised water in the saucer, the ointments, the waste bin full of cotton buds.

She said goodnight to Gerry and, on her way to the bedroom, passed their luggage in the hall. She switched on the late night news on the small radio beside her bed and got into her pyjamas. Quickly, because the bedroom air was cold. She saw no point in paying good money to heat a room all day for a minute's comfort last thing at night.

Before getting into bed she turned off the electric blanket. Now and again she'd fallen asleep with it still on. By the time Gerry came to bed she felt and looked awful. 'Like fried bacon,' was the way he described her.

She loved this hour to herself – this separation at the end of every day. Her hot-water bottle, the electric blanket, the radio voices. Gerry, out of action, in another room listening to music on his headphones. Having a nightcap, no doubt. Or two or three. The storm doors locked, the windows bolted. The place safe. Sometimes after the news she read for a while in the silence. The sound of a page turning. The absence of talk. But of late she'd been too tired to read, even to hold a book. Hardbacks were out of the question. There was a tipping point when she knew she was going to 'get over'. Her head would go down on the pillow, her hand creep out from under the covers to get rid of the book or to switch off the radio. The duties and the menus and the lists melted away. Responsibilities were such that nothing could be done at this hour. They were hidden behind a curtain but would return with a swish first thing in the morning. And before she knew, she was sound asleep.

Her insomnia, if it came, happened in the middle of the night. Anywhere between three and six she could be seen curled on the sofa sipping hot milk, nibbling a biscuit. And her wakefulness could continue for hours. In bed or pacing the floor. At such times her worries and angst were on full display. Magnified, like the mirror. A worry in the wee small hours was a different beast entirely to a daylight worry. And that would keep her awake. Maybe she would get over again in an hour or two but there was no guarantee.

There was a blast of music. Her eyes opened. What in the name of God . . .? She closed them again, compressed them. Burrowed her right ear into the pillow. Pulled up the duvet to cover her other ear. But still the music pounded. What in the name of God was he up to?

Gerry sat staring ahead. The television was off and the place silent. There was a cone of light above his head which left the rest of the room in darkness. He considered the sofa a defensible space. It had a concavity which fitted him exactly. Everything he needed was to hand – favourite books – music and film guides, CDs. His architecture books were shelved in the study. In the bathroom Stella had just gone through her pre-bed routine. He heard the snap of the bolt as she came out.

'Goodnight,' she said. She came to the end of the sofa smelling of toothpaste and finger-waved a little before going. 'Don't forget we have an early start.'

He waited until he heard the bedroom door close then went to the drinks cupboard. In the kitchen he filled the Kilkenny jug. Back at the cupboard he poured himself a whiskey in his favourite tumbler and topped it to the brim with water. He liked the heaviness of the Waterford crystal, the heft of it – it made the drink feel more substantial, more potent. He went back to the sofa and set the drink on the bookshelf. It glowed yellow in the light. The shelf was lower than the arm of the sofa so that if his wife came in again she would not see it. Not that he was trying to hide it from her – he would say to anyone and everyone, 'At night when Stella goes to bed I have a substantial dram and listen to music.' But with the glass out of sight she could not see the volume. For her, a small glass of wine with a meal was 'a sufficiency'. And good for the heart.

The central heating was set to switch off at Stella's bedtime. The radiators ticked as they cooled. The place creaked and the wind moved outside. He smelled the flowers on the table. Stella had bought stargazer lilies and now that it was night they were sending out their fragrance. He sipped his drink. It was unlike her to have flowers that would waste their sweetness on the desert air when they were away.

He chose a CD. His headphones were marked L and R but the letters had all but worn away. He slid them on. Although the music came loud and utterly clear he turned up the volume. He drank again, lowering the level, savouring. The whiskey was gold and the facets of the cut glass, silver. It would make him sleep give him a good night's rest and he'd be ready for

3

action in the morning. There was nothing worse than setting off on holiday feeling lousy. Of course he would need another couple of these to get him over.

Headphones cut him off from the real world and, sometimes, even here on the sofa he felt vulnerable. Anybody could slip into the room behind him – even though the front door was locked and all the windows bolted. Was it another leftover from Belfast? *Loyalist murder gang kill retired Catholic architect in Scotland.* He could be garrotted from behind. So much for defensible space. He turned up the volume even higher. It was a wonderful noise – with the horns going full blast and the kettledrums thudding. He congratulated the composer and the musicians with frequent sips from his drink. Then there was a violent flashing. For a moment he thought it might have been lightning – or an explosion.

'Gerry.'

He looked up. Stella was in the doorway in her dressing gown, her hand on the light switch.

'Sorry,' Gerry shouted above the din of the music. 'My fault.' He jumped to his feet and snatched the headphones off. It had happened before but even *he* looked startled at the volume in the room.

'Holy fuck.' He bent over and switched off the main loudspeakers.

'I don't know which is worse – that expression or the racket,' said Stella. 'If you want to end up living on your own you're going the right way about it.'

'Sorry, I didn't realise.' The room went silent except for the tinny sounds coming from the headphones around his neck. 'I didn't know . . .'

'You'll damage your hearing. Next door'll be in to complain. It's half twelve,' Stella said. 'And we've an early start.'

4

'Everything packed?'

'What are you talking about? I was trying to sleep.'

'How long were you standing there?'

'A minute or so.'

'Why didn't you say?'

'You wouldn't have heard,' she said. 'Didn't want to give you a fright, maybe a heart attack. Then I'd have nobody to go on holiday with.'

'I'll not be long,' he said.

She went back to bed. He poured himself another whiskey.

'Just a smidgen.'

But he poured another smidgen on top of it. Two smidgens make a bigger smidgen. The world seemed to recognise only drunk or sober. What about the in-between – the spectrum, the subtle gradations? The first drink brings a little distancing – a concentration on another world – an ironing around shirt buttons, a smoothing of wrinkles. Stella would laugh at him. 'You never ironed a thing in your life – you'd only burn yourself. To say nothing of the shirt.' But he had ironed enough to know. The sharp prow nosing around, the material flattening in the heat. More drink and he began to soar. To spread his wings, rising on the thermals of the first couple of glasses. Later he unleashed what was tied down. Freed what was trapped. He began to listen sharper. To see more. To love better. Tomorrow – they were off again. A midwinter break. How privileged! Despite having retired years ago, his life was punctuated with visits to places around the world which *seemed* like holidays. A talk here – a paper there. Architectural jurist, receiver of honours, a taker-up of freebies. And most of the time he insisted on having Stella with him.

*　　*　　*

He wakened. Almost pitch-black, but not quite. His mouth was dry and his nose cold. His eyes adjusted. There was a faint outline of the pulled curtains – outside a little less darkness. It would be somewhere between five and seven. Every time he woke it was the same stupid debate – would he or would he not get up for the bathroom? He knew he wouldn't get back to sleep if he didn't. He eased the bedclothes to one side, sat up and took a mouthful of water. The bedroom was like a fridge. The sound of Stella's steady breathing. He inserted his feet into his slippers and stood. Sudden chandeliers in the darkness. Only for a second. Jesus – he thought they'd gone away. Spiders of light, sparks, flashes. A prelude to a stroke. He backed out of his slippers and lay down again beneath the duvet. They could be something else. The result of too much drinking? How much was too much? He knew he was doing himself harm. After Hogmanay he'd made a resolution to give up. But not yet, O Lord, not yet. He'd told his optician about the sparklers the last time she'd tested him for replacement glasses. Left them at his backside somewhere and even though he'd stuck a label with his name and address inside the case, nobody'd had the generosity to send them back. What use would they be? All glasses were bespoke. If somebody else wears *his* glasses they won't see a bloody thing.

'Better or worse?' the optician asked.

'Better.' Another lens inserted.

'Better or worse?'

'Worse.'

No matter what, it would be another hundred and twenty quid.

'If you could rest your chin here . . .'

'On the chin rest?'

'Yes.'

The stare into this woman's eyes, the fear that she would smell his old man's breath, being only inches away. Glimpsing his own retinal veins like blood-red winter trees. Déjà vu the confessional – the lowered light level, the proximity of the listening face. How long has it been since your last eye appointment, my child? Alone or with others? Better or worse?

The optician dismissed his worries about the chandeliers – everybody gets them at your age, she said. It's when you stand too quickly.

He still needed the bathroom. Rising from the bed, slowly this time – no fireworks to speak of – shuffling forward, finding the door. He knows how to walk his home in the pitch-dark. Turning the handle in such a way it would not click and waken Stella. He walked along the hallway avoiding the packed and ready cases. The air in the bathroom was so cold it stung. The heating was normally set to come on at eight. But her ladyship would have turned it off because they were going away. No sense in heating the place just to leave it pleasant for the burglars. Breakfast in your overcoat with the fog rolling off your tea. As he drained into the bowl he closed his eyes and continued as far as possible to remain asleep. Maybe his doctor would have a different story to tell. 'Yes, light spiders are inevitably precursors of a stroke. Hypochondriacs die too, y'know.'

He pressed the flush and headed back along the hallway. A faint glow came from behind the study door. The place was dark except for the winking coloured lights of the router and the various add-ons and extensions. Like a fairground. Their mobiles charging side by side. Stella must have been up earlier when he was in his first sleep. He sat in front of the screen. She had been online checking something and had not closed down properly. Very bad, she was, at covering her tracks. There was an unpronounceable name on the screen superimposed on a lawn surrounded by trees and houses in sunlight. In the middle of the lawn was a religious statue. Looked a bit like the Sacred Heart. Beneath it the words, '*It can be difficult sometimes to find the gate but when you do, walk through and you will find yourself in another world.*'

Because they were going away he shut down the computer. Then all was cold and dark. He shivered and rose from the chair.

In the bedroom the breathing was long and slow. He walked around to his own side. In his absence she had moved to the middle. The warm cave, with the person lying soft at its centre. His pillows seemed to fall naturally into the gap between his cheek and shoulder. The cave was redolent with cotton smell. He aligned himself to her. Her heel to his instep, knee to back of knee, bum to lap. They were as soft, stacked chairs. Momentarily the steady breathing stopped. She was aware of his arrival and softly ground herself backwards against him. In response he put his arm over her. Her pyjama jacket had ridden up and his now cool fingers accidentally touched the scar on her stomach. Hollow like another navel, a skin pucker. With another one behind her to match. Marked fore and aft, she was.

'Move over,' she said.

Both of them paced the flat in their coats looking out for a taxi. It was a large Victorian tenement with stuccoed ceiling roses and egg-and-dart cornices. When they first moved in Gerry had said the ceilings were high enough to keep giraffes. It had been built on a corner so that it overlooked two streets. There was a small narrow garden with bushes and green ground-cover around the perimeter. Stella had brought back plants from her walks in the woods – she thought nothing of carrying a soup spoon and a plastic bag with her. A bunch of her snowdrops had just come out. Later there would be imported bluebells and daffodils.

Gerry was in the bedroom inspecting the glass telltale affixed to a crack in the wall. It was claimed the building was subsiding because of old mining works. There were normal settlement cracks where inner walls had moved relative to outer ones over a century. At such junctions the wallpaper had been pulled into sags and wrinkles. 'A bit like ourselves,' Stella had said. 'It's not only dogs that get to look like their masters.' Occasionally in the night there was a trickle of mortar, between the wall and the window boards. Chimney debris and soot sometimes appeared on the tiled hearths in the mornings.

'Well?' Stella came into the bedroom. 'Any sign?'

'No movement. Look for yourself.' He pointed to the telltale.

'I meant – of the taxi. I wouldn't know from that thing if there'd been an earthquake or not,' said Stella.

'Do you have the passports or do I?'

'Everything's in your shoulder bag,' she said. 'Where you put it.'

The taxi was now six minutes late.

'If I was going to some boring architects' meeting it'd be five minutes early.'

'Calm yourself, Gerry.'

He pulled everything out of the shoulder bag and set it on the bed while she looked on. His mobile, passports, tickets, both his and hers, cheque cards, medication. She checked in her leather handbag for *her* washbag, purse, eye drops, artificial

9

tears, a half-packet of Werther's Original, the wallet of family photographs, her Filofax, her mobile.

'Jesus – the Filofax?' Gerry rolled his eyes.

'For phone numbers,' she said.

'Who do we know in the Netherlands?' She ignored him and went on stirring the depths of her handbag.

'We know people *here* but not their phone numbers. Emergencies happen. Did you remember your shampoo?'

'And conditioner. All measured. Twenty-five ml of each. Dandruff-free terrorism.'

'What's the limit?'

'You can take a hundred.'

He was wearing a red angora wool scarf knotted at his throat. He looked at himself in the full-length mirror.

'Somebody said I was flamboyant wearing this.'

'Who?'

'I don't like flamboyant.'

He went to the cloakroom and found a navy scarf. Back in the bedroom he looked at himself.

'Midway between flamboyant and dreary,' he said.

Stella held him at arm's length.

'You could try another knot. An Oxford, maybe.'

'Do knots have names?'

'The splice. The hitch?'

'That's the language of the building site.' She undid the knot and began to tie another, more elaborate one.

'I can't do it on you – only on myself.' She turned him around to face the mirror, stood behind him on tiptoe.

'Down a bit,' she said and pressed on his shoulders. He bent at the knees and remained that way until the knot was tied.

'You know all there is to know about the language of the building site, Gerry.'

'It's my fucking profession.' He began to fiddle with the scarf, pulled the longest leg and the knot fell apart. He tied it as he always did.

'Suit yourself,' she said and walked away.

'I'm going to phone that taxi.' He went into the study and picked up the receiver.

He heard the sound of hoovering. He looked out into the hallway. Stella was pushing the upright vacuum cleaner to and fro across the carpet. She saw his head poke out.

'It's on its way, sir,' Stella shouted.

The voice on the phone said, 'It's on its way, sir.'

'Thank you.' Gerry put the phone back on its cradle. 'What are you doing?'

'There was just a black bit of I-don't-know-what there.' She nodded to the carpet. 'They say that every time.'

'What?'

'It's on its way, sir.'

'So you want to have it nice for anybody breaking in?'

Stella switched off the whine and wound up the lead. She went into the front room and came out with a black plastic bag in one hand, a bunch of stargazer lilies in the other. She thrust them into the bag and tied the neck.

'Put them out,' she said. Gerry did as he was told. He went once again to look out the window.

The taxi dropped them miles from the main terminal. When they asked the driver why there, he said, 'Regulations. Since the airport was car-bombed.'

He lifted their large suitcase out of the boot and set it in front of Gerry. Stella retrieved her own and they extended handles simultaneously. Both set off, their cases growling behind them. The strap of Gerry's shoulder bag cut into him like cheese

11

wire. They approached the main terminal, protected behind stainless-steel bollards.

'This must have cost millions,' Gerry shouted above the noise of their cases. 'What's to stop a motorbike bomber going *between* the bollards?'

By the main entrance three or four people were smoking behind a plastic hedge. Excluded, like lepers. Inside the doors Stella checked the monitors and they joined the correct queue. Each time the line progressed they shoved their luggage forward with their feet.

'It'll not go without us,' Stella told him.

'Don't you bet on it. Everybody here's got more luggage than sense.'

They eventually got through security – after the security guy had thrown away Gerry's shampoo and conditioner. Liquid in open vessels was not allowed, he said. They had coffee to calm themselves.

'Was any comment made about your digging spoon?'

'I don't carry it all the time. Only on walks.'

She minded their stuff and Gerry went for a wander in duty-free. Nothing but perfume. And adverts for perfume. The place reeked of the stuff. Slim sales girls dressed in black offered to spray samples onto upturned wrists. Gerry refused.

He came to the spirits section. Stella had warned him not to buy anything. A bottle of his favourite Irish whiskey would be cheaper in Amsterdam, she said. The Traveller's Friend, he called it. Because it helped a man get over to sleep. But there were too many imponderables about buying drink in Amsterdam. Did they sell it in supermarkets? Was there an off-licence system? Maybe it was like Norway or Canada and you had to go to a Government Liquor Store which, if he remembered correctly, stayed open only during office hours. Best to get it here and now when it was available. He tried to buy a bottle of Jameson but the girl asked him for his boarding card. He reneged on the deal and stomped off back to where Stella was sitting.

'What is it?' she said.

'They want my boarding card.'

'Who does?'

'I don't know what her name is. Deirdre from Airdrie.'

'Get me some Werther's – if you can remember.'

He got his boarding card and took his passport, just in case. The girl slid the bottle into a white foam lattice before putting it into a plastic bag.

'Why did you need to see my boarding pass?'

The girl smiled. She rang up the purchase and handed the bag over.

'Regulations.'

Standing with other men at the urinals unnerved him – he preferred a cubicle. He set down his bottle of whiskey to wash his hands. Even in its plastic bag it chinked on the marble surface. The dryer was of a new design and was amazingly powerful – a roaring, supersonic noise which startled him. The skin on the back of his hands rippled.

A man came in with his wee boy. Gerry watched them in the mirror. The father approached the urinals and the child was going to follow him.

'Stay there,' said the father. The child did as he was told. But a moment later he moved under the hand dryers and immediately set one off. With a howl it blew hot air down onto his head. His hair threshed and flickered and the wee fella screamed with fright. He didn't know where to run. Gerry stepped forward.

'He's okay, okay,' shouted the father above the noise. But the child's tears and panic were obvious as he screeched his head off. Gerry squatted to be at the same height, put an arm around the child, patting his back, while his father finished. But the boy twisted away towards his dad. The father smiled and picked him up – touching the top of his head to feel if it was hot. 'You're okay. You got a fright. It was just a big noise.' Gerry made a sympathetic face.

'Och, the poor wee man,' he said. Then to the father, 'I've a wee one that age myself. A grandson. You couldn't protect them enough.'

'He's all right, aren't you, son,' said the father, leaning back from him. The child stopped crying but was distressed and shy at being the centre of attention in a toilet full of grown men. He nuzzled into his father's neck as they backed out the door.

In WH Smith's Gerry bought a packet of Werther's Original. He'd kid her on that he forgot. Then surprise her just before take-off.

In the huge hallway Gerry joined his hands behind his back as he walked. He stared up into the ceiling of the new extension.

'Hi,' he said and sat down beside Stella.

'What did you get?'

'The Traveller's Friend.' She rolled her eyes a little.

'What about the Werther's?'

'I forgot.'

'You'd be a great one to send for sorrow.'

'Have you what'll do you?'

'The remains of a packet.'

14

Gerry stretched out and put his hands behind his head. He told her about the toddler and the hand drier.

'Designers and architects should take responsibility for stuff like that,' he said. 'It's just bad design and shouldn't happen.'

'The poor wee thing,' she said over and over again.

'I held onto him till his father had finished at the porcelain.'

'Too much information,' said Stella. 'It's your turn to hold the fort.'

'So I've time to waste,' said Gerry. 'Where's the paper?'

She pointed, got to her feet and wandered off. He followed her with his eye. She went into the duty-free area. It was a huge concourse and she looked tiny at the far side of it. Architecture was about the size of things compared to the human. He opened the paper and began to read.

She came back sooner than expected.

'It says *Boarding*.' They walked the carpeted corridors for ten or fifteen minutes. Stella said, 'If you'd told our parents carpet would be laid in miles, they wouldn't have believed you.'

The plane sat roaring on the runway, waiting its turn. Stella particularly disliked both take-off and landing – that race to build up speed, the parting from the ground and then, at the end of the flight, the thump of the tonnage of aeroplane coming into contact with the earth. The way the wings shook and opened up like they were broken, followed by the roaring of the reverse thrust. Now she closed her eyes and gripped the armrest. Gerry put his hand on hers. He tapped a little rhythm on the back of her hand to comfort her.

'What's this?' said Gerry.

'Wristbands.'

'Where did you get them?'

'In duty-free.'

'What are they supposed to do?'

'Keep me from being sick.'

'How?'

'Pressure points.' She showed him a white bead which touched her wrist on the inside. 'It presses here – near your pulse point – it stops nausea. They've worked for me in the past. On ferries. Remember?'

'Look, I've been flying for years and not once have I seen anybody throwing up. There was a child one time – probably had a feed of bad oysters and dodgy stout before he got on. You'd be far better off saying the rosary. For a special intention.'

'Which is?'

'God, don't let me vomit on this flight.'

Stella smiled and said, 'We used to say the rosary in the car going to dances.'

'You did not.'

'The driver was a lot older than us but he was kind. Did it for petrol money. He gave out the rosary as he was driving.'

'Poor horny guys going along, paying their money, hoping like mad for a bit and you're saying the rosary on the way there?'

'Ireland in the fifties.'

'Was nobody ever carsick?'

'Not a one.'

'So you'd be far better off saying the rosary than throwing your money away on bloody armbands . . .'

'Wristbands. Armbands keep you from drowning.'

Gerry produced the packet of Werther's.

'Like a sweet for take-off, *modom*?'

'You said you'd forgotten them.' She pulled out another tube of Werther's. 'So I bought my own.'

16

'You're so organised.' Gerry put the sweets back in his pocket.

The plane's engine note rose and it javelined down the runway, pressing them into their seats. Then the rumbling under-carriage noise stopped.

'We're off.'

Stella smiled and opened her eyes.

'Have you brought a book?'

'I'm on my holidays.'

She snuggled back in her seat.

'I'm really looking forward to this,' she said. 'There's some things I want to do.'

'Like what?'

'My own concerns.'

Gerry hooted as if there was something mysterious in what she'd said.

'Me likewise.'

'So we don't necessarily have to do them together.' She smiled an exaggerated smile.

'Why didn't we go somewhere warm?' he said. 'Like to a nearby hemisphere?'

'Too much hassle.'

The plane rose and began to judder as it entered cloud. Again he put his hand on her hand.

'How come you were in Amsterdam and I wasn't?'

'A conference. With teachers.'

'*When* was this?'

She shrugged.

'I think it was the eighties? Anyway I thought it would be good. To remind myself.'

'It's a very elaborate piece of storyboarding.'

17

'How do you mean?'

'Planning ahead. Mapping it all out. The way you want things to happen.'

'Storyboarding?'

'It's a movie term. They draw a comic first – then film it. It's a way of setting out exactly what you want to happen.'

'I like that word,' said Stella.

It wasn't a long flight. Stella did two crosswords. Both cryptic. One in the morning paper, the other – kept flat in her Filofax – clipped from Sunday's paper. She had a theory about crosswords: that they would keep her mentally active in her very old age. Press-ups for the brain, she called them.

The plane turned on its side and below they could see Amsterdam.

'It was summer last time,' said Stella. 'We flew over tulip fields. From the air they looked like freshly opened plasticine. Rows and ridges. All primary colours.'

'Looks very grey now.'

'If it's raining I wouldn't mind a snooze when we get as far as the hotel.'

'In the middle of the afternoon?'

'Last night I discovered what bad sleep is.'

'What?'

'Lying awake. You and your music,' she said.

'You never go to bed in the afternoon at home.'

'Away is different.'

The first smell in the airport building was of flowers. Hyacinths in January. Stella drew some euros from a hole-in-the-wall machine after checking the exchange rates. It shelled out high-denomination notes only and she tut-tutted. She gave half to Gerry and he slid them into his wallet. As they made their way to the train station Gerry pointed at her wristbands.

'You can take those things off now.'

'They keep me nice and warm.' Stella's face was turned up to the huge noticeboard.

'Look.'

'What?'

'Europe,' she said. 'Does that not do something to the hairs on the back of your neck? To be on the same piece of land? Rome, Warsaw, Berlin, Prague. Moscow, even. You could get on a train . . .'

'Let's get to Amsterdam first.'

The board changed with a roar and a flutter of individual letters and in an instant the whole board trembled and all the information leapt up a line.

'Double-decker trains,' said Gerry.

'You're such a boy sometimes.'

They found a place in an empty carriage and got settled.

'Which direction are we going?'

Gerry pointed. Stella changed her seat.

'You're a forward-looking woman.'

'Always have been.'

The train pulled out and cleared the terminal. It was grey and raining. Stella wriggled her hands out of the wristbands and put them in her bag.

'We should jump in a taxi,' she said. 'Around the station can be a bit unsavoury. Last time we were lugging our cases through junkies and ne'er-do-wells. In the days before cases had wheels.'

19

'It's all going far too well,' said Gerry. 'A bad omen.'

In the main station pigeons crossed their path, cooing and speeding up to get out of their way. Gerry stopped to look closely at them.

'Have you ever seen their feet?' Stella shook her head, no. 'They're nearly all deformed. In Glasgow Central, it's exactly the same. Wee red clenched fists, missing toes, running around on their knuckles . . .'

'So they are,' said Stella. 'I've never seen that before. Poor things.'

A couple of the birds rose in front of them and they felt the wind of their wings as they passed. Gerry ducked, thinking of germs.

Gerry paid the taxi. From nowhere, Stella produced an umbrella and led the way through the rain into the hotel, hoisting her cabin case up the steps to the large revolving doors. The clerk checking them in spoke good English.

'Perhaps you want to go out separately?'

They were given two plastic cards for room keys. The door-man reached for their cases but Gerry said, 'It's okay – we can manage.'

In the lift when the doors slid to Gerry consulted the little paper envelope containing the card.

'Three nine six,' he said.

She pressed the button and when the lift began to move they kissed. It was a habit they had developed, to kiss lightly when alone in a lift. Between floors.

'It's so embarrassing – making a flunkey out of someone.'

'Gerry, it's his job.'

'And then there's the tip. He'd stand around hoping.'

On their floor they followed the arrows to the room number. Gerry slid the plastic into the lock and plucked it out again. The room was dark because the curtains were pulled. He inserted the card into the wall slot and said in a booming God-like voice, 'Let there be light.'

The television screen welcomed them by name.

'*The Hotel Theo wish you a pleasant stay. If there is anything we can do to help, please let us know.*'

'A free drink would be nice,' Gerry said.

Stella went first to the window and drew back the dark curtains. She lifted the inner nets. Their room faced into the centre of the hotel. Opposite were windows up and windows down like a crossword. Gerry came to join her, looking over her shoulder, putting his arms around her waist. There was a flat roof below.

'Would you look at that rain?' said Stella. Lying on the wet roof was an empty Gauloises packet beside a child's plastic seaside bucket.

'Wonderful,' said Gerry.

Stella set the big case on the king-sized bed. The lid, when she opened it, cast off droplets of rain onto the coverlet. She began to unpack. Gerry went around the bed and lay down full length on the opposite side.

'Perfect,' he said. 'Hard as a brick runway. Soft beds spell danger to my back.'

'D'you like these?'

She held up a cellophane pack from Marks & Spencer.

'What are they?'

'New pyjamas.'

'Black?'

'As sin.'

He raised an eyebrow and looked up at her.

'Why? Did you think it'd be a turn-on – like sleeping with a priest?'

'Priests usually have enough independence to choose their own pyjamas.'

Stella stripped them of their packaging. She threw it all in the waste bin and slid the pyjamas under the pillow. In the bin the bundled cellophane crackled softly as it tried to regain its shape.

She handed Gerry the remote control.

'Get me English News.'

He began flicking, watching the changing screen – hearing the riffle of European languages. Then BBC News appeared. A reporter was on a beach interviewing a man who had come ashore from a heaving and crowded boat. The migrant's English was broken but good enough. Behind him was a woman holding a baby. The reporter ended with a shrug. 'A man and his wife with their infant son changing countries to escape from war.'

'On and on it goes,' said Stella. She carried her washbag into the bathroom. Gerry could see her reflected in a mirror opposite the doorway. She tore off the pleated paper from a bar of soap and inhaled it. 'I'll have the luxury of a bath or two in here,' she shouted. She took out her plastic bag of creams and tubes and artificial tears and set them on a ledge.

Gerry was still on the bed with his shoes on when she came back into the room. She kicked off hers and folded herself into the coverlet beside him. From her bag she produced her Amsterdam guide and began to flick through it. One restaurant boasted of 'robust stews'. She tried to find it on the map but fell asleep.

Stella awoke to a knocking. Her watch told her they'd slept far too long.

'Who is it?'

She opened the door. Two shy girls in uniform. They smiled and the one nearer the door said something in Dutch.

'English?' said Stella.

'Turn-down service,' said one of the girls.

'Thank you,' said Stella. 'But we can do that ourselves.'

'Chocolate?' The further-away girl held out a platter with tiny gold-wrapped bars. Stella still had the Amsterdam guide in her hand. She awkwardly took a handful of chocolates with her left hand and nodded her thanks. She closed the door with a push of her shoulder.

'We've just turned down the turn-down service,' said Gerry, laughing. 'Anyway, it's just more subservience. Carry your bag, sir? Turn down your covers, sir? Some chocolate to rot your teeth, sir?'

There was a knock from a door further along the corridor and the whole spiel began again in the distance. This time in Dutch.

At seven o'clock they put on scarves, hats and overcoats.

'Have you got your plastic key?' said Stella.

'Yes.'

'When you take the card out of the thing all the lights go out.'

'Your electrical engineering degree has stood you in good stead.'

They went down in the lift, kissed with pouted lips. Stella consulted the man at the desk about somewhere good to eat nearby. At a reasonable price.

'Do you like Asian spice?' the man asked. 'Taiwan?'

They both nodded. He produced a single sheet map from beneath the counter and X-ed the restaurant.

'What's it called?' asked Stella. The concierge shrugged. The three-way translation was beyond him. English, Dutch, Taiwanese.

'Is good,' he said and smiled. They thanked him and turned away. Gerry half whispered to Stella, 'A map is useless if you don't know where you are on it.' She turned back and said to the concierge, 'Hotel?' And he put another X on the page.

'Sorry,' he said.

*   *   *

24

Outside it had stopped raining but it was bitterly cold. They walked by the night canals and she hooked onto his arm tightly for warmth. The water was alive with lights and ripples. Fairy lights fastened to the undersides of bridges made hoops with their reflections. There was an icy wind cuffing here and there, darkening the water. Gerry looked down.

'Come away from the edge,' she said. 'It gives me the weirdest feeling.'

'What does?'

'The blackness of the water. How cold it would be.' He extended his elbow so's she could hook on again. 'It's the thought of suicide in there – when death is an improvement of your situation.'

'Hey – lighten up. We're on holiday,' said Gerry. 'We're going out to eat a meal. Perhaps a drink or two. And we just passed an Irish pub.'

There was the ring of a bell and a warning shout. Stella looked over her shoulder. A girl on a bicycle swept by.

'Wow,' said Gerry, 'would you look at her go. She's something else.'

Stella looked down at the pavement markings then up to the figure cycling into the gloom.

'This is a bicycle track. In the middle of the footpath?'

The waiter who served them was extraordinarily handsome and Stella was very taken with him. He even shook out the red paper napkin and surrounded her with his arms as he allowed it to descend gently onto her lap. His English was excellent. Stella, in mock shyness, fanned her face as if to cool it while at the same time raising her eyebrows to Gerry.

The food was fine and they shared a Rioja – Stella had a glass and Gerry manfully finished the bottle. She praised its temperature.

'The tepid-er the better,' she said. He had a couple of ice-cold Heinekens to accompany his starter.

As he paid the bill Gerry saw Stella take the leftover biscuits from his cheeseboard, wrap them in her napkin and put them in her handbag.

To get to the Irish pub they had to cross a main road. He always took her hand when crossing – she had little sense of the speed of approaching traffic. Also, to be looking the wrong way in Amsterdam was a positive danger. At home, on her own, she always used pedestrian crossings. But Gerry thought of the hand holding as an intimacy – different to 'hooking on'. It was skin to skin. The snugness of the fit. The hands made for each other.

In the pub they found an empty table. The barman's accent was from Dublin and the place was filled with Irish junk from the 1950s. Opposite them, a wall of Guinness adverts. Calendars of Irish writers. Railway posters with Irish paintings. Pictures of overnight boat crossings from Belfast to Heysham and Liverpool.

'There's a company who supplies the whole paddywhackery kit,' said Gerry.

A group of musicians was setting up near the door. There were fiddles, a bodhrán, beards, a forest of microphones on upright stands.

'Sometimes I find easy listening hard going,' said Gerry. 'These are diddley-dee specialists.' They sat looking at one another. 'Stella, you haven't bought me a drink in years.'

'I am always too slow,' she said. You're like lightning up to the bar.'

'I'll have a whiskey – a Jameson – and I'll leave the measure up to yourself. Kill them if they try to put ice in it. And some water on the side.'

Stella took her purse and approached the counter. She returned carrying Gerry's drink and a jug. Gerry lifted his glass and looked at the measure.

'A well-built ant could piss more.'

'I asked for a double.'

'You're learning.'

'Killing you with kindness.'

She went back to the bar for her fizzy water. When she sat down Gerry was diluting his whiskey.

'Alcohol is the rubber tyres between me and the pier.' He held up his glass to her. They chinked.

'What gets you by,' she said and took a sip.

'You and me.'

'Me and you,' she said. 'I suppose we're lucky to have each other to ignore.'

'You look preoccupied.'

'Storyboarding my life.'

'Are you okay?' he asked.

'Yes – fine.'

'No, I don't mean that way. I don't mean . . .'

'What?'

'In yourself. You seem quiet. Very inner.'

'I'm not aware of it.' After a while she said, 'Given the world today. Right now there's probably a boat somewhere in the Mediterranean full to the gunwales with poor people. Ready to sink. And we're here.'

'I keep saying – we're on our holidays.'

27

Gerry looked past her at the posters. He pointed out a picture by Paul Henry – a scene of lake water and bundled-up creamy white clouds. '*Lough Derg – Ireland for holidays.*' Stella had been on pilgrimage to Lough Derg several times – three days of praying and fasting. Bare feet in the rain, no sleep, black tea and burned toast. Gerry put on a voice: 'I'll report yis to the Tourist Board. How dare you call that a holiday.'

But Stella defended it.

'It's a step back from your life to concentrate on what really matters. And in those days a lotta cigarette smoke.'

'The Jug of Punch' started up and there was a lot of toe tapping.

'The arrogance of amplification in a space this size.' Gerry had to shout to make himself heard. Then they were asked by the singer to join in the choruses. The guy's accent was from Northern Ireland.

'Isn't it strange,' Gerry said, 'that Ireland's biggest export is a lesson on how to enjoy yourself. That and the car bomb.' The band launched into 'Will ye Go, Lassie, Go'.

'Oh, I love this one,' said Stella. The music seemed to get louder. Most of what Gerry said got lost despite Stella leaning her ear towards him and him cupping his hand to shout into it like a loudhailer. But then the band began to play IRA rebel songs. 'Sean South of Garryowen', followed by 'The Patriot Game'.

'I hate this stuff.' Stella pulled a face. 'Let's go.' Gerry nodded.

'They just assume we support violence. A wink and a nod. Ireland's fight for fucking freedom.' Gerry drained his whiskey.

'I'm looking forward to my bed,' Stella roared. 'And my hot-water bottle.'

*   *   *

They walked a different route back to the hotel, shivering. The moon was racing through clouds, sometimes disappearing completely.

'Is that a gibbous moon?'

'I've no idea,' said Gerry. 'I'm a stranger here myself. Chic Murray.'

'I know.'

'It's sandpapered off on the right-hand side a bit.'

'It was full a couple of nights ago.'

'So was I,' said Gerry. 'God, but it's cold.'

The sky was alive with seagulls underlit by the street lights – soaring and cackling, sometimes mewing like cats high in the night air – ghostly, their wings arched in the dark. They cruised looking this way and that, as if from a cockpit, gazing down for any scrap, any morsel. One bird crossed the moon.

'You forget Amsterdam is by the sea,' said Stella. 'Until you see the gulls.'

They put their heads down and shouldered into the wind, getting to the hotel as quickly as they could.

They were stopped by a strange object on the pavement in front of the hotel steps.

'What in the name of God is that?'

Stella was sure it had not been there earlier.

'Search me.' Gerry bent over and looked down. It was a solid block of white ice, about the size of a microwave oven. There were indentations here and there on it. He could see frozen streaks beneath its surface.

'It's waiting for its *Titanic*,' said Stella.

'It's one of those Rachel Whiteread sculptures. Her that won the Turner Prize.'

'Who?'

29

'She does inside-out houses. Like casts. Negative space rendered in concrete. Except this is ice.'

Gerry put his foot on top of the block and gave it a push. It trundled forward heavily – downhill into the gully of the pavement.

'Reminds me of a curling stone the way it moves,' said Gerry.

'That's your heart, that is.'

'That's for your drink, that is.'

Stella, in the hotel's towelling dressing gown, tidied her hair into a plastic shower cap while water plummeted into the foam. Gradually her reflection in the mirror misted over. She rarely had a bath like this – but loved the Hollywood idea when she was on holiday. The air filled with the smell of lavender. She hung the dressing gown on the back of the door and slid beneath the foam. Good to be on her own for a bit. And now that the tap was off there was a wonderful silence. From outside she could dimly hear the television. She lifted her hands clear of the suds and examined them. Handling luggage, she found, invariably resulted in damage to the fingernails. On her left hand, her rings. Both wedding and engagement. A little foam clung to them, reminding her of cuckoo spit, with a tiny gleam of gold at its centre. There was a faint hiss as the suds began to disappear. Her knees and the outline of her body began to show. Her stomach, still bearing the track of her pants. Elastic and skin like tongue and groove. And the scar near her navel. Above the pale line of her C-section. To see the scar on her back she would have to corkscrew herself in front of the mirror. On beach holidays she always wore a black one-piece. And after all these years Gerry had ceased to comment. Ceased to do most things. Except drink.

How could changes be made at her age? To even think of leaving seemed such an impossibility. There was too much to be done. But she was known as an organiser – that kind of woman. She accepted challenges – was chairperson of the residents' association for their tenement, had accepted the position of Eucharistic minister in her parish, organised jumble sales and sales of work. Over the years she had bought and sold flats for their son, Michael. Gerry referred to her as his 'transport captain'. Organising complex journeys, booking hotels, contacting people to meet them, seeing the whole journey in her mind's eye before they ever left home. She had university degrees, for goodness' sake. If *she* couldn't stand up for herself then who could? She rehearsed inside her head what she would say to him. Different ways, different tones of voice.

Tomorrow. How would things work out? It could be a place of sanctuary.

Most people broke up because they'd met someone else – but this was not the case. It was becoming simpler now that both sets of parents had died. Their son Michael was the only one who'd have to be told and he was in Canada making a life and family of his own. He'd understand – knew what his old man was like. The drinking genes he'd inherited were Stella's, not his father's. If Gerry was going to continue to live in the same bibulous fashion she would prefer to be elsewhere. A Room of One's Own. She unwrapped a bar of soap and began to wash her arms and shoulders. And just as she was beginning to enjoy the sensuousness of the soap it was away, slipping between her fingers. She had to sit up straight and search below the dwindling froth with both hands.

'I would fain be prone,' said Stella, coming out of the bathroom. She wanted to watch the BBC News.

31

'You saw it earlier.'

'Something new might've happened. That's the definition of news.' Gerry found the remote and began to press buttons. She boiled the kettle and filled her hot-water bottle.

'Turn it down, Gerry. You don't want anybody thumping the wall.' She rummaged in the case for her book.

'I thought you were never coming out of there,' he said. He went to the bathroom but didn't bother to close the door. The bathroom mirror reflected another mirror in the bedroom. He could see Stella now in her white nightdress on bended knees at her side of the bed. At first he thought she'd dropped an earring or something – then, when he looked at her hands, he realised she was praying. He was about to speak out, to say something comical to her, but stopped himself. This was a thing he didn't often see. At home they went to bed at different times – allowing each other their own space, in current jargon. He didn't know she was still doing this.

Stella brought her joined hands up to her face. The hotel's hand lotion was good, not sickly sweet. She had a mantra so she would not be distracted, a framework to keep her from drifting. It involved praying for the people she loved, a glide over the family, briefly touching them all with her mind. Her parents, her brothers and sisters at home and in different parts of the world. Like Master Ryan's roll call at school. Prayers of thanks for her extraordinary life, for her remarkable survival. To be cradled in the hand of God. She was nine when her father died. His body was laid out in the front room and when she was brought in to see him she was told to say a prayer. Other people were there so the body would not be alone. He was so still. Lying at peace. His hands tied with a rosary. Later that evening there were people in the kitchen and a man sang, 'Shall My Soul Pass Through Old Ireland'. She closed her eyes and rested her head on the hotel coverlet for a moment. Prayer was like a visitation, like checking her child, in the light from the landing, last thing at night. And nowadays she prayed for refugees everywhere, the put-upon, the full of fear, those fleeing from war. But prayers like these were just spiritual tidying. Something to be done morning and night. Before sleeping and after waking. Putting the world to rites. She smiled.

Gerry flushed the toilet and stood looking at himself, waiting for her to get up. To give her more time, he washed his hands slowly. He looked again in the mirror and saw her finish her prayers, make the sign of the cross and stand.

Back in the room he sat in front of the television. Stella stood watching the screen over his shoulder, then turned her attention to the bed. It had been made tight as a drum and she began to dismantle it. First peeling back the heavy cover and throwing it in the corner where no one would trip on it. Then unbuckling the white top sheet, tugging it and releasing it all the way round. She knew Gerry would create a fuss if he felt trapped. Then he would have to get up in the darkness and there would be moaning and cursing as he struggled to loosen the sheets. When all was slackened off she got beneath the bedclothes and leaned back against her stacked pillows. He heard the gurgle of the hot-water bottle as she pushed it down the bed with her feet.

'Oh, this is *so* gorgeous,' she said.

'I'll be in later.'

Gerry poured himself a Jameson. The first dram created a loud liquid popping in the neck of the bottle – something he had to be careful about at home if he was pouring within earshot. He filled a coffee cup with water from the bathroom and diluted his drink. For a long time he didn't touch it – he wanted Stella to think, like James Thurber's character, that when it came to drink he could take it or leave it. After a while Stella stopped reading and turned away from the room.

'Is the door locked?' she said. 'People staggering around drunk in hotels make mistakes.'

'I'm not going out anywhere,' he said.

'Very droll.'

Soon her breathing, long and slow, indicated sleep. It had been a long day.

The mention of locking doors and the rebel songs from the Irish pub brought Belfast back to him. He tried to flinch away from the images. Concentrate on the drink. The first mouthful. The Jameson deserved his attention. He had nothing but praise for it. A whiskey made in the south, a Catholic whiskey. Bushmills was Protestant, made in the North. Black Bush. It was well named. But he couldn't care less. As far as alcohol was concerned he was totally non-sectarian. He finished what was left in the glass and poured another. However, the memory in question would not leave him alone. Indeed the more he drank the less he was able to resist. Something had happened to sensitise him. Like pollen preceding sneezing. He'd just been to lunch with two of the other architects. They all knew they had work to do in the afternoon so they drank only porter. Single X. A pint each. Helped them keep a clear head because it wasn't strong. It wasn't considered drinking – the way gin and tonic wasn't considered drinking – just something to wash down their sandwiches. There were stories of the boys falling asleep after lunch. Propped upright by a clear perspex ruler between

34

drawing board and forehead. But that was myth – a story told to strangers. Nobody at work believed it.

There was somebody waiting for Gerry in the meeting room off the main office. The others went back to their work. There was an atmosphere – everybody looking at him expectantly. Gerry went into the meeting room. A bulky middle-aged man and a younger guy were standing by the boardroom mahogany table. The two men looked round when he came in, and nodded. They declared themselves to be from the RUC. This was bad news – enough to make his stomach swoon. They invited him to sit. It was his place to offer *them* a seat. This was *his* territory. Was somebody dead? But still he remained on his feet. His body did not want to move – his mind was racing. He tried to read the clues. The older man had heavy jowls and a dark moustache. His inability to meet Gerry's eye was disconcerting. It either had to do with the news he was about to break or he had Gerry figured for a Catholic. He was wearing a maroon paisley-patterned scarf and holding the crown of his soft hat between finger and thumb. He was ill at ease – his fingers fidgeting. The younger one again motioned Gerry into one of the chrome and leather chairs surrounding the table. Why was it so important for him to sit down? Why were they insisting on it? There was a clang as the chair hit against the one next to it. Gerry sat down. Then they asked if his name was Gerald Gilmore. He nodded. And they checked his address. This was getting worse. His knees became jelly, ice invaded his stomach. The older man continued to touch the tassels of his scarf.

'There's been an accident,' he said. 'Your wife was involved.'

Then he was waking up in the chair. In a hotel room. With the light from the television changing as the picture changed. Stella's breathing from the bed. How long had he been asleep?

35

Had he drooled? His watch said it was after two. Had he put it forward after landing or was it still British time?

'Better get going.'

He finished the whiskey in his glass.

'Did you say something?' Stella spoke from the bed. 'What are you muttering about?'

'Snuthing. Sallright.'

He sat still until her breathing returned to being audible and rhythmic. He switched off the television and went to the bathroom. When he closed the door he depressed the handle and eased it back slowly so's not to waken her. He aimed down the side of the bowl and after he had finished closed the lid to quieten the flush. He was on statins for his cholesterol. To be taken at night. But pushing one of these brutes out of its blister pack was noisy. So at home he kept them *outside* the bedroom. Now here in the hotel bathroom with the door closed it was okay. Stella would hear nothing – she would not be disturbed. He ran a glass of water, broke out the tablet and swallowed it. In the act of medication he ended up looking at himself in the mirror. The drink was labelling his face – it was a kind of telltale, like the one fastened to the wall at home – to show the subsidence, the undermining. To let people know what was going on. The nose – more than anything else – red or grey or slightly tinged with blue – it'll eventually become pocked like a strawberry. The whiskey sunburn, the tan, the leathery look. This all takes years, decades. The oul habits sculpting away at the finished you. When it first made its appearance he had frequently used the joke 'That rosacea would give you a red face.' His image stared back at him. He was developing a dewlap – a definite dewlap. He waggled under his chin scornfully with his fingers. But if all this stuff was on the outside what the hell was he like inside? Was he shrivelling his liver? Pickling God knows what organs. The finished you. He raised the towel and wiped the corner of his mouth. There was a danger too that his drinking would end the both of them being together. He knew she hated it so much. The answer was for him to keep it to himself – the amount he was drinking. But half the time he didn't know.

The hotel tumbler only held a moderate amount of water but he filled it to the brim. He squeezed the light switch so that it did not snap. Around the bed to his own side. Deposit the glass of water. His spectacles lay on their lenses on the bedside table, their legs up. 'They'll become scratched if you do that,' his optician had said. He pushed the spectacles to one side so that his hand could get directly to the glass of water in the new dark. Stella snored quietly in her nest of pillows.

His bladder woke him. For some moments he didn't know where he was. No light anywhere, except the red glow from the television standby. An hotel room. Amsterdam. No outside light whatsoever. The curtain overlap was perfect. It was Stella in the bed with him. She was silent but he thought she was awake. He didn't want to arouse her to find out whether she was asleep or not. When he got up, immediately the chandeliers came. Stars against the night sky. Marcasite jabs and darts. An imminent stroke – probably *before* he reached the bathroom. Blood pressure and alcohol. *The Diving Bell and the Butterfly*. Marooned in the outer space of no speech. Nurses changing him down below three times a day. His hand went out and using the wall he guided himself to the lavatory. He tried to be as quiet as he could but there was no need, because Stella had switched on the bedside light. She *had* been awake. When he came back into the room she said, 'Weet wee-o.' The two words.

37

'What?'

'The black pyjamas.'

He gave a theatrical bow.

'Me next,' she said, getting out of bed.

'Didn't flush – didn't want to waken you.'

'I'll flush for both of us.' On such occasions there was an unspoken pact not to speak, not to waken each other too much. A 'ships that pass in the night' moment. Occasionally one or other of them voiced the cliché.

But sleep would not come back. For either of them.

'First night away syndrome,' she said.

Gerry heard her twist and turn in the huge bed. She switched on her bedside light, got up again and began to rummage. Noises came from the foot of the bed – like crinkling, like crunching. It went on for a long time. Eventually he reared up and saw that she was sitting in the armchair raising a half-eaten biscuit to her mouth with both hands.

'What's with the midnight Mass?'

'Sorry,' she said. 'I felt hungry all of a sudden.'

'You're stopping me getting over,' he said. He lay down again and thrust his head into the pillow. 'Where did weet wee-o come from?'

'Must have been the comics,' she said. 'A bit like your storyboarding. How does somebody wolf-whistle in a comic? There has to be a speech bubble. But it's not speech – so – weet wee-o.'

She came back to bed. 'I could never get the knack of whistling. And the nuns didn't exactly encourage us. On the grounds that Our Lady never did it.' It was not long after she turned out the light that she began shaking with laughter. He felt the vibrations.

'What's so funny?' he said.

'*Getting over*,' she said. 'What a quaint phrase – I haven't heard *getting over* in years. My father used it all the time. My mother'd say, did you sleep well? – and he'd say, naw, I'd a hard time getting over.' By now Gerry was laughing too.

'I'm still half shot,' he said. 'Stop talking or we'll never get over.' And that started them again. But the laughter this time was not as long or as intense. They were silent. He put his arm around her, held her close for a while until she moved away from him in the vastness of the bed.

Rather than turn on the light and risk wakening him Stella reached above the bed and lifted a corner of the curtain. It was still dawn dark but there was a yellow sodium light outside somewhere. She turned back the sheet and swung her legs out of bed. The light was enough for her to find her way to the bathroom. She was glad she'd had a bath the night before.

She knew her clothes in the wardrobe, not by colour, but by shape and touch. The sulphur light neutralised their colour. She chose a navy outfit with a pale silk scarf. It wasn't important because she'd be wearing her overcoat the whole time.

Gerry would sleep for ages. Before she went out she lifted the red napkin containing the last of the biscuits and put it in her bag. In the lift she avoided herself in the mirror. Savoury breakfast smells drifted from the buffet. Yet she felt it would be inappropriate to go in, overcoat and all, to eat by herself. She might be back before Gerry was up and dressed. She shouldered on through the revolving doors into the street.

It was cold and wet. She threaded one arm through the handle of her bag and put both her hands in her pockets to keep them warm. But immediately her nail snagged on the lining. She made fists because she hated that sensation. A pocket lined with silk was like a magnifying glass for the slightest imperfection. The light from the east, rising up between buildings, was white. She had put a bookmark in her Amsterdam guide and stood into doorways out of the rain to consult it. The network of canals on paper was confusing – one looked much like another – distances were deceptive. It took ages to get to where she wanted to go. She walked past the entrance several times without realising. '*It can be difficult sometimes to find the gate.*' There was a brick archway which led into a dark passage. She hesitantly walked its dry length, hearing her own footsteps echoing. The passageway led out into a space which took her breath away. The notion of being born came to her. Moving from the dark into the light, into the world. She was in a new place, had the feeling of being a new person. An amazing born-again feeling. No one remembered the experience of being born. Maybe just as well. She had been born once and given birth once. The first she didn't remember, the second she wanted to forget. The giving birth had been surrounded by such circumstances as to flood her body with panic when she thought of it. But she had become expert at nipping the memory off before it could get started by concentrating on the physical world around her. Grass, winter trees, a ring of neat ancient houses with their backs to the world, all looking inwards – like covered wagons pulled into a circle – creating their own shelter. An inner court or Roman atrium. In the centre of the green space stood a Christ-like statue facing a red-brick church. It was the same place she had seen on her computer screen at home. And the silence was the same. The passageway she had come through had edited out the noise of Amsterdam – the trains, the trams, the cars, all gone. As if to emphasise the quiet, some sparrows cheeped within the enclosure of houses.

41

Now that the rain had stopped she walked around the space, savouring it. For a moment or two the sun broke through the clouds and shone whitely on the wet branches of the trees. She turned her face up to it and her eyes closed automatically. So she stopped walking and stood, became aware of the red world behind her eyelids. The same thing happened at night when she couldn't sleep, only then the world was black. And she focused on the thud of her heartbeat as it pressed on the pillow. The body working away without permission. Independent. The heart never taking a break. The bowels never taking a nap. When it stopped, that was the day it was all over. She'd come close to that once. A day she'd never forget. Death had winged her. But some day, somehow she would move into soul. It happened to everybody who had ever lived since the beginning of time. Soul was her, minus her body. Parturition – her, minus her son. Gradually her eyelids darkened, then opened. The sun had moved behind cloud. She should put together another parcel for Canada soon. It would keep her fresh in their minds after the one at Christmas. In Oxfam she'd bought a game for her grandson, Toby. Construct-o-Straws. A bargain, still in its cellophane. Maybe make an architect of him some day – like his grandfather. Her payment, a tiny contribution to charity. For the others – her son, Michael, and his wife – she could buy something here in Amsterdam. Indeed she might do it this very morning if she had time. Without Gerry tripping after her.

The door of the church refused to budge. Only an empty echo of the clunking of the door handle. The guidebook told her this was the English Reformed Church dating from the fifteenth century. She walked around it, trying to see in. Someone she'd studied as part of her degree was Julian of Norwich. A woman anchorite with a man's name – the first female to write a book in English. Her of 'All shall be well' fame. And again, 'All shall be well.' Julian had had a cell constructed against the outside wall of her church, like a wasps' nest. It contained only a hard bed and a crucifix. There was access to the church through a small, unglazed window or 'squint' which enabled her to keep up with Mass and the ceremonies, and through it she'd receive the Word of God and the sacraments. Gerry had pointed out a leper squint to Stella in the outside wall of a church in Antrim. Stella imagined the excluded lepers huddled in the rain, crouched, taking turns to follow the Mass. Julian of Norwich was a contemporary of Chaucer. Stella loved the down-to-earthness of the medieval period, its vulgarity, the language itself with its flat, sat-on vowels and its ability to move in a blink to the religious, the mystical, the compassionate.

She moved to have a closer look at the houses. One was marked 1660 on its gable, the numbers looking authentically old. There was a courtyard with square indentations in the wall. In each was a little Old Testament scene – all of them recently restored and painted with bright colours – Abraham brandishing a sword above his son, the burning fiery furnace consuming the three young men whose names she could never quite pronounce, the flight into Egypt. DE VLUGH VA EGIPTEN. She liked this last one best with Mary protecting her child in her lapis lazuli cloak being led by Joseph.

To her left was a doorway beside a noticeboard with the messages written in Dutch. It too was shut. But there were times displayed. If they were opening times she would not have long to wait. The rain was beginning again. She walked back to shelter in the passageway. Maybe she *should* have had some breakfast. Her hand went into her bag. The softness of

43

the red paper serviette, the texture of biscuit. She nibbled one now as she stood. It was so quiet she could hear the crunching inside her head. That waiter had been such a charmer. With his white teeth and Asian good looks. His professional kindness. His act of draping this very napkin over her lap. When she finished, not wanting to litter, she bundled the serviette into her pocket. Then realised that crumbs had spilled in the lining.

She recalled a time when Gerry had had that effect on her. So long ago. When he was flavour of the month. The first time he swept her away in his car. Even *having* a car, in those days. They drove up the twisting east coast road to the Glens of Antrim. Through a landscape which amazed her. Waterfoot, Cushendall, Cushendun, then on to the seaside town of Ballycastle. She was shy of him at first in the car. They smoked Benson & Hedges. She wasn't much of a smoker but it was nice to keep him company – most of the smoke she blew down her nose. And the day was good enough to have the windows open.

And they talked. Politics and religion. Explored the byways of each other and each other's families. She was one of six, three boys and three girls and they had lived in a small house in a large village. It had no running water and an outside toi-let. It had been her job every morning to fill an enamel pail from the pump in the street outside. But they weren't aware of this as a hardship. They were very *near* the pump. Not all their neighbours could boast of that. They washed in their bedrooms with a flannel in a basin. And he told her he was an only child who collected stamps. When she laughed he claimed it was a way to travel without going anywhere. But no, she said, she hadn't finished her story about the house. The District Council began building an estate of council houses to rent in the village and people were asked to apply. The houses were of varying sizes and styles. One had four bedrooms and when they applied for it there was endless talk of anticipation and hope. How great it would be. As well as the bedrooms, a bathroom and two lavatories for their sole use. Her mother and father prayed and enlisted the prayers of their children, that they would get this house. They all did a novena of Masses, getting up at dawn, walking the hill to the chapel. Later it transpired that their mother went round to the building site at the dark of night and threw a miraculous medal into what would later become the spacious garden of the desired house. It was just one more thing her father wanted – a place to grow stuff – carrots, onions, potatoes. Maybe the odd flower or two. But when the time came didn't the powers that be, Unionist to a man, award the four-bedroom house to one of their own – a Protestant policeman. A widower, a sergeant in the RUC, who lost his wife to cancer. With one teenage son. What need had they of such accommodation?

That started Gerry on the Unionists. Northern Ireland was a country given away by someone who didn't own it. The resulting state was like an extreme Protestant version of Franco's Spain. It would go on for ever because those in power had arranged it in such a gerrymandered way that voting was useless. It was like putting your cross in invisible ink. And it wasn't just Catholics who were disenfranchised – it was the same for anybody of the left. She soothed and quietened him, told him again and again what a lovely day it was. They stopped for ice cream in Cushendall and parked by the golf course so that Gerry could eat it before it melted all over him.

When they went walking along the seafront in Ballycastle she was intrigued to see the grass tennis courts. Emerald green, beautifully kept. The nets looking new and taut. He said that they would be getting everything shipshape for the summer and the arrival of the Scots tourists. Most of the courts were occupied and the players kitted out in whites. The puck and whack of the ball, the polite squeals after missed shots – she found it all a bit intimidating. There was a way of doing tennis and she didn't know what it was.

They walked down onto the beach and lay on the sand. It was a day of intermittent cloud and sunshine. Shadows moving across the headland of Fair Head. The sand was soft and she spilled it from hand to hand while he smoked. Later they walked further along the beach. The dry sand was difficult to walk on so they moved closer to the sea where it had been solidified by the withdrawing tide. The water left fringes of lace. She was always on the lookout for stones. Only white perfect ones would make her stoop. She would show them to him with a little flourish. Look at this one. When they were wet and glistening they seemed special but she knew that when they dried out maybe some yellow or grey would creep into their colour. The perfect ones would end up in a glass bowl on her table. It was their simplicity that she found so attractive. A full-moon shape. And the fact that they cost nothing, that they were not being sold by anyone.

In the landscape he looked better. A man for the daylight – better than in the orange glow of a dance hall. Good-looking rather than handsome. He seemed thoughtful, concerned, the kind of guy who would do anything for you. Above all he seemed interesting – the way he talked about art, about architecture. How could anybody make architecture interesting? Before meeting him she had been barely aware of it. People had to have houses to live in, shops to sell from, bus shelters, schools, churches but, generally speaking, it was a shrug for her. She would present him with white stones and

46

he would reciprocate with pyramids and skyscrapers, ceiling bosses and Lady chapels. When he talked to her about these things he talked close, leaning in, his eyes fixed on her eyes. What came across was his energy and enthusiasm, his turn of phrase and wit. To her ear his speech seemed fresh-minted.

At the far end of the beach they came to a footbridge and walkway. But the tide was out so that the bridge appeared foolish – a leftover, a bridge to nowhere. They climbed the steps and crossed to the middle of the structure. The flooring was of wood and was weather-beaten and bleached. Why was such a thing there? He said, at first, that it was an unfinished bridge to Scotland. Then he reneged on the joke and told her that it was a popular place for rod fishing. At high tide the bridge was necessary to get to the rocks that yielded the most fish.

They must have been downwind from the town because they could faintly hear the music from the amusements and squeals from the rides. She was resting her elbows on the parapet looking out to sea. A lighthouse on Rathlin Island flashed once. She waited a long time and it flashed again. Beyond, Scotland could be seen as pale blue on the horizon. She turned to him to ask a question and he kissed her. When the kiss finished she rested her forehead on his shoulder. He then moved to kiss her again. She extended her finger to stop his lips and left it there, making him feel she was unsure of him. He smiled a confused smile and she felt the movement of it beneath her finger. Then after a moment's hesitation she took away her finger and returned his kiss.

For ages afterwards, every time she wore that coat, she felt a joy of sorts when her fingers encountered the grains of sand in her pockets.

*   *   *

47

She leaned her shoulder against the wall of the passageway in Amsterdam and looked at her watch. Footsteps. She turned and the light was partially dimmed as a figure came towards her. It was a middle-aged bespectacled woman who excused herself in Dutch and walked past, her block heels ringing. She produced a bunch of keys and let herself into the building opposite. Stella moved forward. She hesitated, didn't want to crowd in on the woman if this was just the start of her working day. Give her time to take off her coat – polish the rain from her spectacles. She might have a routine that did not include answering questions from the likes of Stella. So Stella walked another lap of the herringbone path around the garden. It would be impossible to get lost here. She lifted her head to the overlooking houses. Curtained windows – some with plants on display. Aspidistras, just like those at home. And in one window high up, the scarlet of a poinsettia, bright as a sanctuary lamp. The layout of the garden reminded her of a cloister, although there was no covered colonnade, no pillars holding aloft a roof. Anyone walking and meditating was open to the worst of the weather. And therefore distracted. A cloister was a sheltered walk to nowhere. A spiritual gym. The one that stayed most in her memory was in the cathedral at Santiago de Compostela. The shadows of its pillars creating a zebra crossing of light and shade, a place to pass in safety. A place of laps – a place which brought you around to your starting point. An alpha and omega place. Where the mind and the spirit could be freed by being restricted. Exercise for those who wanted to remain within walls. Imprisoned yet protected from the outside world.

Some months later, before the summer ended, Gerry and she went away again. To Galway and the west coast. When they checked into the small hotel the owner looked up from her registration book and asked if they wanted singles or a double room. Stella said, very definitely, two singles.

At dinner they shared a bottle of Blue Nun and praised the food extravagantly. They could see the garden from the dining room and the woman, who also served at tables, pointed out the very herbs which gave so much flavour to the food.

They went into the garden afterwards. The light was changing from evening into night. A crescent moon was in the sky over the sea, creating a path of light to where they were standing in the herb garden. He showed her the trick his father had shown him – crushing the leaves between his finger and thumb, then smelling the aroma, gilding his hand with fragrance. But he was not bold enough to offer his fingers for her to smell. He was relieved when she imitated what he was doing and inhaled her own fingers. She made noises of surprise and pleasure after each plant.

'The smells are getting all mixed up,' she'd said. 'I don't have enough hands.'

The next day – when they praised both the food and garden to the owner – she walked them around and named some of the more dramatic plants. Sage, rosemary, lavender, lemon balm, ordinary fennel and bronze fennel.

Where Stella was walking now had the feel of a place where you could never go astray. A bleached snail shell could be a milestone. A spiky yellow plant she knew as Winter Sun could be a marker. In the corner of the garden was a silver birch, its branches fine and intricate and they had gathered the rain into themselves. The low sunlight caught these droplets and they flashed. As she moved there was a rainbow effect, throwing out little flints of colour. She stopped to look more closely and was amazed that the colour change happened with the slightest movement of her head. In a corner there was a bush in full blossom. It was only January, after all. She saw it long before she came to it – white petals stained with pink – but she had no idea of its name. She moved her face close and inhaled. Such a glorious smell. How could it be flowering in midwinter? Maybe the sheltered nature of the place had created its own climate. All these things were good omens. God's grandeur.

She smiled and approached the door next to the noticeboard. There were now lights inside and people moving about. But still she hesitated. She needed her questions to be clear. Just in case of language difficulties. A middle-aged man came out of the office building carrying a plastic folder. Sensing the rain, he placed the folder on top of his head. His hand was still on the door. Stella moved forward and went in, thanking him.

The woman with the glasses was behind a desk talking in Dutch to some well-dressed African men – two in suits, two in colourful tribal costume. Stella waited and the waiting seemed to take for ever. The longer it took the more apprehensive she became. She wanted to try her voice out loud to see if it would shake – give away her nervousness. At some point a man in a fawn gabardine came in and stood in the queue behind her. She had no way of knowing if this woman with the glasses behind the desk could speak English. Until, that is, Stella asked her question. And she was not sure what the question should be, how she should phrase it. The man in the gabardine smiled at her and she smiled back. He said something in Dutch. She said she did not understand.

'Are you on vacation?' he asked.

'Just for a few days.'

'It is a pity about our weather.' He shrugged his shoulders, 'Winter.' She smiled and nodded. The African party took their leave of the woman with extreme politeness and went out the door. Stella cleared her throat and stepped up to the desk.

She walked back up the dark passageway into the noise of the city. No need to consult her guide. There were shops everywhere. Many of them didn't have doors but instead had a curtain of hot air separating street and shop, hawing down on the top of her head when she entered. The gifts she wanted to buy had to be small – simple to wrap, simple to post, when she got back home. Making a family parcel with the Construct-o-Straws for Toby. She hated paying more for the postage than the gift. A postcard from Amsterdam would be nice. Wherever did the mother get a name like Tobias? Of course, Danielle was French. More correctly, French Canadian. 'Toby' was a kind of compromise that Grandmother was allowed and she only got to use it on the phone these days. The last time they'd gone back to Canada after a visit to Glasgow she'd talked to Toby on the phone. He was three. She was trying to get him to say something. Did you like visiting your grannie? Silence. Then she heard Michael's voice faintly in the background, 'It's no good nodding your head, Tobias. On the phone you have to *say* yes.'
'Yes.'
'Of course you did,' Stella said.
And she had a picture of the child at the other end of the phone standing silently holding the receiver nodding his head. It nearly broke her heart.

*　　*　　*

She found a large and classy department store. Like any other city, Amsterdam was full of shops which sold things that nobody wanted. Or the kind of things some people wanted but nobody needed. She chose a tie for Michael – a little too colourful, but she didn't want to seem conservative – and a scarf of black and white stripes for Danielle. All she needed now was a postcard to go with them.

When Gerry wakened, the roof of his mouth was like corduroy. He lay still and stunned. Last night – why had he remembered the two RUC men coming for him at work? That stuff should stay in the past – should be well and truly buried. But it was a waking thought and for Gerry first thoughts were always bad ones. The dry mouth happened every time he was in a hotel. He blamed the air conditioning. There was never any way of opening a window to moisturise the air. The fact that he had an awful lot to drink the night before had little or nothing to do with it. There were nights at home when he drank as much and he didn't wake like this. The RUC man's face was still there but he couldn't recall the younger one. In the unmarked blue Cortina the older one was twisting in the passenger seat to look round at him. Saying that Gerry was lucky they happened to be going that way. Special treatment was something they didn't believe in. The young one driving. The older man had set his hat on the dashboard. The track of it was still visible on his hair. From behind, Gerry could see that the older man had a bald spot – like a monk's tonsure. A little of his scarf appeared above his coat collar. The paisley pattern, complex, coloured, closely interwoven. Now nobody was speaking. Eventually the driver said something to his colleague in a tone of voice which excluded Gerry. Something about what they ought to do later on. When they finished this job. Gerry looked from one to the other. He realised he was 'this job'. Done under sufferance. Not meeting his eye. There was a fibrillation continuing in his stomach. He sat forward as if looking at the traffic would clear it. But he didn't speak.

When they reached the hospital the driver dropped them outside Casualty but stayed with the car. The older man, who hadn't bothered with his hat, ushered Gerry into reception. The place was busy – all bustle and plastic doors which slapped shut, trolleys with or without patients being pushed here and there, nurses in sensible shoes seen through an open door whipping curtains around bed spaces. A nurse in an apron came out of the door half running, half walking. The plain-clothes RUC man queued behind some other people waiting at the reception desk and nodded to him to sit down. Gerry got the distinct feeling he was being treated like a second-class citizen. It had something to do with his name. From the very start they knew he was Catholic. Gilmore in conjunction with Gerry equalled Fenian. Then there was the eye contact. Or lack of it. Eventually Gerry saw the cop speak through an aperture in the glass to the nurse in charge. He then left, nodding. 'These good people will look after you,' he said.

After a while a nurse led him along a corridor. She walked a pace or two in front of him – or maybe it was that he followed a pace or two behind her. Like a child. No idea where he was going. All the corridors looked the same. Peppermint green above the dado, lower down, bottle green. Two soldiers carrying guns walked past them going in the opposite direction. The corridors became less crowded and they could hear their own footsteps, the starchy sound of the nurse's outfit as she moved. He wondered if this corridor led to the mortuary. Was this the way they broke such news? Perhaps the whole thing was a mistake. The accident involved another woman who had been confused with Stella. He would get in to visit her and the woman would look like nobody he had ever seen before and he would smile and sympathise and pat her arm and leave and tell the nurse in charge – dressed in scarlet beneath a white apron – that that wasn't his wife at all. There had been an error. A case of mistaken identity. But the nurse was walking on ahead of him with solemn determination. She knew what she was about. They came to another area of seating. About half the seats were occupied. The nurse asked him to wait and she went off to another room. Gerry sat down at the end of an empty row. This space looked like a gymnasium – wall bars, ropes, treadmills. The people sitting seemed to be talking quietly, seriously. Nobody was laughing or whistling. But bizarrely there was a brightly coloured toy mounted on a table – a game where the player had to negotiate a wire monocle the length of a metal maze without touching it and setting it off.

His head moved on the hotel pillow. He tapped his tongue against the roof of his mouth to see if he could raise any moisture but there was none. His hand reached out and his fingers closed around the glass. He brought it to his mouth and the water was wonderful.

For a while he just lay there with his eyes closed. Inside the room – silence. Outside – some distant hammering – and always and everywhere pneumatic drills. Probably at the behest of some architect.

The silence inside the bedroom was unusual. He turned in the bed and looked. Stella was gone. Her half of the sheet was neatly folded back in a triangular dog-ear. He looked towards the bathroom but the bathroom door was open – not a habit of hers. She must have gone down for a paper. Or was it a Sunday? And she'd charged off to Mass? He looked at the day on her crossword newspaper – it definitely wasn't Saturday. So today was not Sunday.

He got up and sat on the side of the bed for a long time. Another drink of water was necessary – he had absorbed the first one so totally. Everything that could be done, should be done to make him feel better. He stepped out of his black pyjamas, went to the bathroom and turned on the shower. While he waited he brushed his teeth and hoped the shower would arrive at a suitable temperature. A cartoon he had seen once was a shower handle with only two settings: 'Too hot' and 'Too cold'. Never a truer word. There was no bath mat so he slow-hurdled the side of the bath with great care and barely let go the chrome handle on the tiled wall as the warm water poured down on him. He used the two toy-town bottles of shampoo and conditioner supplied by the hotel. The towel was the size of a toga when he wrapped himself in it. He gingerly got out of the bath and shaved.

When he was dressed he sank into the armchair. It was just after nine. Television at this time of the morning sickened him. The very fact of it. And it was the wrong time for his iPod music. So he endured the room's silence. Outside there were occasional voices – other hotel guests, domestic staff, the bump of a fire door closing. Maybe Stella had gone down for breakfast – had said something to him, thinking him awake when in fact he'd been asleep. He tried her mobile but it went straight to voice message. Maybe he should look in the dining room. He stood and plucked the plastic key from the power source on the wall. In the corridor the girls in lilac housecoats dodged in and out from room to trolley to the sound of vacuum cleaners. They all seemed to be foreign – from Thailand or Puerto Rico. If he made eye contact with any of them they smiled. Their lovely faces lit up.

There was a mirror in the empty lift and he saw that his white hair was sticking out all over the place. Like he'd slept on it. The hotel's conditioner had not agreed with him. Cheap rubbish, no doubt, bought by the gallon to fill their own expensive tiny bottles. He tried to smooth his hair with the palms of his hands, swore death to the security man at the airport, the bastard, who had relieved him of his own Rolls-Royce conditioner. Walking across the foyer he wondered if he might approach the female desk clerk, 'Did you see my wife going past here without me?' He was laughing at his own joke when the desk clerk looked up. She smiled at him and it did him good.

The breakfast room was large and ornate. Stucco and cut-glass chandeliers. Victorian. But that word didn't apply here. Did they date periods in the Netherlands by who was on the throne? King Billy-an? He stood at the head of a shallow marble staircase overlooking the place. Stella wasn't there. The plan they had worked out for such emergencies didn't apply. 'If we get separated, return to the last place we were together.' That meant bed.

He gathered himself some cereal from the buffet and proceeded to a table set for two beside the window. Since Belfast, he always sat in a chair facing the door. Prunes on top of cornflakes. Good for the bowls and jugs. The sucked prune stones transferred from spoon to plate had a disturbing similarity, in colour and shape, to cockroaches.

Now that they had mobile phones, theoretically it should have been easier to keep tabs on one another. But practically it had not helped. In the first instance you had to remember to bring the bloody thing with you. If you had it with you, invariably one or other of the mobiles was switched off or needed charging. And then, even if you did get through, Stella's phone had some mysterious setting which diverted incoming calls straight to 'Leave a message'. And her phone did not ring. And she did not answer it. They were of a generation who had used crank-handled phones in Donegal.

A waitress came to his table – her hair, like watch springs, piled high on her head. Young people. There was something about the glint in their eye, the cut of their jib, their enthusiasm, the resilience of their skin.

'Tea or coffee, sir?'

How had she guessed his language group right away? Did he look *so* British? But he was Irish. And proud of it. Despite the pub last night. Despite the last fifty years.

'Black tea?' he said.

After the waitress brought his pot of tea he walked to the buffet. He normally avoided fried foods but felt that because he was on holiday he could indulge himself a little. And Stella wasn't there to protect him from the saturated fats. Or was it unsaturated fats? Trans fats were even worse, it seemed. But he didn't know where they resided, so they were difficult to avoid.

Where *was* she? She'd never done this before – wandered off on her own. Was it to meet somebody she'd met the last time she'd been here with the teachers? An affair? At her age? Who conducted pre-breakfast affairs?

He was almost swooning with pleasure as he forked the bacon and eggs into his mouth. His own little affair. Fried potatoes and two eggs at breakfast. When he finished he had another cup of tea, taken leisurely. All the papers in the rack were in Dutch so were of no use to him. He just stared around. It was such a rarity for Stella and him to be apart. And before he knew it, he was back in that waiting room in the Belfast hospital. An older woman in a pink overall had

57

brought him a mug of milky tea. She sat down and updated him on the situation but could say little more than that his wife was in theatre. She explained she was one of the 'pink ladies', volunteers who helped in A & E. Her name was Mavis. All he could do was shake his head. When he asked if his wife would live, the woman said she had no way of knowing. It was someone he loved, he said, as if to explain his persistent questioning. The woman put her hand on his arm. She seemed concerned about whether he took sugar or not. He hadn't the heart to tell her he didn't take milk. Still, after she walked away, he drank the tea and smoked another cigarette. Rubber-soled shoes squeaked as people walked to and fro. The woman came back to him again. She said that she had just had a word with one of the nurses and that his wife left a message for him when she was being prepped. She said to tell you that all shall be well. The woman said that his wife had said it twice. That all shall be well and all shall be well. Said you would understand. They would keep him informed the Pink Lady said. Gerry nodded. A teenage boy came out of one of the doors with a white sling and a bright new plaster on his arm. He left with what looked like his mother and father. The boy was very pale.

It must have been more than an hour later and Gerry was still sitting there smoking cigarette after cigarette, listening to ambulance sirens. Seeing lights flashing from somewhere. Difficult to distinguish incoming from outgoing, difficult to know if it was a bomb or a heart attack. The real danger of course was no sirens. That meant no warning. There would be dead and wounded. Plenty of work for the big scissors. He'd heard a nurse friend of Stella's use this phrase at a party. She didn't work in Casualty but knew nurses who did. Talked about cutting people out of all their clothes. He tried to remember what Stella had been wearing when he left home earlier that morning.

At one point a little girl and her mother came in. The child made a beeline for the other side of the room where the brightly coloured toy was. Again and again the toy buzzed as the girl failed. Her mother was taking no interest in what the child was doing except to say occasionally, 'That's enough now.' She sat sideways on her seat and stared off in the direction of the window.

He asked the waitress for a toothpick. Bacon always did that to him. When he finished his tea he went up to the room. The place had not yet been serviced. He'd left the bedclothes mountainous at his side. The bath towel lay on the floor. He glanced at his watch. Almost Ailment Hour. It was Stella's idea to allot no more than sixty minutes a day to their various illnesses. But he had nothing new to report. He noticed hairs, approaching luxuriant, growing from beneath his watch. So much so, that he took it off and inspected where it had bitten into his skin. That might be something he could report. He smiled. Sub-watch hirsutism. With concomitant angst.

He pulled back the curtains. Light flooded in. It was not raining. The packet of Gauloises and the yellow child's plastic bucket. They might have been there for years. And will be, for years into the future. Unless the hotel changes hands.

He didn't want to show he was inadequate when on his own so he tied his navy scarf around his neck and put on his hat and coat. Stella had left last night's map on the desk. He pocketed it and went downstairs. She wasn't in the lobby or the coffee lounge.

Outside, the block of ice was still there. The street iceberg. He surmised somebody had done exactly the same thing as

59

he had done and pushed it, because it had moved several metres since last night. What was it? How had it got there? Something square had filled with rain, which had frozen and been emptied out or cut free. There was no sign of it melting. He toed it gently again and it slid unsteadily, rumbled a little. He stepped around it. Then stopped and looked more closely. There was a faint blue tinge to it in the daylight. Maybe it was frozen piss dropped from an aeroplane. That blue disinfectant flush. He could kid Stella about it – tell her that's what it was.

He followed the signs northwards towards the station. A girl in denims and red anorak cycled towards him, her mobile to her ear, steering with one hand. She rang her bell at him. Gerry stepped back and looked down to see bicycle path markings. He thought she was amazing, sitting high in the saddle, her hair streaming out behind her. Indeed all of the girls cycling were amazing – like Valkyries, Amazons. Who needed a red-light district?

He had to cross a main road rumbling with traffic and reached out to take Stella by the hand before realising she wasn't with him. His hand went to his pocket to disguise the empty gesture. The traffic lights changed. The green man was universal. The Irishman. This one had a little green pork-pie hat.

Having negotiated the road, he wondered *when* he had first held Stella's hand. But he couldn't remember. It was certainly not to cross roads, that service came later. Logic told him when it would have happened. The first time he had laid eyes on her was at a dance in Fruithill, a Catholic tennis club. One shirtsleeved summer night. His memory manufactured or filled in the details. Her pale frock. The gold cross at her neck. And when he saw her, he had to dance with her. And to dance with her he had to hold her hand in his. One of the first things they established was that neither of them played tennis. And they laughed and made jokes about this. She was from Dungiven, a small town in County Derry, taught English in a girls' comprehensive in Belfast, shared a flat on the Antrim Road with some civil servants. He was so taken with her that he asked her to dance a second time – which was quite forward of him – and she had been sufficiently taken with him to consent. Usually when a set of three dances finished everyone returned to the crowded margins of the hall. But having agreed to dance together again they stood at the edge of the floor waiting for the music to start. And it took a long time. And, as they waited, he must have taken her left hand in his right and gone on talking. Who knew what they talked about? It was a matter of not frightening her away, of not causing embarrassment, of keeping her face to face, of retaining her. And to do it by entertaining. And when his second dance with her started they changed hands. The band was a showband and played a set of three songs before the dance was over. He remembered this particular set as slow – a waltz or slow foxtrot. He had devoutly wished for it to be slow but, really, the sprung floor was so crowded that there was very little dancing going on. People moved when and where they could. It was a licence to be close to someone you didn't know. 'Spanish Harlem' was very popular at the time. And the Everly Brothers' songs. All showbands did covers. Nobody wrote their own stuff then. Even after all this time Gerry could remember the sensation of his hand on her back through the material of her frock and the mix of perfumes and scents that filled the hall. And her hair – he remembered smelling her hair when they were dancing. After the second dance he offered to buy her a mineral. He smiled, remembering Catholic dances which didn't serve alcohol. She took an orange juice. And he had the same. And the hall had become so hot and smoke-filled that they stepped outside onto the balcony with their drinks. Into the night air – not quite dark because it was June – which was filled with the smell of lilac from the bushes around the clubhouse. The red clay courts had been closed down for the night but there were still a few lights left on. Insects were whirling around the bright bulbs. In the dusk he could see the pale of her neck as she looked down at the courts. Her skin was amazing – flawless, translucent, smooth. It seemed to have light coming from it in the dark. He asked her to go out with him. And she smiled with her eyes and nodded that she would like that.

'Ever been to Ballycastle?' he said.

He walked the streets of Amsterdam his fists closed against the cold. The architecture was unique. In strange cities he was always looking up. At first in Glasgow he had been amazed at the number of spires. Here it was the different gables – neck and bell gables, ornate and plain gables, enough to form ramparts against the sky. Some were stepped, which he felt was Scottish. All of them with a hoist beam for moving furniture in and out with block and tackle. All of them roofed with orange terracotta tiles. He loved the houses reflected in the canal water.

In the bracing air he began to feel better. Except for Stella's absence. Was she all right? He'd seen movies – thrillers – where somebody near and dear to the hero disappears. On a shopping trip – last time glimpsed, she was pushing a supermarket trolley. Kidnapped. He'd read of weird things in Holland. Those cartoons. That well-known guy who'd been slain on the street – a member of parliament or a film producer or something. He consulted the map then headed north along the Spui. There was an icy wind coming from the North Sea, down along the canal, brushing the water to darkness. His whole body was clenched against the weather. If he relaxed he wouldn't feel so bad, but it was hard to relax in such temperatures. Stella had a theory that if you had courage and stretched your feet down to the bottom of the bed then they would warm quicker than if you lay there 'like a half-shut penknife'. He lowered his head to avoid the wind and saw his shoes pace the pavement beneath him. Nowadays wind brought tears to his eyes. When he blinked, tears spilled and he had to mop his eyes with a hanky before he could see clearly again. Unlike Stella whose problem was no tears at all. She had to carry hers about with her.

He arrived in a large square full of shops and cafés. Different establishments had different-coloured tables set out on the stone flags in front of them. There was a Waterstones book-shop on the corner. He liked the familiarity of the big W and the black frontage. The same in every city. Like the way Mass used to be before they dropped the Latin. He crossed the square to it.

The Art and Architecture sections were on the second floor. He climbed the stairs and browsed for a while until he got his breath back. Then he went to the window and took in the view beneath him. It was an impressive space. His gaze travelled around the square until he saw something familiar out of the corner of his eye. It was Stella.

It gave him such a jolt. Such a strange feeling. Like when he saw her across the space of Glasgow airport going into the duty-free area. She looked so tiny in the distance – like a stranger, like a woman seen through the wrong end of a telescope. He remembered meeting her once in Glasgow by accident. He had left the drawing office to go on an errand of some sort – biscuits, maybe – and on St Vincent Street he'd met her coming out of John Smith's bookshop, now no longer there. She was supposed to be at home. In the picture he had of her she was wearing a plum-coloured coat with a scarf to match and it was a moment or two before she noticed him – she was looking over her shoulder at some books in the window display. They were about five paces away from each other when she turned and their eyes met. Her eyebrows went up with delight and she smiled her smile. He was elated and stood there blushing because he felt such elation. It was like the first time they'd met. And yet they'd been married about twenty years. She had come to him with her hands out.

'What are you doing here?' she'd said.

'Admiring you.' He took her offered hands and held her close so that their cheeks brushed. 'I might ask the same question of you.'

He tried to remember what had happened next. Had they gone for a coffee? Or lunch? But the picture was lost. What remained of it was the shyness and admiration which existed between them after such a long time together.

He noticed now that at the far side of this Amsterdam square she was standing, her head looking down. Then she began to nod. She was talking to a man in a fawn gabardine standing next to her. Gerry set his book on the windowsill and watched. Was it somebody she knew? Maybe somebody she'd met – the last time she was here? She had a memory for such stuff. But what if it was something more? Not a matter of recognising – but somebody she knew well. He dismissed the thought and went down the stairs. When he came out of Waterstones he could still see her. The man

64

walked away from her and disappeared. Stella set off across the square with Gerry following. People were walking in all directions and he had to keep his eye on her in case he lost her again. He had perfected a two-finger whistle at school – the gym teacher had taught them how to do it – loud enough to referee basketball matches. *Weet.* And knowing it, Stella turned. In a square in Amsterdam. Like a bird on a crowded beach who knows the sound of its own chick.

'Do you fancy a coffee?' he said.

'Only if it's a small cup.'

Gerry sat down in an empty seat by the window and Stella went to the counter. Coffee places were so noisy. This one sounded like they were making the *Titanic* rather than cups of coffee – the grinder going at maximum volume, screaming on and on – making enough coffee grounds for the whole of Europe while another guy was shooting steam through milk with supersonic hissing. A girl unpacked a dishwasher, clacking plates and saucers into piles. A third barista was banging the metal coffee-holder against the rim of the stainless steel bar to empty it – but doing it with such venom and volume that Gerry jumped at every strike. Talking was impossible. It was so bad he couldn't even hear if there was muzak or not. And still the grinder went on and on trying to reduce a vessel of brown-black beans to dust. Stella had to yell her order.

Gerry looked out onto the square. Pigeons pecked and waddled after crumbs in between the green café tables and chairs. Stella eventually came to the table.

'In the coffee shops of heaven they will not grind coffee beans,' she said. 'But coffee will be available.'

She'd ordered a croissant for herself, with butter and strawberry jam. She began to eat almost immediately. The coffee was good, the croissant even better. Through bites she said, 'I assume you had breakfast.'

Gerry nodded.

'That size of cup okay for you?' he shouted.

Stella sipped her latte and nodded. The coffee grinder ceased.

'Thank God for that,' he said. His ears now sang in the absence of noise. 'So where did you get to?'

'I went for a walk.'

This did not seem a sufficient explanation.

'I woke early and you were sound asleep – snoring your head off,' she said. 'So I figured I'd leave you to it. Grinding coffee and snoring are some of my least favourite sounds.'

'I've missed the Ailment Hour.'

'We can do a two-hour stint tomorrow. If you feel well enough.'

'I've got these strange hairs growing beneath my watch . . .'

'I was only joking.'

'So was I. Did you not have breakfast? In the hotel?'

She shook her head – no.

'Where did you go?'

'A walk. It was glorious. To see a city starting the day. Then I ended up in a wonderful place. Over there.' She pointed to the far side of the square. 'You walk down a passageway into a quadrangle place – trees, houses all around a green, with their backs to the world. You remember in Cromarty the fishermen's houses had their backs to the sea – they preferred shelter to a view. That's what these houses were like. And an old church. But it was shut – too early in the day.'

'Does God work office hours?'

'He's on call, I'm sure.'

'And the man?'

'What man?'

'The guy you were talking to. In the square. In the cream raincoat.'

'He was behind me in the queue. He was very patient.'

'What queue?'

'In the place – in there – they have an office.' Gerry looked at her, his head on one side. Stella smiled and said, 'No. He was just being friendly. His English was very good.'

'What's the office?'

'Deals with the organisation. Don't ask me to pronounce its name. To do with the Beguines. In there.' Her voice was becoming sharp and she was aware of it.

'And this afternoon?'

'This afternoon I will endure a gallery.' She smiled. 'But only if you let me show you this place.'

'Which place?'

'The place I've just been.'

They gathered themselves and left a tip of some small change, unsure whether it was an insulting sum or an unbelievable generosity. As they crossed the square a flock of pigeons feeding on the ground blocked Stella's path.

'Hello, pidge,' she said to one that had strayed out from the melee. Then in an explosion of wings all the pigeons rose and took to the air.

'Why do they do that?'

'What?'

'The simultaneous thing. One goes, they all go.'

'They must be Catholics.'

The sun came out and no sooner were they in brightness than Stella led Gerry into the darkness of the passageway. In the tunnel space their voices sounded strange and vibrant, as did their footsteps. They emerged into the sun and Stella gestured with her hand. Look, see, behold. Above all, listen.

Gerry stared, his head back, his mouth slightly open. There was something familiar about it. The impression was of a bowl, a secluded place filled with light surrounded by buildings in the old Dutch style. Elaborately decorated gables – full of swags and scrolling – each house different by design and time.

'A great space,' he said. 'I like the about-to-fall-down nature of the houses. The way they lean against each other – like a lot of drunks. And the hoist beams – like unicorns.'

'That's where I made my enquiries. In there.' Stella pointed to the doorway opposite the passageway.

'What about?'

'Matters of life and death.'

'And other trivia.'

'The person I wanted to talk to wasn't there. But she'll be in on Monday.'

'Will we be here till then?'

'Yes – how many times do I have to tell you?'

At the centre of the grassy area was a stone statue of Christ with hands pointing inwards towards his stone heart. Now Gerry knew where he had seen it before. It was what Stella had left on the computer screen the night before they came away.

She showed him the colourful biblical plaques and the ancient church. There was another statue. A woman, her head covered with a veil. Stella had not really noticed it on her first visit. She went closer. And then realised the statue was of one of the early Beguines. A woman – was she of stone or bronze? – in the act of walking, her left hand lifting the hem of her dress.

'In the early days this place was below sea level, the guide-book says. Flooded all the time,' said Stella. 'She's a woman who's getting things done. Isn't she great?'

They continued to wander along the path. Gerry pulled a face.

'There's a feel of Van Gogh's prison yard here.'

'Nonsense.'

'This path. Round and round. Like Albert Speer.'

'Who?'

'Hitler's architect. Remember the story about him in prison?'

Stella shook her head, no. Gerry told her about the time Speer had spent in the garden at Spandau after the war. Each day, as he took his daily exercise, walking in circles, he wondered about the distance covered. He measured his own stride and the length of the path and calculated the mental journey as if he was walking around the world – visualising all the places. He read everything in the library he could get his hands on about what lay ahead – the geography, the cuisine, the culture – so that he would know what to imagine when he got there.

Before his sentence was served he'd got as far as Mexico – about 20,000 miles.

Somewhere a door slammed and a young woman strode towards them. She smiled at Stella.

'Is the church open yet?' Stella asked.

'Wheech church?'

'Is there more than one?'

'There is two.' The young woman pointed to the brick church, 'This is the Scots Kirk,' and then to a doorway which seemed to form part of a terrace of houses. 'This is Roman Catholic.'

'Is that a church?'

The young woman nodded and gestured for them to enter.

'You must like us much.' She smiled and walked on, keeping the smile on her face.

'What did she mean by that?' said Gerry.

'She was in the office earlier,' said Stella. 'And now I'm back.'

'You're definitely well in here.'

'We talked a bit. She was nice.'

'And what, may I ask, was the nature of your enquiry?'

'Oh, it wasn't with her. She was just being friendly. My enquiry was spiritual – and would be of little interest to you.'

Stella walked up to the row of houses. She reached out to the door the young woman had indicated and pushed it open. There was a faint squeaking noise. Gerry stepped into the porch behind her and followed her into the dark space of a church. The altar was, unusually, on the long wall. A sacristy lamp gleamed red – a sure sign that the place was Catholic.

Stella blessed herself and knelt briefly to say a prayer. There was no one else in the place. As they walked around, their footsteps bumped and squidged on the boards of the floor. Stella found a rack of leaflets in different languages. She skimmed the one in English.

'I remember hearing of this when I was last here,' she said. Because they were on their own she didn't whisper but read the words aloud. In the 1600s, it seems, Catholic worship was banned by the Protestant powers that be. No public Masses were allowed so they resorted to using their own houses.

'A bit like the Mass rocks in Ireland?'

'That's why it doesn't look like a church outside,' said Stella. 'It's camouflaged. Last time I remember going to a church in the red-light district called, Our Dear Lord in the Attic.'

Gerry raised his eyebrows. 'Brothels with a sanctuary lamp?'

He was gazing upwards at a series of painted panels on the wall. The whole thing seemed to be telling a story. The largest image was of a woman sitting on a wooden chair in front of the fire. She was leaning forward, lifting something from the flames under the watchful gaze of two angels. The thing she was lifting resembled a white sea urchin, spiky with light. The other panels showed a man sitting up in bed being given communion by a priest. Then another man – or was it the same man? – what was he doing? Being sick? Gerry waved to Stella, beckoning her.

'What's all this?'

'I've no idea.' Stella's head moved, following the narrative.

'That priest is doing your job,' said Gerry. 'Giving out communion. Can you make out what's happening? Spewy street in this one.'

'What?'

'He's throwing up.' Gerry pointed. 'It's a graphic novel – a storyboard sequence.'

Stella put on her glasses and began to read the leaflet aloud.

'*In the year 1345 in the city of Amsterdam a man lay dying in a house on Kalverstraat.*'

'A good opening sentence,' said Gerry.

'*A priest came and gave the man communion. And after he had gone the sick man felt unwell so the maid brought him a bowl and he vomited up the sacred host.*'

'Lovely,' said Gerry.

'*At a loss to know what to do with something so sacred afloat in something so vile – something so divine in the midst of something so human – the maid consigned the contents of the bowl to the fire . . .*'

'Must be a translation,' said Gerry. 'Nobody consigns contents.'

Stella looked up over her glasses at him. She read the rest silently to herself. Then told Gerry.

'The man, it seemed, died later that night. But in the morning when the maid was clearing out the grate she saw the host – still there – untouched by the flames.'

'Fireproof, sickproof wafers. Might be a market for . . . '

'Stop it, Gerry.'

'And then . . .?'

'The priest had a church built to commemorate the miracle.'

'Which was?'

'The indestructible host.'

'Minor league, that.'

'Miracles come in all sizes. I should know.'

'What happened to you was not miraculous. It was within the bounds of possibility,' said Gerry. 'Miracles seem easier to believe in the Middle Ages. Glad about the church, though. Keeps us architects going, that kind of thing.'

Gerry wandered to the back of the church where it was dark. The wood was old. Blackened floor planks and roof beams were of irregular sizes. There was a book on a wooden shelf.

Buch der Gebete
Book for your prayers.
Liver por vows prières

A ballpoint pen lay beside it. Gerry looked at the page and the various hands and the different languages and colours of ink – some were pencil. French and German he recognised easily but could not follow the meaning. He turned pages, looking into the past. Most of the entries were short, a line or two. He laughed out loud and Stella shushed him. He pointed to the book and read, 'May Arsenal win just one piece of silverware this season.'

Stella smiled. Gerry turned the pages and his eye was drawn to a longer entry. It was in English but the style of handwriting was American. Characteristic slanted loops and downstrokes in ballpoint. Immediately he knew it was a girl because she says she is pregnant. She asks God for help. Further down the page there were other entries in the same hand. For three days in a row this girl had come and prayed. In the second entry she is critical – *Yesterday I prayed and nothing happened. The miracle of Amsterdam, indeed!!!* Three exclamation marks. This woman was obviously in some distress. Two exclamation marks would have been enough. But it wasn't the baby which was the problem. Her lover had abandoned her. By the third entry she has become indignant: what sort of a God was he to pass up this chance to bring three such beautiful people together – her, her lover and the unborn baby. She was close to despair – the child's father was not willing to take up his responsibility. He was running away. And it was not as if she was pursuing him. What sort of a God would make him feel that way? Was there a God at all? *We haven't done anything to You.* In this entry she sounded confrontational and at the same time sad. *Make everything right and I'll believe in You,* she wrote.

Gerry called Stella and pointed out the sequence to her.

'Poor thing,' she said, after reading it. She patted the written surface of the paper like it was the girl's hand then returned the book to the most recent page.

They walked back along a canal in the direction of the hotel and came to a bridge where hundreds of bicycles were parked or abandoned. It was as if they had silted up during some massive flood – as if they had been unable to negotiate the ram-stam rush through the eye of the bridge and had ended up snagged by its side. Some of them appeared to have been there for years. Flat tyres, rusted frames, twisted front wheels – frames with no front wheels – poor bare forked animals, Stella called them. Gerry offered her his hand and she took it.

'You're freezing,' he said. He put their joined hands in his pocket. 'The other two hands will have to fend for themselves.'

A girl cyclist rattled past them over cobbles. Then in what could only be an act of bravado she reached up both hands and adjusted her ponytail.

'Wow,' said Stella. 'If a car and a cyclist have an accident here, the law *always* blames the car driver.'

'You're kidding.'

'Always.'

'Looking at the state of some of these bikes . . .'

'Bread-carts,' said Stella, 'bread-carts of bicycles. Things left over from the last war.'

'Or the one before that.'

They came to a main road and waited to cross it. He took her hand from his pocket but still held onto it.

'You're a good deal warmer,' he said. A gap opened up in the traffic and he walked her to the middle. There was a black four-by-four approaching but they had time to cross. Gerry strode forward but Stella was nervous and held back. He tightened his grip on her hand but she had frozen in the middle of the road.

'Come on.' She wrenched her hand away from his. Her whole body was immovable so Gerry walked on across the road. He waited for her on the far pavement. She stood in the road looking this way and that. The black four-by-four cruised past her and she came almost running to Gerry's side.

'Some day you'll get us both killed,' he said.

'I can judge for myself,' she said. 'But you can't judge for me.'

They stopped and looked at lunch menus in windows. Some displayed their fare in English. One place looked promising but just as they were about to sit down music started up. Frenetic pounding. American rap with the occasional mutha-fucka. They turned and left. On the street Gerry said, 'That stuff is *so* relentlessly the same. I don't give a fuck about the fucks. It's the volume.'

'Just as well. They have cups the size of chamber pots.'

'The whole idea of size is American. To sell twice as much as you wanna drink. And charge you half as much again. Paying for what you throw away.'

'My mother had a mantra about Mister Coleman – how he became a millionaire from the mustard left on the side of your plate.'

'And popcorn. In buckets. Big enough to annoy your neighbour throughout the *whole* film.' Gerry mimed furi-ous hand-to-mouth eating. 'Another American stunt – eating watching movies. In every cinema your feet are stuck to the ground. *It's such a waste sitting here watching the screen – we could be getting fat at the same time. Go get another. Gasometer size. And bring me a ten-gallon Coke.* It's no wonder American arses are the biggest in the world. *What size Levi's, madam? You got two measuring tapes there, baby? One ain't gonna be enough.*

They eventually found somewhere that pleased them – off the Amstel Canal.

'Gooood-sized wee cups,' said Gerry. The place was a cross between a club and a hostel. No tablecloths. The staff were friendly.

'It's so nice to sit down,' said Stella. 'I've been on my pegs all morning.'

The waitress brought menus and Stella and Gerry produced their reading glasses.

'Some wine?' Gerry said.

'At lunchtime?'

'We're on our holidays.'

'Are there no half-bottles?'

'Not that I can see. Where does that leave me?' said Gerry. 'Finishing the bloody bottle, that's where. Priests drink more wine saying Mass than you do – just a wee splash.'

'They have small carafes.'

Gerry ordered one of house red and when it came he sipped his glass and made noises of pleasure. Stella joined him, sipping a half glass. They chinked.

'Moderation in all things,' said Gerry. 'Especially moderation.'

Music was on faintly in the background. Something familiar.

'It's an improvement on the muthafuckas.'

'Have you *noticed* the muzak?' said Stella. 'Apart from that last place all the stuff they play seems to be from the fifties and sixties. "A white sport coat and a pink carnation", "Bye bye love", "Just a-walking in the rain".'

'Bill Haley and Elvis.'

'And Buddy Holly.'

'Things so old they could be from "the hit parade".' They laughed a little at the dated words. 'Hit parade.'

'We always listened to stuff like that in the dark,' said Stella. 'Hugging cushions. "The Great Pretender" was the first time I ever got the shivers on the wireless.' She smiled.

'I thought you were too poor to have a radio.'

'Daddy got an old one from somebody. I remember the day it came into the house. The Platters.'

'They were the boys.'

'And the words – you got to know them off by heart. She half sang, half spoke the opening of 'The Great Pretender.'

A waiter arrived with their food and they stopped talking. They ate quickly, taking the edge off their hunger.

'The child would be two,' Stella said.

'What?'

'The pregnant girl in the comments book.'

'Are you still thinking about her?'

'According to the date of her entry.'

'Or nine months after it.'

Stella ignored the remark.

'The sadness in some people's lives,' she said.

'We can't be responsible for everybody's grief.'

'That's the only way forward.'

'Stella – don't be daft.'

'I don't mean responsible – I mean, take it into account, somehow. Maybe even try to do something about it. I like John Wesley . . .'

'John who?'

'The founder of Methodism. *Do all the good you can, by all the means you can, in all the places you can,* and so on and so on.'

'I can go along with that. Except for the definition of *good.* Your friend the pope . . .' said Gerry.

'Pope Francis? He's doing his best.'

' . . . he might see *good* as banning condoms. But others would see it as just more people to feed. More suffering. More

77

AIDS. More death.' Gerry wiped his lips with a paper napkin. 'But we're on our holidays. Spare me the gloom.'

'Just before we lighten up – where do you want to be buried?'

Gerry rolled his eyes and shrugged.

'And you? At home or in Scotland?' he asked.

'Scotland *is* home now,' she said.

'Would you mind if I, or my ashes, was buried with you?'

'If you're still drinking I don't want you next nor near me.'

'I'll definitely have given it up by the time I'm dead.'

'In that case . . .' She smiled. 'I'll move over.'

'Thanks.'

Gerry poured the remainder of the carafe into his glass. Stella was trying to mop up the tiny bits of salad with bread.

'How did you end up in . . . that place?'

'Which place are we talking about?'

'Where we were – just now.'

'The Begijnhof?'

'How do you know how to pronounce it?'

'The woman told me. When I started asking questions.' Stella stopped eating.

'What kind of questions?'

'About origins. Medieval times. It began as a home of the Beguines.'

'You're just trying to confuse me now.'

'A Catholic sisterhood who lived alone as nuns, but without vows. They had the right to return to the world and marry if they wanted to. I think the place has a great sanctuary feel to it.'

Because she had been up so early and 'on her pegs' all morning Stella said she needed a rest and a doze before taking on the afternoon. They went back to the hotel and she pulled the curtains to dim the room. She folded herself into the coverlet and was asleep almost immediately. Gerry did not join her. He sat in the gloom watching flickering pictures on the silenced television. News items, unrelated to the scrolling text constantly moving from right to left. Words on a red travelator. A Russian archbishop dressed like a Christmas tree waving his crozier. Agitation, crowds, riots of some description. Guns being fired. A reporter and his microphone ducking away.

Gerry sought out his ancient iPod. It was one of the first – big, like a white enamel washing machine. The knack of getting the music he wanted mostly eluded him. He couldn't swirl his finger properly, couldn't leap to the piece of music he was after so he just listened to whatever came on, through the headphones. But he had chosen the pieces in the first place so it didn't feel completely random. He slipped the iPod into his pocket and, with great care, poured himself a whiskey. Nothing obstreperous, just something to keep him going. He sipped. The music on the headphones became Bach.

Once, in a mammoth session, a friend had warned him against drinking on his own. Other people act as brakes, he said. People like you and me set the pace. Nobody'll be as bad as us. This man had been in to dry out – several times – so he knew what he was talking about. This friend had said that people who drank the way *they* did hated themselves. Getting drunk was a form of temporary suicide. But the good thing was you got a chance to begin all over again the next day. How could he avoid drinking on his own when Stella hardly drank at all? He mock-toasted her. Here's to you. Remember the time in Germany? Was it words spoken aloud? Or thought? Some conference or other. Or an architectural jury. Maybe Stella wasn't with him. Weimar, was it? And a trip to the concentration camp at Buchenwald had been arranged. And everyone got off the train and there was a tour bus waiting.

79

It was so hot and the bus full. Everybody sitting silent and afraid of what they were going to see. You could hear people breathing. And Gerry heard a wasp. It flew amongst them – and everybody leaned back or moved their face to one side to avoid it. It nosed up and down the windows, bouncing a bit, and nobody had the courage to whap the bastard because of where they were going and what had happened there. The Bach ended and he switched the thing off. Pouring from the bottle was dodgy – it had to be angled – so too the receiving glass. Or the time in Spain. It was a wedding – outside the cathedral. Stella was more interested in the bride's dress than the medieval architecture. There was a burst of machine-gun fire. Incredibly loud with flashes and smoke all over the Plaza del Obradoiro. Who would want to murder such a couple? Not good for people coming from Belfast. Time for a change of underwear. Smoke drifting close to the ground. Fireworks, not machine-gun fire. Jumping jinnies, squibs. Just like at home in Ireland – the firing of shotguns at country weddings – to scare away evil spirits.

The TV picture had turned again to news. Violence. Buildings had grown flames and black smoke. There were tanks. Where was it? Beirut? Syria or Iraq? Religions'll fight among themselves till all's no more. He didn't want to turn up the sound and waken Stella. He'd seen his fair share of that kind of stuff. When he worked at the office in the Diamond in Derry, it was firebombed. Who or why was never found out. Maybe a couple of fourteen-year-old Savonarolas, egging each other on. He drained his drink, heard his teeth hit the glass as it upended. He resisted pouring himself another and tried to imagine how the petrol bombing could have happened. The Provos were prone to that kind of nonsense. They even tried to burn down the Linen Hall Library in Belfast. Before he realised it, he had poured himself another drink. Accidentally. Apologies. Since when did a fight for Irish freedom include the burning of books? The destruction of buildings. The IRA were disarchitects. Destroyers. *Show me a building and I'll turn it into a car park.* A smashing of window glass followed by a whoosh as the contents of the bottle caught. *How many houses are you getting to the gallon these days?* He imagined it as cinema. The burning of a whole city of scale models. What fuel, what tinder. Plan chests. Rolls of trace, T-squares, set squares and protractors, templates and stencils. Cars the size of Dinky toys, trees as small as interdental brushes. Not only would there be the real fire but there would be the fire reflected in the cellophane windows. Tiny trees would hiss and disappear, leaving only blackened wire. Aflame the way Bombay Street had been aflame. From end to end. Catholics burned out by a Loyalist mob. Both men and women figurines melting. Like the chocolate on the biscuits in the Victoria biscuit tin they all gathered round at coffee time. The box bulges then bursts, flinging biscuits everywhere. The dry balsa wood catches instantly and there are streets and churches and schools and halls of residence roaring and sizzling because now the curtains have become hanging flames and the venetian blinds twist of their own accord. Models of architecture. Burt Chapel itself with its copper roof an inferno – apple-green flames leap. The labels scorch, then finally ignite. Steeples topple, bell towers collapse. The heat moves into drawers, the handles become red-hot, the trace drawings curl and brown, become *millefeuille.* Strata, layer upon layer of work. Hour upon hour, day after day. The architects, both Scandinavian and local, their inspiration and ideas, ruled plans and freehand work all reduced to ash. Cupboards full of pages of materials, of notes, of quantities, of measurements. Changed by flame to nothing. In the name of a struggle, in the name of religion. Creating an absence. Figurines are not important. They melt away. Like the fire's perpetrators. When Stella heard, all she said was, 'Nobody was killed, thank God.' The next morning Gerry picked his steps through the devastation, seeking something to salvage. The blackened wood looking like alligator skin, the light shades draped like Dali watches on the desks, the venetian blinds – the ones which survived the melting – buckled and warped. Some biscuits at the toe of his shoe looked good enough to eat. A place of creation savaged. And the smell. Nothing like the smell of work wasted. It took weeks to leave his clothes. And even then he wasn't sure whether it had gone or not.

'Gerry, are you still on for the museum?'

Gerry pulled away his earphones. He'd nodded off, Stella was coming out of the bathroom. She straightened the coverlet the way one would smooth out a dog-eared page in a book. And pulled back the curtains.

'Yes,' he said. 'Yes, of course. Why not?'

The Rijksmuseum was far enough away to travel by tram.

'How do you pronounce it?' said Gerry.

'Like in *Casablanca*. Rick's Café – Rick's museum.'

Stella bought a *strippen* of tickets from a machine at the stop – enough to do a couple of days.

'Maybe we won't punch them, just hold onto them in case an inspector gets on. He'll see our foreignness.'

Gerry paced about, trying to keep warm, looking down at the tracks and up at the overhead wires.

'Remind me,' said Stella, 'to buy a *Guardian* for the crossword.'

'Will that not cost you?'

'Yes. But it's my mental gym.'

A blue and grey tram pulled in with a rumbling rubber sound. It was crowded and people looked up at them when they got on. They had to stand. Stella made an extravagant gesture of looking around for the device that would stamp or validate their tickets. Finding none, she shrugged at Gerry. He shrugged back at her,

'How terribly inconvenient,' he said.

'Would you look at that,' Stella said. She nodded towards the front window of the tram. Two cyclists – a boy and a girl – sailing along in front of the tram, weaving in and out.

'Like a couple of dolphins in front of a ship,' she said. 'They were holding hands a minute ago.'

'We were being romantic, your honour.'

'It *is* romantic,' said Stella. Gerry hung on, steadying himself against the stops and starts of the tram. He shouldn't have had the whiskey.

They took the lift to the top floor of the Rijksmuseum. Gerry's technique was to work his way down through the galleries, moving always to his left, until each room was accomplished. In the beginning they walked together. But sometimes Gerry discarded whole walls of pictures at a glance and Stella wondered why as she walked behind him.

'Self-satisfied burghers,' he said. 'Dutch still lifes – paintings of vegetables like faces . . .'

Many people wore earphones and carried audio controls but Gerry whizzed past and around them.

At other times he was much slower. He would linger in front of a painting that took his fancy, bend over and look at it more closely, right down to the very brushstrokes, while Stella stood and moved her weight from foot to foot. Occasionally his hand would go to his pocket and produce his glasses case and he would put on his glasses and read the painting's label. Once he leaned close to her, 'Every time I open my glasses case nowadays,' he said. 'I am pleasantly surprised to find my glasses.'

Sometimes he wanted to retrace their steps so he could show her some detail.

'We don't have the time,' she'd say.

'On our holidays?'

'Or maybe the inclination.'

84

He succeeded in persuading her back to look at *The Jewish Bride.*

There was a crowd gathered around it. It was huge, big as a hoarding, a great slash of browns and yellows and reds. Two figures, a man and a woman on the edge of intimacy, or perhaps just after, about to coorie in to one another. Hands. Hands everywhere. A painting about touch. Stella joined the crowd and wormed her way to the front. Gerry watched her bite her lip as she gazed. She became aware of Gerry watching her. He excused himself and threaded his way to her side.

'Well?'

'There's a great tenderness in him,' she said. 'You can see he cherishes her.'

'Look at that hand of his,' Gerry said. 'And the sleeve. Like a big croissant. The way he's put the paint on.'

'And the faces,' she said. 'But *she's* not so sure. Shy, yes. Sure, no. What sumptuous clothes.' She pointed out the groom's hand around the woman's shoulder and his other hand resting on her breast. The bride's touch of the groom's hand.

'She's allowing him to have his hand there,' she whispered. 'And her other one's protecting her stomach.'

'Yes.' Gerry nodded.

'Somehow the hands seem too big.'

'Nonsense.'

'It's the subject of the painting – the woman's permission – and it's in the hands,' she said. 'He can do what he likes with them, Rembrandt can.'

The next time she saw a vacancy on one of the centrally placed sofas she moved quickly to take it, slotting herself into a niche between strangers. It was a buttoned leather affair, firm but comfortable. Her feet ached.

She signalled to Gerry that she was having a rest. He indicated that he would come back for her and she nodded. She put her head back, closed her eyes and listened to the floorboards creaking all around her.

Stella had noticed that the woman in *The Jewish Bride* wore pearls. Also earrings. Maybe that was why she looked so intimately self-assured. Stella hadn't had her ears pierced until her sixtieth birthday. She'd been squeamish about it but thought the pain would be balanced by the confidence the look would give her. She would become – finally – a woman taking her own decisions, a woman with authority over herself. She felt herself drifting. To be caught snoozing in such a place. Especially after a nap at lunchtime. She opened her eyes. Opposite where she sat was an image of an old woman reading. From a distance she let her eyes roam the picture. She didn't know who it was by. The old woman's face was in shadow and the book large – so big that it appeared floppy and awkward. Her hand was on the page steadying it or keeping her place. Stella, without noticing, closed her eyes again. Reading was so important – it so enriched.

When she was a child her parents encouraged her even though they themselves read very little. She remembered waiting for the library to open. Stamping from one cold foot to the other. The village didn't have a real library. But a volunteer, Mrs Brownlee, came on a Tuesday and Thursday evening, from six until eight, and opened the municipal hall. It was a place where people voted, a place where men in suits gathered for meetings, a place where children did their eleven-plus exams. Stella only knew it as the place where, after the war, she'd been sent to collect free orange juice. On winter evenings she'd shelter from the rain in the doorway, protecting a pile of books beneath her coat. Mrs Brownlee was a Protestant and she would drive up in her car and come walking quickly, her keys jingling. The building was empty and cold and full of echoes but everything changed when the light was switched on, the store cupboard opened and Mrs Brownlee dragged out the cardboard boxes of books. The pulling of the boxes was not always easy – they snagged sometimes on raised knots on the old wooden floorboards – and Mrs Brownlee would groan and tut-tut and ask Stella for help. There was a box for men – Zane Grey and cowboy stories and, for the women, love stories. And a box for boys and a box for girls. Stella liked to rummage in both. She read the Just William books because of Violet Elizabeth Bott. It was *she* who made her laugh, not William. And Enid Blyton – any of the Adventure Series. Or the Famous Five. Every so often a new shipment of books arrived. Those nights Stella dropped to her bare knees and was speechless, uncovering one new book after another. Sometimes she flicked a book open and read a line or two. The first words of every story tasted fresh. In each new book, at the front, was a white library insert and because it was blank she had the thrill of knowing she was the first to read that book. Like making prints in fresh snow. In old library books this insert page, stuck with Sellotape which had gone brown, was untidy with date stamps. They just put the return-by date anywhere, sometimes even upside down.

At home the only book they owned that was not to do with religion was *Virtue's Simplified Dictionary*. It was American and no one could give an explanation as to how it had come into the house. It was fat and had along its fore-edge little indentations – twenty-six of them, each containing a letter of the alphabet. The book was grubby with use. It had illustrations, some tiny line drawings, some colour plates, one of flags of the world, one of the flowers of North America. It was a book which could be relied upon, a book she only later realised she loved. People talked of being in difficulty and of opening the Bible for an answer but Stella played the same game with the dictionary. Closing her eyes and randomly inserting her finger into the little cave index, choosing any word on the page. There were some words she couldn't understand the explanation for because the words that did the explaining were unknown to her. So she had to look *them* up. Trace them back and cross-reference them. This had happened to her in her early teens with the word *spermatozoon* – God knows where she'd read it. She followed the trail until she had unravelled, more or less, what life was all about – although the dictionary was silent on the practical side of things. And she was left floundering in a pool which, according to the priest in confession, may have been of bad thoughts. An occasion of sin brought on by *Virtue's Simplified Dictionary*? When she looked up 'occasion' it turned out to be 'a favourable chance or opportunity'. This did not sound appropriate.

In some ways it was unfortunate that it was an American dictionary and it spelled some words the American way. Her homework occasionally had a word with a red ink strikethrough and the correct spelling written nearby in Master Ryan's flamboyant but legible hand.

Stella opened her eyes and saw Gerry approaching across the gallery floor.

'Is it time for a coffee?' she asked. 'Have we done enough to earn it?'

Gerry nodded. He tried to put away his glasses.

'This bloody case is too small. My legs are hanging out of the bed, so to speak.'

*   *   *

After they visited the museum shop they drank good coffee in sensibly sized cups – none of those steam-heated ones so heavy you couldn't lift them, so hot you daren't touch them to your lips. Stella had Dutch pancakes, he *biscotti*.

'The last time I was here,' she said, 'there was an exhibition of religious relics. "A Stairway to Heaven", it was called. Lovely gold and silver stuff. But I saw people – mostly old people – who were awestruck, not by the art but by what it contained. Bits of bone, shreds of cloth, locks of hair. You could see it in their eyes – the possibility of a cure. Their very own miracle.'

'Utter superstition,' said Gerry. 'I'm sure there were enough bits of the true cross to make another Forth Rail Bridge.'

She stared at him, not wanting to continue. Instead she rummaged in her bag and produced a postcard she'd bought in the museum shop. *Old Woman Reading*. It was not the painting she had seen but a different one. When she'd asked for the postcard the assistant had shrugged and said they were out of it. There are many old women reading, she said.

'Isn't that a wonderful state of affairs,' said Stella.

The assistant had offered her another, even better, card. An old woman, cowled in some dark material, looking down at a book. It was so lovely – the concentration in the eyes, the luminescence of the ancient face reflected from the page, the interior light from reading whatever was printed there.

She unscrewed the cap of her pen and wrote a message on the back then handed the card to Gerry for his signature. He added 'Love Granda' and capped and returned her pen.

'My feet are throbbing,' said Stella.

'Don't tell me you're chickening out. The best is yet to come.'

'What?'

'The Vermeers. There's three of them.'

'Aw no.' Stella's head dropped to her chest. 'A whole family?'

'No – three *paintings*.'

'Thank God. I thought there was a room for each.'

'I want to see what Vermeer's sesame seeds look like up close.'

'If you drank less at lunchtime, it might help.'

'It has no effect on me,' said Gerry.

'That's the danger. You have developed a tolerance.'

'You'd rather I was intolerant?'

'You think you're not that too?'

Gerry smiled and dipped his *biscotti*. He leaned forward to bite off the softened end.

'That place you went this morning, down the passageway – what's going on there? What do you want to see this woman about?'

Stella looked at him. She sipped her coffee.

'I'm tired. I'm tired of living the way we do.'

'What do you mean?'

'There are important questions to be answered. How can we best live our lives? How can we live good lives?'

Gerry gave a slow shrug.

'And there's somebody in there with the answers?'

'No. These are questions you have to answer for yourself.'

'Do unto others?'

'There's a word you never hear nowadays, a word from my childhood – *devout* – I want to live a more *devout* life.'

'And how do you do that?'

'I don't think you'd understand. If you're not a believer. It's to do with charity, to do with prayer. I'm just exploring.'

'And if you find what you're looking for?'

'It'll be good.' She shrugged. 'But I know it'll lead to other – more difficult – questions.'

'And where does that leave me? Us?'

'In different places.'

When they got back to the hotel room Gerry flung himself on the bed. Stella dropped the *Guardian* on the sideboard and it slithered off but she couldn't be bothered to bend and pick it up. She sank into the armchair with her legs straight out in front of her and her head flung back. Both made little noises of expiration.

'We've gone past ourselves,' she said.

'Overdone it by a mile.'

'A kilometre, maybe. Multiply by five and divide by eight.'

There was silence for a long time. Still lying flat Gerry undid the laces of his shoes and toed them off. They clunked onto the floor.

'Would you look at what these socks have done to me.'

For going away, along with the black pyjamas, Stella had bought him a pack of three pairs of socks to match his shoe size. What she hadn't paid attention to was the elasticated top. Normally he insisted on loose ones.

'I'm trying to think of a word,' he said, screwing up his face. 'Oedematous.' He was fumbling at the pale skin beneath his trouser leg. 'It's these bloody socks. Leg liquid increases. And it swells – after a hard day's Art. My socks are leaving Guinness rings on my legs.' His hand was massaging the ridges. 'Want to feel?'

'I can forgo it for the moment. Maybe later.'

He stared at her and said, 'Later they might be gone.'

'I'll be disappointed then.'

'They've made egg-timers of my legs. Look at the way they've nipped me.'

She glanced over at the bed and saw what he meant.

'Don't blame the socks – it's you. Your skin's gone spongiform – you poor thing . . .' she made a clucking kind of noise with her mouth. 'Where should we go tonight?'

'And they itch.'

'Don't scratch. It only makes things worse.'

'Hmmmm?' He had his eyes closed and was raking his ankles with the pads of his fingertips. He was making little moans of pleasure. 'The only thing that feels better than this is . . . You know you shouldn't but when you give in . . . ohhh, when you give in.'

Gerry raised both hands away from the area of temptation and clenched his fists. He stayed like that for a while then said, 'I liked the sound of that place – the one that said it was good for robust stews. Washed down with a robust bottle of wine or two.'

'Stop – you'll draw blood.'

'I'm not using my nails.'

He held up his hands as if he didn't know what to do with them. He reached out and touched her. Like the husband in *The Jewish Bride*.

They made love. Afterwards it began to get dark and Stella switched on the bedside light. The room was warm. Gerry put his arm around her.

'Look,' she said, 'still on the elasticity of skin. Look at the depression your watch leaves.'

'It'd take the best part of a week for that to disappear – looks like a moon crater.'

Gerry reached out to his side of the bed and began to strap on his watch, embed it in exactly the same depression on his wrist.

'Now you've seen the evidence of my sub-watch hirsutism.'

'Why do you take your watch off?'

'Habit,' he said. 'So's not to hurt you. Maybe a scratch . . . The same reason footballers aren't allowed to wear jewellery.'

'I didn't know you cared so much.'

'I would not beteem the winds of heaven to visit your face too roughly. Or some such.'

'You know what I love about this?' She was staring at the ceiling. 'Not having to think of what's for the dinner.'

'You flatter me too much, methinks, m'lady.' They both smiled.

'You know what I like, being away?' said Gerry.

'What?'

'You don't have to remember anyone's name.'

'As long as you remember mine.'

There was a long silence.

'I'm trying my best.'

Stella gave his bare shoulder a slap.

He joined his hands behind his head and propped himself higher on the pillow.

'I love those guys who *give* you their name. In conversation. They make themselves a character in their own stories. "And he said to me – says he – Ronnie, don't be such a fool – take it while it's going." And I say "Ronnie, I know what you're talking about." As if I knew his name all the time.'

'Sneaky,' said Stella.

'What'll happen when . . . this stops?'

'What?'

'This.'

'Then there'll be no more.' She smiled.

'I'm not looking forward to that,' he said. 'What'll be the point?'

'What was the point *before* sex came along?'

'I can't remember a time like that.'

'When you were eight or nine? Did you not think life was great then?'

'I think I felt sexy even then. Women undressing on the beach – Irish Catholic towel writhing.'

'That's just curiosity – not sex. For a boy with no sisters.'

'Say what you like. I was interested. A sneeze'll be the most physical pleasure I'll get from now on.'

'Wait,' said Stella, 'if some force was to come along and say – you have to live your life all over again – except that this time you are a eunuch. Would you opt for that?'

'With some reluctance.'

'So sex is not the be-all and end-all? There are other things.'

Stella went into the bathroom.

'The way I feel at the moment I could stay in tonight. Do my crossword.' She raised her voice so's she could be heard. 'But a robust stew has its attractions. Followed by lemon cheesecake. Have you an opinion on this matter?'

She dried her hands and came out. On the bed Gerry had begun snoring.

'Your fallback position – Gerry – is, in every instance, to fall back.'

Gerry woke. It was dark even though the curtains were open. The only light was a tangerine diagonal on the bed from the sodium lamp outside. Stella, wearing a dressing gown, was in the armchair sound asleep. The novel she'd been reading had slipped to one side and she was curled upright like a prawn. Gerry swung off the bed and planted his feet on the floor. He padded quietly to the sideboard, dipped into

94

the plastic carrier bag, found the neck of the whiskey bottle and lifted it up to the orange light source. Replacements were required as a priority. He'd overdone it. There was enough left to do tonight but tomorrow had to be planned for. If only he'd thought the thing through. With Stella out and about on her own that morning at the Beguine place he could have found a shop, purchased a half-bottle of any variety of whiskey – Scotch, even – and had it back to the hotel and into the bottle and the half-bottle disposed of in the rubbish bin before you could say clang! Nice as ninepins. There was a stainless steel bin between the two lifts. But oh no – he'd never thought. Never planned ahead. Storyboarding ability – nil. He'd been too taken up with where Stella was and who she'd run off with.

Without taking the bottle from the bag he removed the screw top and poured a good dram into one of two clean glasses on the tray. As quietly as possible he screwed the cap back on and tiptoed to the bathroom. He closed the door and switched on the light. As he filled the glass with water directly from the tap he looked up and saw himself naked in the mirror. Not a pretty sight. Sly bastard. The water formed a flat film of silvery white on the surface of the drink. To avoid this phenomenon the water should have been rested. Give it time to sit. To de-fizz. He drank the glass of whiskey halfway down, then put on the white towelling hotel robe. The stuff of it was soft against his skin. He tried to avoid the mirror. A shower would be a good thing. He carried his drink to the bedside table and set it on a folded tissue to avoid the click which might have wakened Stella with a start. At the same time he switched on his bedside light. Clothes all over the place. He ignored them and sat down. If she woke he could call it a reviving drink. Something to uplift his flagging spirits. Just a very tiny one. Because we're on our holidays. But she remained poleaxed, her head jerking up and then slowly sinking down again. The whiskey relaxed him. He drained what was left in the glass. At this time of the day it was enough. He got out of the chair, went to the bathroom and washed the glass out, dried it with a tissue. Then brushed his teeth with minty Sensodyne. He upended the cleaned glass on the paper doily, where the maid had set it when she'd serviced the room earlier.

She woke with a start and stared at him as if he was a stranger.

'So?' she said. She exaggeratedly widened her eyes, then rubbed her face with both hands. 'I'll not sleep tonight. Too many naps in the one day. Must be the change of air.'

'What's the storyboard?'

'For this evening?'

'Yes.'

'What time is it?'

'I think it's time for a robust stew,' said Gerry, 'but first a shower.'

'Give me a minute.'

Stella rose and went into the bathroom.

When the toilet flushed Gerry shouted loudly, 'I think I'll have a little drinkypoo – a touch of luxury.'

She opened the door and came out drying her hands.

'What did you say? I couldn't hear with the flush.'

'I'm having a drink.' He held up the glass to her in a toasting motion, 'To make me feel like Frank Sinatra.'

He waltzed past her into the bathroom and diluted the whiskey straight from the cold tap. Again the silvery milk-like surface. He came out and took the armchair and sipped his drink.

'The first of the day,' he said. Stella was tidying the room, lifting clothes and shoes and newspapers and magazines off the floor.

'Except for the wine at lunchtime.'

'Wine doesn't count. Like gin and tonic. Soft drinks all.'

'Get me the News,' said Stella. 'Preferably in English.'

She threw him the remote control. He found the BBC channel.

'I hate the way they've succumbed to that ticker tape streel-ing across the screen. Coat-trailing.' Stella settled herself, sitting on the bed.

He threw the remote to her. 'Another thing copied shame-lessly from the Americans. The mute button is two from the top.'

He went into the bathroom carrying his drink.

'Fly me to the moon,' he said over his shoulder.

'Just don't sing it.'

He closed the door and sat down on the toilet. It was fractionally lower than at home, which meant that he panicked in the last few millimetres of his descent. Out of control. His knees were more bent. Nearer the floor, he was. He drank off his whiskey and half turned and set the empty glass on the cistern. When he finished he stood and flushed, whipped back the shower curtain. The tap ran, cold at first, then he mixed in the hot. When it was a perfect temperature he pushed down the plunger and the water hissed down from the shower head.

He took off the dressing gown and hung it on the back of the door. Gingerly he stepped into the bath, holding onto the metal handles. For a long time he stood letting the water pummel the top of his head. Then he lathered his hair with shampoo from a replaced hotel miniature. Stuff he detested, it was so heavily scented. The perfume equivalent of Mantovani's cascading violins. Totally ineffective against dandruff. He opened a replaced miniature of conditioner and set it on the rim of the bath ready for use. Partners. Salt and pepper shakers. Oil and vinegar. Shampoo and conditioner. Gerry and Stella. He was just turning and stooping to pick up the conditioner bottle . . . and there was nothing. It began *because* there was nothing. A swipe in the air. When there should have been *something*. Some purchase. Nothing except pure air. Flying to the moon. When one strong magnet is aimed at another they refuse, they skid off each other. No contact. No purchase. Frictionless railways have been based on this principle. They bounce away. Like his heel and the enamel surface. Like his wife and himself, skidding off each other. YA FUCKIN BASTARD. Not touching as much as he would like. Down. Not touching at all – even in the slightest. HOLY FUCK. I'm going down. How many promontories, bone ends, cartilaginous dislocations will be broken, damaged, bounced off hard enamel. What was the line about Jupiter and Mars? So many pounds plunging in record time. In the blink of an eye. Vivid in the mind as a road crash. Like losing your virginity. Contact has been made. A gonging sound. That was it. A gong shower. He'd seen such a thing. Bony contact. When the realisation was fully on him he roared. Whether it was on the way down or when he hit the enamel he wasn't sure. But he was there, the right way round with the water from the shower hissing onto his feet, his jaw throbbing, his knees and thighs reddening. His cock askew at ten past two.

'STELLA!' he yelled above the noise of the shower.

In the distance, 'What is it?'

'I've fallen.' She burst open the door and came running to the bath and half screeched, laughing at the sight. He just lay there stunned, his heart pounding. Hammering.

'Are you all right?'

He reached out and checked each limb. Sought out his coccyx. It seemed okay. The water was slicking the hairs on his legs into straight lines. Stella turned off the shower and suddenly it was easier to hear.

'No laughing matter. I could be dead and gone.'

'But you're not,' she said. 'Are you okay?'

He pulled himself up into a sitting position, moved, felt no pain. Nothing broken.

'I'm okay.' She was laughing. 'No thanks to you. I'm going to sue this place. Where's their rubber mat? Every bath should have a rubber mat. For the elderly.'

'But you *deny* you're elderly.' She took a white folded towel from the rack and opened it to him. He gripped her hand through the dry surface of towelling and she raised him to his feet. He clung to the stainless steel handles and hoisted himself over the side of the bath, groaning.

'Steady. Watch yourself,' said Stella. He stepped onto the bathmat. She enveloped him in the towel. 'You're shaking.' She led him into the bedroom. 'Here, lie down.'

'Could ruin the holiday, that kind of thing,' said Gerry.

'Are you okay? No pains?'

'Lucky – no breakages – just sheer luck.'

'Maybe we should stay in.'

'I'm all right. Nothing a robust stew wouldn't cure. With a robust bottle of wine.' He began drying his hair.

'I'm sorry, I didn't mean to laugh. It was just nerves.'

Gerry lapped the towel around his middle like a skirt and inched up onto the bed. He lay back on the pillow.

'It's a kinda crucial event.'

'What?'

'The first time you fall in the shower.'

'Don't go morose on me, Gerry.'

'The next header is into the grave.'

The lift door slid shut and, being alone, they kissed. A peck. On the mouth. Gerry wore a raincoat and his navy scarf – she, a mustard jacket with a faux fur collar. He frowned and preened a little in the mirror.

'My hair's sticking out.' He tried to claw it down into place. 'In the panic, I forgot.'

'Forgot what?'

'Conditioner.'

'The paparazzi will know. It'll be all over the papers in the morning.'

'And my sore chin.'

'We'll discuss it during Ailment Hour. Oh, I forget to say – the day before we left I met a woman in the bank and I was telling her about Ailment Hour. She said she and her husband did exactly the same thing only they call it the organ recital.'

'I like that.' Gerry laughed. 'Organ recital is good.'

It was dark and he still felt a little staggery going down the hotel steps. He steadied himself on the handrail and immediately felt it sticky.

'Ahhhhh shit.' It had been painted black. He untacked his hand and looked at it. Blackened fingers and a huge black mark on his palm. Like some kind of police fingerprint procedure showing whorls and loops and creases. He held up his hand to

101

Stella. It was only then he saw the warning sign chalked on the steps. PAS GEVERFD. Presumably 'wet paint'. The warning plastic tape drooped uselessly to the ground. The girl on duty at the desk seemed momentarily confused when he held up his blackened hand to her as if taking an oath. Or was it a high-five gesture?

'Paint remover? Or any margarine?' How on earth would she know what margarine was? And if she did know, would she have the faintest notion of its ability to remove gloss paint? She phoned the maintenance people while he washed his hands in the bathroom across the hall from the desk. Again and again soaping and wiping with paper towels, sniffing at the marks to see if they had diminished. But it was no use. It was still there and tacky to the touch.

Stella had come in through the revolving doors, out of the cold. She stood to one side of the lobby as if the problem had nothing to do with her. Gerry was now leaning on the marble counter, waiting.

It was nearly five minutes before the maintenance man arrived with a rag and a plastic bottle of white spirit. The outside of the bottle was splashed and stippled with different-coloured paints. Gerry looked at it – smelled the whiff of it from where he stood. The thought of going out to eat, reeking of this stuff, did not appeal. He didn't want to offend the guy so he took the bottle and went into the bathroom. Looking at himself in the mirror he unscrewed the top. If he used this it would linger on his hands all night – like the way smoked fish lingers. Worse than that. No, thank you. He screwed the top back on the bottle and washed his hands, trying to rid them of the smell of even handling it. He held the bottle in a tissue and returned it to the guy. When he joined Stella and they walked out onto the street he apologised for not taking her by the hand.

'I'm still tacky,' he said.

'You always were.'

She hooked onto his arm and they walked slowly, close enough to try to keep warm. The pavements looked like they were beginning to freeze – areas of grey sparkle – and shops exhaled warmth, creating a small local fog outside each doorway.

'This is not my night,' said Gerry. 'A black mark. Hands stinking of paint thinners, grey hair all over the place, bruised chin, slight limp.'

'Och, God help you.'

Before they went into the place of robust stews Gerry noticed a supermarket next door. In the restaurant their coats were taken and they were shown to a warm table well away from the icy draught of the door. The waiter brought menus and served a basket of bread with little wrapped packs of butter. Gerry lifted a butter square and pointed to his heart. Fluttered his other hand a little.

'Margarine?' said the waiter. Gerry nodded.

'You're not usually so fastidious,' said Stella.

'Wait and see.'

The waiter brought some small tubs of a brand of margarine unknown to them. The packaging was covered with green hills and yellow fields and blue sky.

'The very thing,' Gerry said and lifted one. Stella looked at him. He told her what he was going to do, excused himself and went in search of the toilet. He found it in a corridor behind the front desk. But he didn't go in right away – he went next door to the small supermarket and bought a half-bottle of whiskey – some awful make he had never encountered before. Tyrone Superior, probably made in

103

Bulgaria or somewhere. He'd have taken anything – Dunphy's or Crested Ten or Redbreast, even Scotch – just so long as it came in a flat half-bottle that fitted his pocket. There was no queue and no language problems. The only faint lift of an eyebrow came when Gerry produced a high-denomination note from the back of his wallet. The whole exercise was so easy that he paused – made a stop gesture with the flat of his blackened hand and went back and grabbed a second half-bottle. Better safe than sorry. The girl at the till looked at him askance but he smiled to reassure her. Was she looking at his sore chin? His strangely painted palm? Had this man been in a drunken brawl? Why was he wandering the icy streets without an overcoat and with a wallet full of high-denomination notes? Should she phone the police? She swept his second purchase through and gave him his change from the whole transaction. He slipped the first bottle into the right-hand pocket of his jacket, the second into the left. He was nothing if not a well-balanced individual. He patted down the pocket flaps. When he'd bought the jacket he had thought them unfashionable but Stella had assured him that pocket flaps would come back in again. Now he was glad of them. He put his shoulders back and headed next door to the restaurant toilet.

For all its boasting of robust stews it was quite a sophisti-cated place. A cinemascope mirror was surrounded by pearly bulbs like in an actor's dressing room. It filled the wall above a series of elegant wash-hand basins. He paused to look at himself. Touched his sticking-out hair. There was a mark coming up on his chin and he touched it to see if it was tender. It was.

He raised his eyes to look at himself. It was letting the side down, buying two. He saw his image in the mirror shrug. What's done cannot be undone, it seemed to say.

He took the margarine tub from his trouser pocket. It was hard to open. He had to bend the tab and peel back the plastic skin to get at the contents. When he did, the little yellow plop was pleasingly shaped, like a four-leaf clover. He hooked it out with his finger and applied it to the hand that had been stained. He made washing movements, watched his hands glisten and twist in the light – like some sort of polyunsaturated Pontius Pilate. The remaining traces of the black sheen seemed to melt away. He pressed the hot-water tap with his elbow and rinsed his hands. The grey and yellow gloop disappeared in a swirl down the plughole. Then he soaped his hands and did it all again. He felt proud of himself. The affected hand was now as clean as a whistle. And smelled only of soap. And he had two Traveller's Friends – companions, you might say, with their reassuring weight, stowed in his pockets. All within about four minutes.

On his way back into the dining room Gerry saw Stella through the glass doors. She had her elbows on the table, looking down almost as if crestfallen. And it struck him as *so* unusual that he paused before pushing open the door. What was this aloneness? Her natural state was to relate to people. At parties she entered the room and joined the first person she came across. At the same party Gerry would move around talking to different sets of people, joking here and there, listening as hard as he could without cupping his hand behind his ear. An hour or so later he would look back and Stella would be engrossed and still talking to the same person she'd started off with. She found all people equally interesting and seemed unable to reject anyone. Gerry accused her of being a 'bore magnet'.

'It's because I listen,' she said.

'It always ends up an unscheduled Ailment Hour.'

'How could it not, with hypochondriacs like you around?' she said. Here she was in a restaurant in Amsterdam, sitting by herself, staring down at the place setting in front of her, looking like she was on the verge of tears. Maybe she knew.

Now that he was back they ordered, and when the waiter left them Gerry tried to tell her of the success he'd had with the margarine. He showed his clean hand. She couldn't care less. Nor was she impressed by how little time it had all taken. There was silence between them.

'Gerry – I want to talk about something.'

'Fire away. Have you ordered the wine?'

'Yes. The Tempranillo looks good.'

When the waiter brought the wine Gerry dispensed with the tasting ritual. He filled both glasses and left the bottle on the table.

'*Dank ya*,' said Stella.

'Good man,' said Gerry. The waiter smiled and backed away. 'When I was going down in the bath all I could think of was "a gong shower" for some reason.'

'What?'

'Something to do with the noise I made hitting the enamel. Were you not with me at the gong shower?'

'Not to my knowledge.'

Gerry lifted his drink and held it out for a toast. Stella chinged his glass.

'It was Leamington Spa. A fair on the green – on a Sunday morning.'

'I was probably at Mass.'

'Alternative peace kinda stuff. The Warwickshire Badger Group. Indian head massage, tattoos. And gong showers. I'm sure I've told you this.'

106

Stella shook her head. No.

'Unless I've forgotten,' she said.

'There was a bearded hippie and his woman kneeling, waving people into their tent. And there's this big brass gong – like the one in the films – with the half-naked guy. Twentieth Century Fox? Gaumont?'

'Rank,' she said.

'It *was* Rank – definitely J. Arthur. And they get a woman customer and sit her on a chair in front of the gong and the hippie begins to make it vibrate by beating the hell out of it.' Gerry began demonstrating with both hands. 'It's roaring like a jet plane. Goes on for ages and ages. Then fades – the guy's arms must have given up – and your woman emerges, washed with sound. And pays her money.' Gerry put on an American accent. '*I could literally feel the negativity leaving my body, said Martha.*'

'They use ultrasound to clean jewellery. Shakes all the atomic dirt particles off,' Stella said. 'Rings come out pinging clean.'

'Well, so did your woman. I think she had to say one Our Father, three Hail Marys and a Glory Be to complete the ritual.'

Stella seemed irked, looked away from him. Gerry lifted the bottle and filled his glass again. Stella wiped her mouth on her serviette and leaned forward.

'I want to talk about that place we saw this morning,' she said and looked down at her hands. 'We're not getting any younger. I find I'm at a loose end – aimless. There's no role for me. The one grandchild is in Canada and it doesn't sound like there'll be any more.'

'Och, you never know . . .'

'That's not the point – hear me out.' She stopped and turned the knife in front of her to face inwards. 'I want to do something better. In what time's left to me.'

'There's nothing wrong with you, is there?'

'Not that I know of.'

'I thought for a second you'd planned this whole trip to break bad news to me.'

'No.' She smiled at his concern and continued. 'The last time I was in Amsterdam – all those years ago – I heard about that place . . .'

'Which?'

'Where we were this morning – the Beguine place – whatever way you pronounce it. *Begheenov.* The talk was that it was a good place for women who wanted to live a religious life. And I wanted to talk to them about it. Wondered if there were any other places like it. Closer to home.'

'Uh-huh.'

'Are you listening?' she said. 'Because this is important.'

'Of course.'

'Not a convent. But a religious community. Not seclusion. Women can have a place of their own to live but they don't have to take a vow of poverty or anything. That's what they said.'

'What are you talking about? I don't know what's going on here.'

'I made an appointment for Monday with the Spiritual Director – or whatever she's called . . .'

A young Asian flower seller came into the restaurant and began to move between the tables. He came to Gerry and laid out his wares across his forearm. Small cellophane-wrapped red roses. Gerry shook his head. Stella looked up and smiled.

'No, thank you.' The boy returned her smile and continued moving among the tables.

'He doesn't ask old men eating by themselves,' said Gerry.

'Who would they give it to?' said Stella. 'If they bought one.'

As she spoke she was failing to meet his eye and that was not like her.

'I've been marking time,' she went on. 'The family is raised – the work's done. That can't be it, can it? There's ten or twenty years left over, as it were. We've cut the cloth of our lives wrongly. It doesn't fit. I have, at least – but I don't know about you.'

Gerry shrugged. Then it struck him she was being ironic. She didn't say anything more for a while.

'I'm confused,' he said. He challenged her to look at him directly. 'What are you trying to say?'

'We believe different things.' Still she looked at the tablecloth.

'We've always known that.'

'But now things are different. I have a sense of drift. I want to do something with the time I've left. Other than watch you drink.'

'Am I anywhere in your storyboard?'

'Not really.'

Stella was definitely asleep. Her book was too close to her face. Gerry stood and moved it to the bedside table – and on the way back dipped into the right-hand pocket of his jacket, which he'd hung in the wardrobe. He produced a half-bottle and went into the bathroom, closed the door. What had she been talking about? He coughed to cover the snap of the screw-cap opening and poured a drink. His image in the mirror showed him the bruise was darkening. Back in the bedroom he sat down with his drink.

Her breathing from the pillow continued to be long and slow. She wasn't usually that outspoken. Now he looked into his glass and saw that it was empty. That was quick. He refilled and topped up with water.

He'd nearly been caught out in the lift. When it had jerked to a halt at the third floor there'd been a sound from his pockets – somewhere between a glug and a gurgle. But partially smothered by his raincoat. And he'd wondered if she'd heard. If she had, he could not think of a good excuse. What was that noise, Gerry?

Shrug. How would I know?

Sitting in the hotel room now, relaxed, he could think of excuses. He could have blamed the noise on brake fluid. She'd no idea how anything mechanical functioned. Overhead waste pipes? He could have blamed it on borborygmi – tummy rumbles, to you and me. The singular was borborygmus so the plural was appropriate. From two sources. But Stella hadn't remarked on the noise, hadn't said anything except, 'I'm looking forward to my bed.' Did she really mean he wasn't in her storyboard? How could that be? What would he do? He took another drink and was about to set the glass back on the table but reneged. He reached out for the blank pad beside the phone and used it as a shock absorber. Silence when he put it down. But he knew the next time he lifted it there would be a wet ring on the phone pad. A shining zero.

The sounds from the bed changed. Now she was definitely moving into deep sleep. There had been something different about her tonight in the restaurant. Distant. Other. He didn't know whether it was his fault or not. He just saw her as if from afar. Like someone he did not fully know.

The only time he'd felt something like this recently was at Christmas, when he'd accompanied her to midnight Mass. He didn't like the thought of her walking the dark streets alone at one o'clock in the morning. Normally on Christmas Day she rose early and went to church by herself.

He knew the whole Mass drill from childhood. But he also knew that things had changed. Settled in the pew beside her, he was comfortable not to be involved. The church was mock Gothic – like thousands of Victorian churches all over the country – built by some clone of Pugin's. Pointed arches parading up and down both sides of the nave – the altar like an iced wedding cake. As a child he'd been made to look towards the altar. His mother would scold if he looked anywhere else. So he stared intensely at whoever was in front of him. The backs of grown-ups' heads. The mark of a man's hat on his hair, the pattern and colours of a woman's headscarf.

He poured himself another whiskey.

'A small one. A nightcap,' he whispered. 'Just a smidgen.' Lots of water. To render it harmless. What was the point of this remembering? He was trying to get to a place but had forgotten the destination. Why was he back at Christmas? It was something to do with seeing Stella differently. Seeing her as if he didn't know her well. Then he remembered. The priest's microphone voice saying, 'Let us offer each other a sign of peace.'

After he'd kissed Stella and shaken the hands of strangers around him, Stella had whispered, 'Sister Francis and I are Eucharistic ministers tonight.'

She had left him and walked up the side aisle. A nun joined her at the main altar and the priest gave them both com-munion. Then it was the people's turn. Occasionally through the moving crowd Gerry saw Stella on the altar dispensing hosts from a gold chalice. Beside her, Sister Francis was doing the same thing. Stella was above those who approached her, stooping a little, to give them the host. Each time her shoulders rounded, Gerry thought of her as old. He was seeing her as someone he didn't fully know.

When communion finished, Stella returned to her seat, knelt and put her face in her hands. The choir began 'In the Bleak Midwinter'. Then he heard a sound – a shuddering intake of breath. She was fretting about something. All this only a couple of weeks ago. Probably about being separated from their son and grandson at that time of year. But if she was, he did not want to intrude. She took one hand away from her face and produced a hanky and blew her nose. Did her eye condition prevent her weeping? Was she beyond actual tears?

'Are you all right?' But she turned away from him, as if he had no right to see her in grief.

The Tyrone Superior was anything but. However, it was getting the job done.

On their way home from midnight Mass they walked quickly to warm themselves. When they came to the hill she eased her arm through his. She pulled against him a little. 'What's the hurry?' she said. 'We've neither chick nor child waiting for us.'

Gerry slowed.

'I just want to get out of the cold. Get some central heating in,' he said. 'Feel any better?' She smiled a tight-lipped kind of response. 'Tell me again – about the eye thing.'

'There's no lack of tears, God knows. It's just that they're of such poor quality. According to the doctor.'

'Poor-quality tears . . .?' he said.

Gerry waited to hear the cause of her crying but she offered nothing.

112

They had to watch out for slippery patches underfoot and there was fog in the air. Cones of light beamed down from lamp-posts. Their own breath showed in front of their faces.

'I didn't know you were a . . .' Gerry paused, trying to remember the word – 'a giver outer of communion.'

'I have been for a couple of years now. *Eucharistic minister* is the title you're looking for.'

There was a silence. Gerry shrugged.

'You want me to keep you informed about such things?' said Stella.

'I just didn't know.'

'They asked me and I said yes. I wanted to help in any way I could.'

'It's a kind of honour, I suppose.' Gerry squeezed her hand with his elbow. 'I'm proud of you even though I don't believe a word of it.'

'Don't say another thing, Gerry. It's Christmas and I feel good.'

The streets were lined with parked cars, their tops and windscreens whitened with frost. Some people had pinioned newspapers beneath their wipers. In their own street they took to walking in the middle of the road where cars' tyres had darkened the frost.

'It's really strange stuff, frost,' Gerry said. 'It falls straight down, like rain – like the opposite of shadow – white, not black.'

'I wouldn't like to argue.'

Inside, the flat was full of warmth and Christmas smells. The pudding had been boiled, the gravy stock had been made with giblets, a potted hyacinth sweetened the hallway.

'A drink?' said Gerry.

She produced some ham sandwiches wrapped in cling film which she'd made in the afternoon. Gerry poured her sherry and an Islay malt for himself. Stella raised her glass and they toasted.

'Happy Christmas.'

'This arrived today,' she said, handing him an envelope. 'Not your real present. You'll get that in the morning. This one's for both of us.' He ran his thumb beneath the flap. 'The tickets for Amsterdam,' she said, before he could remove them from the envelope.

'You could have booked online,' he said. 'Saved a couple of quid.'

'I wanted to be sure – so I got the travel agent to do it.'

'And put them in the Christmas post?'

Stella smiled and shrugged.

'Wait a minute,' he said. He came back with a tiny un-labelled parcel, glinting with Sellotape.

'You'll get your real present tomorrow.' He kissed her.

'You wrapped this just now,' she said, laughing. There was a small black domed box beneath the loose paper. She opened it.

'Earrings,' he said. She kissed him.

'Thanks.'

'You said you didn't like the idea of an eternity ring so I thought you might like those. Eternity earrings.' She lifted one from the pledget of cotton wool and looked at it closely. 'You were so pleased about getting your ears pierced . . .' She took off the earrings she had worn to Mass and began fitting the new ones.

And now here they were in the middle of the trip, in Amsterdam, in a hotel room, him with an empty glass on the table in front of him. What was her phrase? 'I would

114

fain be prone.' He hoisted himself to his feet. The half-bottle had not been finished but a fair dent had been made in it. He opened the main duty-free bottle, still standing in its poly bag, and poured what remained of the half-bottle into it. The empty went into his left trouser pocket. He should decant both half-bottles while he was at it. His jacket hung lopsided on its hanger until he removed the other half-bottle. He performed the task in the bathroom with the door closed.

A constitutional would have to be taken. Indoors. The second empty he slipped into his right trouser pocket. He checked her position in the bed – not an inch had she moved. With great care he sought out the extra plastic key card so that he could get back in again if the door accidentally closed. Nor would the room be plunged into darkness in his absence, frightening the life out of Stella. So he was proud of himself for using the extra plastic key. A very adult thing to do. He left the door open a fraction to avoid clicks and clunks which would wake her on his re-entry. It was only when he was halfway along the corridor that he realised he was in his stocking feet and his shirt tail was out. He made it to the lifts without bumping into the wall too much. The waste bin had a silver lid and a round hole in its side. He dropped one half-bottle into it. It made a loud metallic bang.

'Sorry.'

He thought of an Act of Contrition. A firm purpose of amendment. Never again. So he bent the knee – the old much-lamented *mauvais genou* – genuflected so's he could insert his arm into the bin – and slid the second empty down the inside until it reached the bottom – quietly. When he straightened up he staggered forward a little, then turned and retraced his

115

steps – at least that is what he thought he was doing. At a T-junction of corridors there were signs pointing to the room numbers. What was theirs? He consulted his plastic key. There was no number on it. The number was on the white bit of paper around the plastic and he had left it in the room. He was sure his room was on the left-hand side. But the corridor was endlessly the same and each magnolia cream door was the same, except for the number. Most of them were silent now that it was late – just the occasional sound of a television and, in between, the padding sounds of his stocking feet over the carpet as he wavered along. The corridor was a relatively recent arrival on the architectural scene. Round about the end of the nineteenth century. Before that, people used to go from room to room. How embarrassing would that be nowadays? He began to select landmarks – the ice-making machine in an alcove. Trays, outside some doors, with half-finished meals, glasses, bottles, white crumpled napkins. One with a half-eaten wedge of pizza covered in grey-green artichokes. He was sure this was the second time he had passed it. Because he remembered thinking he was peckish enough to finish it off. Nobody would know. But the adult in him made him refrain. A firm purpose of amendment. That was just a fancy Catholic way of saying 'I'll never do it again'. Him on his teenage-boy knees in the dark. The priest breathing on the other side of the mesh. Some kind of eye test, Father? Nobody ever said he'd go blind. And the funny thing was – at that time – he *was* resolved never to do it again. And he momentarily joined the angels, felt good about himself. Was uplifted. It could be like that with the drink. If he got help. Or if he really *applied* himself. Eating apples. Or was that just for giving up the cigarettes? The idea of sin had disappeared. The nearest equivalent was hurting other people. Stella was other people. To resolve to give up the

116

drink when you were pissed was completely the wrong time. There was no door fractionally open to him. He turned and proceeded to retrace his steps, back past the ice-maker, past the pizza with artichokes. He began to laugh – this was one way to leave your wife. In the middle of the night, in a hotel in Amsterdam. They would find him at breakfast still padding around, his socks worn through, his feet bloodied with carpet friction. But maybe they wouldn't find him. Maybe he'd never be seen again. He would die and mummify and disintegrate in a corner behind the ice-maker. End up as dust motes. Sucked into a Hoover operated by one of those lovely girls, in a lilac housecoat, from Thailand or Puerto Rico. Sounded vaguely like a perversion. At the T-junction he tried to orientate himself. Try the other way. Plan B. He set off to the right. Warm – he was getting warmer. He recognised a print on the wall, of a ruined Greek temple. Hot. Funny how he never forgot a building. In this rampage along corridors he felt like something from Greek mythology. Theseus or the King of Crete. Maybe it was Daedalus, the architect and builder of mazes and labyrinths. He'd fit the bill. If he'd built it, he'd surely know the way. When he came to it, totally by accident, the magnolia door of number 396 was slightly open. Very, very hot. A sliver of faint light at the door jamb. He pushed on the door and it opened. Their familiar case and his own coat on the chair. In the bed the familiar head on the pillow. Odysseus, home at last. After ten eventful years. Now to lay my weary bones. Maybe a nightcap. To celebrate the fact that he had stowed the empties. He poured himself a drink.

It seemed that no sooner was he in bed and asleep than he was awake again. Cramp. In the dark he flings aside the bed-clothes and swings himself out of bed. His mouth tightens

117

in a noiseless scream. His right foot and lower right leg wants to warp but can't. It feels like a just-caught mackerel arching this way and that. And he's trying to pacify it. Watch your step, this is not life-threatening but it feels like it. I'll walk on you, ya bastard. I'll flex you. Stride up and down trying not to wake the dog-tired wife. It's not extra time at Wembley with his team mates trying to bend the foot while he lies on his back and gets on with the screaming. There's no glamour here. No, this is a pitch-black hotel bedroom in Amsterdam, at three or four o'clock in the morning. Even an ouch would be frowned upon – out of the question. How do you pronounce *ouch* anyway? Nobody ever said *ouch* in their lives. Aaaaaaah fuck – but never *ouch*. *Ouch* is for comics and storyboards. Make it to the toilet and all will be well. Relief is only steps away. Both bladder and leg. The route now familiar in the darkness takes him to the bathroom. Pull the light cord. But the foot will not flatten – it remains like a hockey stick. With all his might he tries to break the arch of it by flattening it against the floor. The pain is a steel hawser. He presses down on his knee – the old *genou*. Hops on his good foot once or twice. The back of the affected leg is as hard and white as ivory. He punches it, clenches his teeth, whinnies as silently as he can, presses his foot to the floor in hope. His toes are bending up and splaying out. Fucking hell. Bend, ya bastard. Flexitime. Flat to the floor. Ninety degrees. Eventually he masters it. The pressure of a single step. The good foot propelling him. A second flat step and he is by the toilet bowl. One foot on either side like a hole-in-the-ground *pissoir*. Relief comes. Thanks be to God and his holy mother. When the pain is finally gone he is terrified it will return. Little wisps of it come back as he climbs into bed. Greatest fear comes when he assumes the leg position which started the attack in the first place. Careful. Turn on the other side. In case heat would be a factor in keeping the cramp at bay he wrests the hot-water bottle from between Stella's thighs.

When they went in to breakfast Stella, who knew their room number off by heart, gave it to the woman behind a desk and they were both shown to a freshly laid table by a waiter.

'Do you want me to show you the ropes?' said Gerry.

'No – not really. Why?'

'You haven't eaten here before. By this time yesterday you'd skedaddled.'

'At my age I think I can manage the concept of the buffet breakfast.' She went to the cereals table. 'And skedaddling is not in my nature.'

Gerry followed her.

'Roughage,' he kept saying. There was a choice of full fat or skimmed milk and he felt a surge of self-congratulation to have worked out which was which from the printed labels. *Volle melk – halfvolle melk*. Something called *magere melk* made him uneasy, so he avoided it. Was it 'mother's milk'? Couldn't possibly be. But they were, after all, in Amsterdam.

They returned to the table, each with a bowl of cereal, Gerry's full to overflowing, Stella's covering the bottom of her dish. When she faced him across the table she looked concerned.

'How do you feel?'

'Okay.'

'You really did give yourself a whack.'

120

She reached out and was about to touch the bruise on his chin but he recoiled. He wondered how much his fall in the shower could be blamed on the drinks he'd had beforehand. They certainly wouldn't have *helped*. And why had he been thinking about Frank Sinatra? Sinatra might have had a drink in the bath if he'd wanted to feel sybaritic. But a drink in the shower? Stella looked at him as he spooned and spooned the last scrapings of his cereal.

'I got terrible cramp last night,' he said. 'You were sound asleep.'

'I'm sorry to have missed it.' Both of them smiled. 'Did you go out?'

'Not that I know of.' Gerry tried to give answers that would cover all eventualities. He had a vague recall of corridors. Of silver bins.

'I woke and you were nowhere to be seen.'

The waiter cleared their dishes and brought tea.

'I'm trying to remember what was said last night,' said Gerry. 'In drink?'

'No – at dinner.' Stella poured their tea.

'I'd like you to spell it out for me,' said Gerry. 'Again.'

'What?'

'The future – as you see it.'

She shook her head, as if to say this is neither the time nor the place, and rested her elbows on the table.

'Today we go to the Anne Frank House.'

'Jesus. School parties,' said Gerry. 'Remember I told you about the wasp on the bus to Buchenwald?'

'Yes.'

'The worst thing was the schools. Children running all over the place with their jotters and clipboards – ticking boxes, getting the answers right. They were quiet enough – their teachers had them well warned. Like in a library. As if the whole thing was a normal exercise. Roomfuls of human hair. Piles of shoes to the ceiling. A crateful of rings. Can you imagine how long it would take to fill a crate that size with golden wedding rings?'

Stella proposed that they walk from the hotel across three canals. Gerry agreed without looking at the map. It was a better morning. The sun shone weakly, not enough to take the chill out of the air, but enough to lift their spirits a little. It was low in the sky and cast long shadows.

'It would be nice to get one good day,' said Stella.

It was noisy. Lorries and cars pounded along the canal banks. Bicycles warned with their bells as they approached and if they lacked a bell the cyclist shouted, which Stella thought quite scary and not at all friendly.

When they reached the Anne Frank House Gerry stepped back and looked at the renovated entrance. It had a whole new modern frontage and gave no sense of being a hiding place. Even at this time of year there was a queue. School parties who had booked ahead went past them into the doorway.

When they finally got into the foyer there were some enlarged black and white photographs. Anne in her school playground before the war. Anne in the street with friends, smiling. Anne at a desk, writing.

'How did they know this tragedy was going to happen?' said Gerry.

'Are there any photographs of you as a child?' said Stella. Gerry nodded. 'Well, there's your answer.'

'But not at a desk, writing.'

'They must have been reasonably well off. When we were that age,' said Stella, 'it was only people with money who had cameras.'

It was good to be in out of the cold. The school parties had gone elsewhere in the building. There was a strange quietness – a church-like reverence. People purchased their tickets in whispers. Stella got out her purse and did the transaction when it was their turn. She refused to pay extra for the black audio guides.

They went into the cloakroom and considered hanging up their coats but decided against it. The visit would not take long. There was an old man putting a small skullcap on his head. He had sallow skin and dark intense eyes. His shaving had been careless and there were wisps of grey at the sides of his mouth. He was affixing the cap to his head with a kirby grip without the aid of a mirror. Probably the same way he shaved. Gerry whispered, 'He looks like a cellist.'

Stella whispered back, 'A kippa – good for crosswords. For the synagogue or prayer.'

They were ushered to a door and when they went through it they found themselves in the actual house away from the new frontage. But it was hard to orientate themselves. There was a bookcase with ring binders and files which opened into a secret doorway. Once through it they were faced with a steep stairway. They climbed with care, Stella going first, and arrived in a room. Some of the windows were covered with semi-transparent patterned glassine. From another clear window was a view of the canal.

Again Gerry was aware of the silence, the sound of creaking as they pressured the floors. They did not speak between themselves. Except perhaps to indicate something with a nod or react by moving an eyebrow. Sometimes a nudge, if they were close enough. The weight of the sorrow grew with each room they passed through. If there was anything that lightened the mood then it also had the effect of making the end of the story darker. The toilet with the inside of its bowl ornately patterned in Dutch blue. In one bedroom, pin-ups of the time – Deanna Durbin and Ray Milland – names Gerry had heard from his own parents' mouths. He stopped in front of an innocuous-looking wallpaper of ochre and white petals. Stella came to see what had attracted him. He did not need to point out the pencil lines which registered the height of the Frank children as they grew. She saw them immediately and bit her lip. It was because she had performed the exact same exercise with their own child that the horizontal marks were so familiar. 'The shoes, the shoes have got to come off. That's cheating. Now heels together, as close to the wall as you can get.' 'Does the thickness of socks count, Mum?' 'Naw, don't be daft, be still.' The calling out for a book – any hardback book – to square off the top of the child's head, to rule the line. The comparison with the previous mark. See how much you've sprouted in three months? The verb used was always 'sprouted'. She wondered what the Dutch equivalent was – the word for sprouted that would have been used to Anne and her sister, Margot.

They moved from room to room, looking at the quotations – black lettering on white walls – reading the translations, absorbing the photographs. They became separated at one point. Gerry was always lagging behind, taking longer over each exhibit.

Stella, in a new room by herself, read: 'April 5th 1944, I can shake off everything if I write. My sorrows disappear.

124

My courage is reborn.' She turned next to a photograph before the war of a line of girls – Anne's tenth birthday – with their arms around each other's shoulders, eyes narrowed in the bright sun. Oh, the dresses. The buttons and shoulder straps, the hemlines, the white ankle socks, shoes and sandals. And the hair. Although these girls were ten years before her time Stella recognised everything. Fads and fashions in those days didn't change much. And she was brought back to her own growing up in her own village in the north of Ireland. In her house they didn't have a lot of clothes. Style was what you wore. More likely, what someone else wore. Cast-offs and hand-me-downs. Her brothers had the best of it because of a generous Protestant family who lived nearby – all boys. For the girls there were very few shop skirts. They had to make do with 'remoulds' – tweeds and summer dresses handed down by aunties, made and fitted by Mrs Johnston. Stella standing there, on the small wooden stool, Mrs Johnston on her knees going around pinning the height of a hem, putting tucks in the waist, her mouth bristling with pins. 'Aww, I mind when I had a waist that size.' When she had pins in her mouth Mrs Johnston's words were distorted. She said them sideways. 'The day I was married I had an eighteen-inch waist. Can you believe it?' And she'd make a hoop with her fingers and thumbs the size she imagined herself to have been. 'But you're the spit of your mammy's side of the house. You're exactly what she was when I first met her twenty years ago. Such a beautiful girl. Being chased by half the men in the country.' There were pins everywhere and while one sister was being fitted the others played with the horseshoe magnet. Stella loved the way the pins and paperclips clung to it, hanging down like some sort of a plant. Mrs Johnston kept the magnet to look

125

for missing pins so's nobody'd suffer, she said, running about in their bare feet.

Then parcels came from Canada. Stella remembered a dirndl skirt – such a lot of material that flared out when she spun around. And belts made with tiny coloured beads in Native American patterns – zigzags, totems, triangles – of such bright colours that nobody would dare wear them outside the house. And underskirts – acres of tulle to better display the material and shape of the dress. Unheard-of sweets, like Lifesavers. Unfathomable flavours like sarsaparilla.

Gerry caught up with her and she showed him Anne's birthday photo, told him about Mrs Johnston and the dress-making and her magnet.

'You never told me that before.'

In the last room they stood at a glass exhibit cabinet for a long time, staring down. The handwriting of a different language was a mystery – but to see its carefully formed letters looping on the yellowing pages was enough. The feeling was similar to the handwritten American entry they'd found in the book in church.

Something else caught Stella's eye and she moved to the corner of the room. There was a narrow mantelpiece and on it was a line of things which at first she could not understand. Mostly ordinary stones. But there was a glass marble with a yellow twist at its centre, a tiepin which looked valuable, some euro cents, a cheap glitter-covered hair clasp – the kind of thing a child would wear – more precisely, the kind of thing the man downstairs had used to fasten the kippa to his head. She raised her eyebrow quizzically. Gerry gave a slow shrug.

'I've no idea.'

'Remember *Schindler's List*?' said Stella. 'At the end. They lined up pebbles on the gravestones. As tokens.' Gerry remembered the violin soundtrack more than the visuals. He nodded and led the way out of the room.

'Coffee?' he said over his shoulder. But when he looked round his wife was not there.

She had the room to herself now, still staring at the little line of objects. It looked informal – like it had not been there for long, as if some schoolchild had just started it and others in the party had followed suit. It was a showing forth. A salute to, and an identifying with, those who had suffered. She wanted to make a contribution. To the victims of war. To the dead and the wounded. Coins seemed too much like a tip for a friendly waiter. What was involved here was Anne Frank and her religion, although her Jewishness seemed not to weigh too heavily on her. But her subsequent death in a concentration camp was the result of it. Also Anne was filled with yearnings that Stella recognised. The suffering involved in her death – about which there was not a word written – must have been unimaginable. Stella's hand moved up to her earlobe and with a little manipulation the earring and its keeper fell into her cupped right hand. It glistened there – a tiny golden circle reflecting the room and its windows – an eternity ring. As a child of ten the notion of eternity had terrified her. Lying in bed unable to reach, in her mind, the end of time. The futility of trying to count to a million. The Catechism was full of it. Life everlasting. For all eternity. She reattached the keeper and set the earring on the mantelpiece at the end of the queue of tokens. The ring part of it rocked to and fro a little, then stilled. She looked around and saw that the room was empty. She bowed her head and said a prayer. It seemed easy to wish someone well, to show gratitude and appreciation for a life

127

tragically cut short. It wasn't so much a prayer, more an expression of solidarity. You and me, Anne. Our different faiths, our common humanity. The way we suffered. Twin souls at the opposite ends of life – you a girl, me an old woman. A young casualty and an old survivor. I make you this offering. Prayer was a summoned intensity, held there in the head and in the heart. Something good, something spiritual. Articulated, spoken inwardly, wished to the point of aching. The moment came to an end and she backed away from the mantelpiece towards the door.

Gerry stood in the hallway looking around him. To one side were the treads of the descending stairway worn thin by the Frank family feet and others before them – not by tourists. The hollows had been sealed and protected by Plexiglas. There was a newly built staircase for tourists.

'Now I'm ready,' Stella said. He reached out and touched her arm through her coat. She seemed in another world.

'Are you okay?'

She nodded.

In the café of the Anne Frank House Stella sat at an empty table overlooking the canal. She was too hot and began to wish that she'd left her coat in the cloakroom. She untied her scarf and let it hang loose. Gerry stood over her.

'Do you want me to get the coffees?' She nodded and combed her hair with her fingers. 'Are you sure you're all right?'

'Yes.'

The sound of ducks on the canal mixed with the yells of children playing in the distance. Not all that different to what the Frank family would have heard.

At the counter Gerry ordered the coffees and a slice of cinnamon apple cake. As he waited he kept his eye on Stella.

Her elbows were on the table, her head in her hands. Maybe it was a bad idea to come to this place. It was enough to knock anybody sideways.

When he appeared with the tray she was putting in her eye drops – head back, elbows high, aiming the white dropper bottle, fingers holding open the lids so that the liquid would enter the eye, rather than be wasted. He set her cup in front of her and his own beside it. There was water on her cheeks. He'd remembered to bring a knife to bisect the apple cake and two forks to share it. She wiped her eyes with a tissue. He sat beside her and slid the tray onto an adjoining table. She lifted her coffee and blew on its surface but set it down again.

'No, I'm fine now,' she said. 'I used to do that book with so many classes in school.'

'It still gets you?'

She nodded. 'I saw those tokens. On the mantelpiece. And I was so . . . so gutted by what we've just seen. The house, the pictures of Anne, its memories and all that . . . and I thought why don't I leave something.' Gerry waited. 'So I left an earring.'

'On the mantelpiece.'

'Yes.'

Gerry looked closely at her, first at one ear then the other.

'The gold eternity ones?'

'Yes.'

'That I bought you for Christmas?'

'I'm afraid so.'

'What's wrong with that?'

'I shouldn't have.' She bunched her fists.

'Why not?'

'I've no right to. It's arrogance, given what that family went through. I'm not Jewish. I have not been involved in anything like their suffering.'

'Come on, Stella.'

'No, really. I'm not a fully paid-up member of the Pain Club, as you call it.'

'If *you* aren't, then who is?'

'I was just doing something to make myself feel good. Swanning in and saying, "I understand your pain." I can just hear them – how dare she?'

'No, they wouldn't. All you've done is made a gesture, expressed admiration. Don't take things so seriously, Stella.'

'If you can't take the Holocaust seriously . . .' She smiled at Gerry. 'They can have my little token. It's no great sacrifice. A single earring can be fashionable these days.'

Stella cut the section of cake in two. The knife was not sharp and the pressure squeezed out a little of the apple between the layers onto the plate.

'You cut, I get to choose.'

'Fair's fair.'

'Anne Frank would be amazed to know you could get good coffee and cake a few feet from where she was so hungry.'

Gerry ate, making little noises of pleasure. Nothing was said for some time. Their forks clicked against the plate.

'I'm still embarrassed about it.'

'What?'

'My gesture.' She rose and edged her way out from behind the table. Gerry looked up at her and rolled his eyes a bit.

'What are you doing?'

'Wait.'

'I've not finished my coffee,' he said. He watched her stride out of the café, back the way she had come.

She stood on the threshold of the room. It was empty. She walked to the mantelpiece, her coat and scarf now hanging

130

loosely about her. The little line of trinkets shone, reflecting the ceiling lights. Now it reminded her of a child's game. How dare she take part in it – her, a rank stranger, a person from elsewhere? She would not have them say – how dare she. Solidarity, my backside. Who was she anyway to think such a gesture was necessary? Just because Northern Ireland had had its thirty years war, its share of suffering. Just because she herself had been involved in that suffering. She lifted her earring from the mantelpiece and slipped it into her pocket. When she turned the old man with the kippa was right behind her, staring at her. He was looking over his rimless glasses at her. Straight into her, then down at her pocket. He was shaking his head, his mouth slightly open. Again she noticed the scrawny way he had shaved. And as she walked back across the floor she distinctly heard a gasp from him. He tried to speak but Stella could not make out what it was he was trying to say. It was only then that she remembered she was in a foreign country and she would not understand what was being said anyway. But his face and arresting eyes said it all as he reached out to steady himself on the glass top of the exhibit beside him. And in a flash Stella understood. She knew she was retrieving her own earring but the old man thought she was stealing. Something of value, whether from the Frank family or from the museum or from something left in the museum – this woman was stealing. Grave-robbing.

And there was no remedy so she kept going. Gerry was in the café and stood when she came in. He drained his cup, knotted his scarf and put his arm out for her to hook onto. She brushed past him and hurried down the stairs. He followed her, calling her name, but she took no heed. She was quicker on the stairs than he – he heard her feet running through the brightness of the entrance and into the sunlight of the street.

'Stella – what's the matter?'

She strode along the canal with Gerry following.

'Take it easy. My knee's not good.'

She came to a bench and sat down. When Gerry sat beside her she was in some agitation.

'There was an old man in there – the one with the cap – the Jewish cap. He thought I was stealing.' She was on the verge of tears.

'What?'

'My own earring,' she said. 'He was very old – looked like he could have been in the camps himself. We saw him in the cloakroom. Putting on his kippa.' Gerry stroked the back of her hand. 'He stared at me *so* much. I have never felt that way in my life before. Jesus've mercy, I'm so totally mortified.'

'It was a mix-up. He had the wrong end of the stick. Those things on the mantelpiece – they're not official. Somebody just started that . . .'

'But I had no right to add to it.'

Some ducks were curious and swam towards the figures on the bench, expecting to be fed.

'You bought me those. I liked them but I didn't like them enough. That nearly put me off leaving one – the fact that I wasn't in love with them. It should've been something really precious to me.'

Gerry looked at the one still hanging from her earlobe.

'I like them,' he said. 'I mean. I like *it*.' He reached out to touch hands again. Stella unclenched her fingers and the other earring was there, almost embedded in her skin. She had clenched it so tightly there was an indentation in the creases of her palm.

'I've never been so ashamed in all my life.' She sigh-shuddered and stood. 'Desecration. Let's get out of here. As far away as possible. I couldn't face that man again – couldn't explain, even if I did.'

She left Gerry sitting on his own, facing the ducks. He jumped to his feet and followed her, only catching up on the main street.

They walked together.

'Where next?'

'I don't want to be inside,' said Stella.

'Let's just walk. You know the way to the hotel?'

'I have a map.'

'Knowing the way and having a map are not the same thing.'

They crossed a metal suspension bridge over a canal. Both sides of the structure bristled with padlocks.

'Looks like they've something to do with bicycles,' said Stella. She stooped to look more closely. The locks did not hold anything. They had just been snapped closed on a hawser or a section of wire mesh. Some of the brass locks had felt-tipped names written on them. 'Don + Gwen', 'Micky & Minnie', 'Leo n Leonora'. One had a message written on it. 'Graham and Vickey. I love you more than Coco Pops.'

'It must be some kind of love fest,' Gerry said.

'Clamped for ever.'

'Have you seen this kinda thing before?'

'I've heard of it.'

'It'll be the young ones.'

'Trendy ones.'

'Just like the ones who started the tokens on the mantelpiece.'

'Me trying to join them. Serves me right.'

'When it comes to a declaration of love,' said Gerry, 'a padlock is a small price to pay. Compared to a tattoo.'

Stella rested her elbows on the bridge and looked down into the black water.

'I cannot tell you how distressing that whole episode was.' She gave a great sigh. Gerry shrugged and put one arm around her. 'Every time I see these earrings I'll think of it and cringe.' She opened her hand and forced herself to look at the earring. 'For all eternity. Were they very expensive?'

'A paltry sum.'

She smiled and he laughed.

'Would you mind if I got rid of them?'

'They're yours. Do what you like with them.'

She closed her mouth tightly and tilted the palm of her hand so that the little gleam toppled into the canal. Both of them watched as the earring see-sawed down through the water, jinking out of sight into the muddy bottom. Before it had gone completely she began to unscrew the keeper from behind the one that was still in her earlobe. She reattached the keeper and dropped the whole lot into the water with the same tilting motion of her hand. Again the movement through the water was the same – a slight zigzagging followed by darkness. She turned to walk away.

'Now I feel guilty,' she said.

'You can't win.'

'I could have pawned them when I got home. Given the money to charity.'

'Hey.' Gerry turned her around to face him and held her close. Hugged her. She leaned her forehead on his shoulder for a while. Then they began walking again. Gerry said: 'I love you more than Coco Pops.'

They came across a little park and went into it. There were very few people about on such a winter's day. The occasional dog walker. A young mother and her child. They sat on a bench in the shelter of a box hedge, hunched against the cold. There was a children's play park just across the path from them.

'It could only be January,' said Stella. 'Snowdrops and crocuses together.' A couple of men in overalls were working in the garden. One was listlessly digging, turning over the soil. Sinking the spade with a foot on the lug, breaking and slicing the turned-over sods. The other man was pruning rose bushes with secateurs. A series of little snaps.

'If I'd known it was going to be this cold I'd've brought a rug,' said Stella. 'Or my hot-water bottle.'

The young mother and her little girl went to the swings. From behind, the mother pulled the swing up to chest height and let go. She sang out the noises she thought her child should make and the child copied the sounds. After a while the child quietened and the only noise was the squeak of the swing as it moved.

'They have it easy nowadays,' said Gerry. 'Look at the ground, it's practically carpet. Non-scratch if the wee ones fall – a way of recycling old tyres.' He ceased to sit hunched against the cold and stretched his legs out in front of him. There was silence between them until Stella said, '*In spite of everything, I believe that people are really good at heart.*'

'I agree.'

'Do you really believe that?' Stella smiled.

'Yes. A quote from Anne Frank,' said Gerry.

'Even in something like the texture of a playground. Scientists think, "Let not the wee ones be hurt."'

'You've a drip.'

Stella rummaged for a hanky and wiped her nose.

'It's the icy air,' she said.

135

A flock of pigeons wandered among the stanchions of the swings. Then, like a handclap, they took off – whirring up in a great arc. This mass flapping seemed to frighten the child. She cried in alarm and her mother lifted her out of the swing. They came past and Stella leaned forward and smiled down at the wee one who, close up, seemed about three or four. The mother and child sat on a bench further along. A plastic ball was produced. She gave it to the girl, then meshed her fingers, holding her hands out from her body to form a hoop. The child threw the ball and scored a basket every time because the mother minutely adjusted, swayed, coaxed the ball into the circle of her arms.

'The mother's cheating,' said Gerry.

'The mother's teaching,' said Stella. 'Encouraging the wee one not to feel a failure. Anyway, teaching's an anagram of cheating.'

'It's like the guy who shot arrows and drew the targets round them afterwards. Where they stuck. That way he got a bullseye every time. Do you feel close?'

'To the end?'

He laughed.

'No, do you feel close to me.'

'We're side by side.'

Gerry smiled.

'Come on. Answer,' he said.

'Let me put it this way,' Stella said. 'If anybody asks me how long we've been married I just say, "For a protracted period."' They both smiled. There was silence, which was interrupted now and again by the noise of the secateurs and the spade moving through the friable soil.

'In every relationship,' said Stella, 'there's a flower and a gardener. One who does the work and one who displays.'

'Nice one.'

'Which do you think you are?'

'I have no doubt I am – one or the other. Maybe both. All my life I've been putting the cornflakes on the table. Coco Pops, even.' He lowered the timbre of his voice. 'But because work involves creativity I'm inclined to display a little. To flamboy, as you call it.'

'It's the daily grind I'm talking about.'

'Like what?'

'Never-ending stuff,' said Stella. 'Whereas you do man-work. Build something and it's there for hundreds of years. I cook the food, do the dishes, hang out the sheets, pay gas bills, electricity bills and it all has to be done again the next time. As Virginia Woolf says, "Nothing remains of it."'

'Where would we be without my minestrone soup?' said Gerry.

'Still washing up all the equipment you used. Who does the ironing?'

'You do. Far too bloody much of it, if you ask me,' said Gerry. 'Who ever heard of ironing underwear? Or pyjamas.'

'Who does the hoovering?'

Gerry nodded slowly, conceding.

'Why is it always me,' he said, 'who has to fill the stapler?'

Stella didn't even smile this time. She remained silent for a while then said, 'How would the gardener end a relationship, do you think?'

Stella was hunched with her arms folded. Gerry persuaded her to unfurl, to sit in a relaxed fashion like him.

'Are you all right?' he asked.

'This is not good. I feel very shaky. After the goings-on today.'

'Maybe it's your blood sugar.'

Stella rustled in her pocket and produced her Werther's. There were only two left. She offered one to Gerry and took the last one herself.

'Calm me down,' she said, rattling the sweet about her mouth.

'Maybe we should have some lunch.'

'No, I couldn't face it.'

They stood. Stella went out of her way to dispose of the sweet papers in a waste bin. Back on the street they came to a place where flowers had accumulated. Bouquets lay on the pavement, in cellophane wraps – some blackened, some withered, one or two fresh and brightly coloured. There were cards and tokens. They were also heaped in bunches on the adjoining traffic island protected by zinc barriers.

'They treat flowers the way they treat bicycles,' Gerry said. 'Just leave them lying around. Think how many gardeners it took to produce this lot.'

Stella leaned over and tried to decipher what was written on the cards. Some of the ink had faded, some had run in the rain. The name of Van Gogh appeared again and again. Stella said, 'It can't be anything to do with the painter.'

'It must be the guy who was murdered a few years ago.'

'The filmmaker,' said Stella. 'He was stabbed or shot.'

'Both, I think.'

'It was a religious thing, wasn't it?'

Gerry watched her. She stood with her hands joined in front of her, her head bowed.

'This is not good,' she said. 'I feel very shaky.'

He took her by the arm and they walked down the street. They came across a taxi rank and Gerry opened the back door of a cab and ushered Stella in.

'Just back to the hotel,' she said. 'I need a lie-down.'

Gerry named the hotel for the driver. He turned to Stella. 'You've gone a bit pale.'

He took her hand and her skin was icy. By the time they got into the hotel lobby she had warmed a little. Still he held her hand.

'Are you going for a sleep?'

She nodded but made no sound.

'Then I think I'll go for a wander. Have you got a key?' Again she nodded. He walked her to the lift and summoned it. It seemed to take ages. She stood watching the red glow of the pressed button, her arms hanging loosely at her sides. The doors slid open and he guided her into the empty space.

'I'll not be long,' he said. He kissed her lightly on the cheek and backed out of the lift.

'Be as long as you like,' she said.

Stella met herself in the lift mirror. How white she was. How exhausted. She flinched, looked at her feet, closed her eyes until the lift stopped at her floor. It shuddered a little and the doors opened.

In her room she stepped from her shoes and lay down on the bed. She did not bother to get beneath the bedclothes but enveloped herself in the heavy bedcover. The luxury of the material, its weight and warmth, made her sigh out loud. But she couldn't sleep. Her head was still racing. Her eyes were closed but pictures were still coming to her. There was an inevitability about them. Trying to sort out the miracle from what was possible. Trying to chronicle the journey of the projectile. The sparrow – in one door and out the other. It was the day she'd first found herself in the Hunterian Museum. They hadn't been living in Glasgow all that long. She'd gone

139

for a walk into the university – which was open to the public – with Michael, who had not yet started school. The rain came on and they sheltered in what looked like a cloister – a forest of columns beneath an ornate Victorian building. They waited but the rain seemed as if it was on for the day. Then she saw a sign pointing upwards to a museum. In the lift she guided Michael's finger to the correct button. When the doors opened into the museum space Michael ran ahead.

In the entrance hall a series of square stainless steel windows contained exhibits. But dominating everything in a central window was a huge book displaying an image which made Stella stop. She did not know whether to look away or to keep her eyes down in self-preservation or to react with horror or embarrassment. The image was almost life size, of a woman giving birth – no – she was not giving birth. She was at full term and had been thrown open to display the child crammed within her womb – in the head-down act of burrowing into the world. Like Macduff. Untimely ripped from his mother's womb. It wasn't how well the artist had captured the grey slipperiness or the violence of the opening technique, what astonished her most was the fullness of the womb. Stella could see herself reflected in the glass, could see how rooted to the spot she was in her pale raincoat. Babies in the womb were like expanding foam. They grew to fit the cavity available. The space was full, the way a Russian doll was full. With another. Full of itself. Not an inch to spare. No room for a needle or bare bodkin to pass through, never mind anything else. And she realised that the flaps of flesh drawn back to reveal the womb's contents would have been scalpelled in the shape of a cross. Four triangular flaps folded back. A container opened. The big scissors not required. There was nakedness and then there was this. Stripped even

140

of her flesh. Her legs agape, her belly and underbelly revealed. What Stella couldn't forgive was the reduction of the poor woman's legs to gigot chops with the bone in. This was the kind of thing the bombers produced in Belfast. She tried to look away from the truncated thighs to the womb itself, bulging with the baby. Somewhere between the baby's right knee and the index finger, there was a gap. A tiny corridor. Or else it was a miracle. There was a label on the exhibit which she stooped to read. *A drawing from William Hunter's The anatomy of the human gravid uterus exhibited in figures (1774).* The word gravid was a mouthful. 'Full to the brim' was what her mother would have said. Within its stainless steel frame the space was gravid with the book on display. 'Enceinte' came up occasionally in crosswords. The models must have been dead, for this dissection and drawing. This poor woman and her baby had been flayed and displayed. For the sake of knowledge. The artist got a mention, the collector and the anatomist got a mention, but there was nothing about the woman. She was without the dignity of a name. And, of course, her unborn child had not yet had time to be named. She was not a jailbird or a hanged woman, just someone ordinary, a woman who had died on the brink of joy. In the eighteenth century such deaths must have been commonplace. But nobody could tell Stella that eighteenth-century people did not feel the same or as much as people nowadays. So she mourned for them, standing in front of their image, and said a prayer for each of them.

She was bending over, reading the label, when she heard Michael coming back. The boy appeared and she put herself between him and the drawing. She walked towards him so that he wouldn't see it and shepherded him back towards the place of dinosaurs and stuffed animals with glass eyes. The questions he would ask. In the time she had taken to look at this drawing she had become it. This was her, had been her. Splayed and wounded. How could she show herself to her own son in such a way.

Other footsteps approached. A security man in a pale blue shirt.

'I'm sorry,' he said. 'The museum is closed on a Monday.'

'Nobody said.'

She took her child by the hand and, feeling glad to be excluded, turned away from the illustration in the monstrous grey book.

On the street Gerry tightened the knot of his scarf and put up his collar. It could be an opportunity – replenish the bottle, maybe. Stella was best left alone when she went quiet. Again he saw the block of ice. It was now cradled in the shallow depression of the dry pavement. Nothing was melting in these temperatures. He tried to remember the direction they had taken to find the place of robust stews. The skyline had the sharpness of an etching, each cornice and gable defined and different – scrolls, pinnacles and garlands precisely delineated. Like cut-outs. The branches of trees, now without leaves, were black against the evening sky. It wasn't a sunset, just an ending of a cold, clear day – turning from blue, to yellow, to blush.

A street of trees was being pollarded. At first all he could hear was the noise – glissandi – ascending from gruff to high-pitched scream. He looked up and saw two men in helmets with chainsaws swinging on a leash from their belts, clambering in the trees. The lower end of the street had just been done, leaving the branches like fists against the sky. In the supermarket beside the place of robust stews he bought more Tyrone Superior. He could do with a drink at this very moment, after such a day. To avoid having to make decisions he went to the Irish bar.

He sat facing the door with a pint of Guinness and a whiskey on the table in front of him. He had watched the Dublin barman pull his black pint and leave it to settle – for the curtains of cream to cascade and form a white priestly collar before topping it off. A poured, but as yet untouched, pint of Guinness has a slight dome to it which reminded him of the faint curvature of the outer wall of Burt Chapel. The Jameson required no interference apart from a drop of water. The Dublin barman was talking quietly to a customer. There was taped Irish music but not at a volume which was irksome.

Gerry's hands lay in his lap and his eye was drawn to the window. The end of the daylight striking the glass obliquely created a glittering, grisaille effect. Like ground glass, a layer of dust activated by almost horizontal light transformed the window into Waterford crystal. No expense spared for the Irish pubs of Amsterdam. The admission and exclusion of light. The double function of windows – to admit light and to provide a view. He was hearing the voice of his teachers again. Dr Rice most clearly.

When he left school in the late fifties Gerry hadn't a clue what he wanted to do. His subjects were mostly scientific. He'd talked to a careers adviser – a rarity in those days – who, as their meeting came to an end, produced a slip of paper from the mayhem of his desk. It was for a summer job in an architect's office. Gerry agreed to give it a go. When the summer was over the firm offered him an apprenticeship. He studied nights at the Belfast Tech – learning on the job – showed promise in everything. He was then poached by a Catholic firm who were well in with the clergy and doing lots of schools and churches. At that time you couldn't cross the threshold of a Catholic church without having your arm twisted to contribute to 'The School Building Fund'. So there was plenty of work. In the early days Gerry spent much of his time colouring prints – brickwork was red, concrete was green, steel was blue. A kind of architectural storyboard. And going messages. Sent out with the kitty money for biscuits and Maxwell House coffee. Also after Vatican Two everything was full steam ahead on liturgical reforms – which meant the buildings in which faith happened had to be changed – 'altared' was the joke at the time – the Pugin-like folderols and backdrops were to be dismantled, the priests had to face the people and the altar rails had to disappear. Then he had the luck to be taken on by Liam McCormick who, at that time, was working on Burt Chapel. Some people – even then – talked of McCormick as Ireland's greatest architect. The chapel was modelled on Grianan Aileach, a circular Iron Age fort further up the hill.

Gerry had just met Stella – must've been the late sixties – and, not long after the Ballycastle trip, he took her to Donegal to show her what he was working on. They had driven up to the Iron Age fort to see the resemblance to the church they were building at its foot – a shape-rhyme with the chapel, separated by thousands of feet, thousands of years.

But Stella was more interested in the view. Give or take some trees and a road or two, she said, it was what you would have seen two thousand years ago. With one slow turn of the head you could see the counties of Donegal, Derry and Tyrone, with Lough Swilly and Lough Foyle in the middle of it all. It made her feel glad to be Celtic. Silence in such a place, at such a height, is hard to come by because the wind is always there bluffing your ears into thinking there is no noise. Maybe the bleat of a sheep and no sheep to be seen. She put her hand in the air to find the wind's direction. Stella. A star with her hair blowing. Eclipsing all else. Her hand in the air.

What was she on about this afternoon about the flower and the gardener? How would a gardener end a relationship? What sort of a question was that? And this stuff about a religious community. She must be serious because she'd made an appointment to see somebody.

He sipped his Guinness. Taste, texture, temperature. Perfect. The whiskey could wait until he had the black stuff half finished. It usually took three visits to the glass, each one leaving its stretch marks. The second half took a lot longer now that the thirst had been quenched. He was reluctant to buy the next one until it could be put off no longer. Then he drained both glasses, rose to his feet and approached the bar.

'Same again.'

He resumed his seat with the two full vessels in front of him. It gave him great satisfaction not to touch them. Enough to know the supplies were in. Their lecturer at the Tech – old Dr Rice – had said architecture was about delivering the services to the client – gas, water and electricity – as elegantly and economically as possible. No more, no less. Oh – it helped if you could draw a straight line freehand and had an eye for what wouldn't fall down. They were in the business of life saving – building structures that would not kill people. It could be St Peter's in Rome or a public toilet in Portadown – the same rules applied. Except that there were no rules in Portadown. He was a great teacher and, as he said himself, he liked to give students enough self-confidence to create, yet instil in them enough knowledge to self-doubt.

The drink was unfurling him. The very place relaxed him with its noises and smells, reflecting the certainty that alcohol was available. Drink made everything easier – easier to feel, easier to find words. Some people he knew were transformed by it into monsters. They became vicious, spiteful and, worst of all, violent creatures. But not him. With a drink or two in him, he loved people, wanted to hug them, not hit them.

He wondered if he was drinking too much. His memory was getting worse – he couldn't recall the ends of evenings, couldn't remember people and their names. Or faces. At home he joked he never would go out again. Indoors he felt safe. Anybody coming to visit him usually made an appointment and their name would go in the appointments diary. On the day, at the appointed time, the bell would ring. He'd glance at the diary and see Jack written there and he'd answer the door and say, 'How are you, Jack?' If it turned out to be someone called Billy to read the electricity meter – too bad. If the meter man *was* called Jack he'd wonder all day how this man had got to be on first name terms with him.

Stella was the opposite. Not only did she remember people's names but she remembered everything about them.

At school he'd loved geometry. There was something about it – its balance, its clarity, the flying buttress of the right-angle sign, the stability of the isosceles triangle. Words like congruent. He loved not only the word but the concept. To be equal, to be the same. There was a time when Stella and he were congruent.

The best present he ever got at this age was a Bayko building set – a toy to build houses with white walls, red roofs, green bay windows. When the whole thing was finished it was the perfect Enid Blyton house, home for the Famous Five. With a double garage for Uncle Quentin's cars.

In the real world with his friends they built huts from dead wood and cardboard and old bits of corrugated iron.

When they were finished they sat in them, smiling with satisfaction, wondering what to do.

It was a career that had let him see the world. Places they would not otherwise have visited. Like Soviet Russia. The land of appalling spalling. In Warsaw Stella wondered aloud why there were so many parks. 'Ask the Germans,' she was told. He loved a city with layers – Lisbon had them – you could even take an elevator from one level to another. Upstairs and downstairs. Gerry thought Edinburgh the most wonderful city to look at, all columns and classicism and cut stone. One of the best things he'd seen there was a street act – a juggler getting above himself. At the Art Gallery on the Mound a young lad pressed his feet against two fluted columns, then inched himself up the building – twenty or thirty feet above the heads of the crowd where he juggled with flaming torches. And as he did so everybody realised that there was no way he could get down. He was stuck up there. For ever. If he took the pressure off his feet – either foot – he would plummet. Of course he made a joke of it – his dilemma was the centre of his act – but eventually he jigged his way down to applause – a stuttering descent, like a toy woodpecker sliding down a vertical wire. He made it look easy.

Gerry ordered himself another drink with a chaser. The barman was good – this time all it took was a nod and a little later the drinks appeared. A thing that really took his breath away was Norman Foster's roof over the Great Court at the British Museum – the audacity and brilliance of it. The approach inside the building from a periphery of darkness into the thrilling light at its centre – the largest covered square in Europe – was utterly wonderful. If it was about anything, architecture was about shedding light.

148

In the presence of such brilliance, having admired it, the next thing Gerry felt was envy. He knew he himself was in League Division Two. Maybe, on a bad day, League Division Three. To have made something which awed people. The pilgrimage chapel at Ronchamp. Light streaming into the space through tunnels in thick walls ending as pools of colour on the floor. Light chimneys above altars. The building itself surprisingly small, halfway between an upturned boat and a grand piano. But wonderful – even down to the small scallop shell embedded in the concrete wall to welcome pilgrims.

Gerry had ended up a university teacher. One who drank too much. Was his failure to make the top to be blamed on his drinking? Or did his drinking come about to take the edge off his lack of success? He finished his drinks and heaved himself to his feet – he swayed – like a rocking skyscraper – but knew he was swaying. He knew his tolerances.

When he got back to the hotel Stella was asleep. He leaned over her in the bed and kissed her temple. She wakened and said, 'I feel the cold off you.'

They decided to eat in the Amstel place again.

'It has the added advantage that we know where it is,' Stella said.

When they had ordered and Gerry had poured the wine he said, 'So are you any easier in your mind about today?'

'No. That kind of thing takes a long time to go away. Ten years from now – if I'm living – I'll groan out loud with embarrassment in the checkout queue.'

He put his hand out and covered hers and shook it gently.

'I'm not talking about the Anne Frank House. But about after it.'

Stella shook her head.

'You learn to live with that,' she said. 'Let me see your chin.'

Gerry turned his profile.

'It's getting yellower, less auberginey.'

They ate quietly.

'Why don't we go tonight,' said Stella, 'and have a look at the red-light district?'

'With my wife?'

'Yes.'

As they were walking arm in arm a fine cold rain came on. Stella looked up at the night sky and hooked onto his arm more tightly. People were coming and going from a very narrow passageway and they wondered where it could lead. It was just larger than shoulder width, so they had to go in single file. Gerry led the way.

They came upon a square with window booths where women posed, sitting with their legs open or walking about strutting their stuff, trying to attract and arouse. Gerry stopped and stared. He unhooked his wife's arm from his own.

'That could be seen as a perversion. A couple looking.'

'Poor things,' said Stella.

They carried on and the passage narrowed again. Gerry took the lead. He turned. 'What'll I do if some bloke tries to squeeze past me with a hard-on?'

Stella slapped his shoulder. The narrow lane led to another, less narrow lane. Gerry stopped and looked up at a building.

'It's a pub, Gerry. As if you wouldn't recognise one.'

'Rembrandt would have had a flagon or two in here,' he said.

Stella cautiously opened the door. A wall of noise roared out – talk loud enough to sound like a train. They edged inside. There were no seats or tables. It was crowded and people stood drinking glasses of draught beer. But it was like no other pub they had ever seen. Low counters, shelved spaces, more like a chemist's shop than a drinking establishment. Gerry raised an eyebrow to Stella and, with a little drinking mime, asked her if she fancied one. She pulled a face. There was a man and a woman in some kind of folk costume behind the bar. A customer in front of Gerry ordered and the barmaid served him with a beer and a short. She filled the shot glass till it overflowed and Gerry thought, 'How sloppy.' The man bent over from the waist and sipped from the glass without touching it. Hoovering up the drink with his lips. The man then lifted the glass and finished it off, draining it for the very last bead, his body language for all the world like Stella putting in her eye drops. When it came to Gerry's turn he hesitated. The barmaid took one look at him and began shouting at the top of her voice in English.

'You like to try? You know about this?' Gerry shook his head. No. 'This is *jenever.* Before you English had gin, we had jenever.'

'I am not English.' He had almost to scream to be heard. 'Irish.'

'With a beer it is very good. With Guinness,' she laughed, 'even better.'

Gerry looked over his shoulder at Stella and mouthed yet another invitation. Again she shook her head. No, not for me.

'Yes,' he yelled to the barmaid. She pulled a yellow draught beer and set it frothing on the counter. Then she produced a sherry glass, grey with frost from the fridge, and filled it to overflowing with the clear alcohol. It smelled like gin. He

151

performed as the man before him had performed, bending over, sucking up the drink. There was a childish pleasure in it – like abandoning table manners, like licking the bowl. Then he picked up the glass and emptied it. Tasted a bit like poteen.

The barmaid waggled her finger at him, then shouted, 'You drink the beer. Then the chaser.'

'Oh sorry. Let me do it right.' She set up another jenever and another beer. Gerry drank one of his beers, supped the top off the gin stuff, then carried the other beer and the gin glass to join Stella.

'It's good.'

'What?'

He leaned in close to her ear.

'It's good,' he shouted into her hair. He didn't like to contradict the barmaid but he thought the beer tasted really good after the jenever. Not the other way around. The beer was the chaser as far as he was concerned. But this was all too complicated to communicate to Stella. She reached out and requested a sip of the jenever. Gerry parted with the glass. Stella sipped and smacked her lips. She wasn't sure. He could tell from her face. She sipped again.

'Do you want one of your own?' Gerry was becoming peevish at her lowering the level in his glass.

'Yes.'

'A beer as well?'

'No.'

When Gerry went to the counter Stella was left on her own. It was such a phenomenon, the noise of this place. Pubs always amazed her with their volume. If everybody kept their voice down then it would be okay. But fuelled with drink their voices rose. And this happened to all the customers, so everyone had to shout to be heard. The whole thing was incremental and exponential. People became hoarse and had to have more drink to soothe their throats, which made them shout louder to drown out their neighbours. And all the drinkers retaliated without realising it. Because of Gerry, Stella had spent too many nights of her life sitting on the edge of a company of drinkers. Especially in the Derry office with the Norwegians. When the Norwegians got drunk they were very hard to understand. The weirdest things became funny to them. They slid down the wall laughing at what would not make them smile at breakfast time.

What were these people talking about? What was so important that had to be shouted? A man was standing beside her. He smiled at her, extended his glass to her in a kind of toast and drank to her.

He was American, by the look of him. He had the top of a *Guide to Amsterdam* sticking out of his pocket so he must, at least, speak English. There were dark spots of rain on his pale jacket. He wore horn-rimmed spectacles. She didn't quite know what to do. This, after all, was close to the red-light district. Maybe it was even *in* the red-light district. Did this man think she was on her own? Was he being friendly or was he trying to pick her up? He leaned forward and said something to her but she didn't hear. Was it a question? Or a greeting? She nodded her head up and down slowly. She was not good at lying. It made her uncomfortable. The American tried again, leaning a little too close. But she could not make out a single word he said. She looked over her shoulder to see where Gerry was.

He was at the counter, bending over. What on earth was he doing with that barmaid? His head was on a level with . . . her haunches. It looked like he was doing something terribly intimate – appalling in public. Just come back to me,

Gerry, please. The American licked his lips and adjusted his spectacles on the bridge of his nose as if he was going to say something else to her. Gerry arrived carrying two glasses, one brimming over onto his fingers. He gave the half-emptied one to Stella. To take the glass Stella turned her back on the American.

'Talk to me. Loudly,' she shouted into Gerry's ear.

'Well, how are you, my poppet,' he cried out. 'Drink your drink. All at once.'

'I'd be sick.' Stella sipped it. Again and again, tiny intakes. 'It could grow on you.' She pulled a face and passed her glass to him to finish. 'It's very strong.'

He sank it in one. She began nodding her head towards the door.

'Let's skedaddle,' said Gerry.

Stella turned her head to nod goodbye to the American but he had moved elsewhere.

'Although skedaddling is not in my nature, on this occasion I will.'

Outside the rain had stopped. Or else the passageway was so narrow that the rain couldn't make it down that far.

'What bliss to be away from that noise,' said Stella.

'And you think I'm enjoying myself when I go out for a drink.'

'I couldn't make out a word that man was saying.'

'What man?'

'Some guy. The one with the specs.'

They eventually came out from the narrowness. To their right was a canal, to their left, a whole streetful of women behind windows in their tiny rooms, touting. Crowds of people were roaming the area. From such a distance the windows were small, bright like television screens. Stella's hand was latched onto Gerry's elbow and she felt him steer her towards the windows. The girls wore impossibly high heels and were half naked. Beribboned and bedecked – bored. Pacing up and down. One was reading a book. Another sat as if on a park bench. Next door a girl was drinking from a polka-dot mug. It was difficult to tell colours because of the harsh artificial lighting. A tall girl had an electric fire at her feet with one bar glowing. Yet another had ventilation problems and she was keeping her window from misting over with a T-shaped squeegee. Again Gerry's arm exerted pressure to go closer but Stella resisted.

'I'm sure they don't want me gawking at them,' she said.

'It's too early. This is cocoa time. About as sexy as Page 3.'

'I just feel sorry for them. God love them,' said Stella. Many of the women were lit with ultraviolet light and their scanty underclothing took on a vibrant purple luminescence.

'UV is what they use to kill flies in the butcher's, said Gerry.'

A crowd of young men came from the opposite direction. Yet another stag party. Gerry and Stella heard them before they saw them – hollering and laughing. They sounded German. They were pointing and backslapping.

'Full of Dutch courage,' said Gerry. 'Believe me – if they're laughing there's no sex involved.'

'Oh listen to you, Mister Brothel Creeper.'

'I hesitate to say what turns me on – but it certainly isn't this. Maybe I could be seduced by a big lassie in woollen tights on a bread-cart of a bicycle. Her knees zinging up and down. Imprinting her pheromones on the saddle. Blonde hair flying. That would ring my bell.'

As they walked, the pavement beneath their feet turned to herringbone. Gerry felt her press him across the road and away from the windows. The ducks and swans in the canal became very noisy – quacking and flapping, standing up and sparring on the surface of the water. The swans arched their wings and straightened out their necks, hissing. Other people stopped to see what it was all about.

'Look who's stealing the show,' said Stella. 'Upstaging the ladies.'

By the time they crossed the bridge the birds had settled. Ice was beginning to form where the water met the stone walls. In corners it had the appearance of grey cobwebs.

The other side of the canal was still part of the red-light district. Stella stopped, pulled Gerry back.

'Look,' she said.

He followed the direction of her gaze. In a narrow side lane were two horses standing under lamplight. He felt her moving him towards the lane. They approached with caution.

'How wonderful,' said Stella. 'What beautiful creatures. I think that gin has gone to my head.' Gerry could see her pouting as she would at a baby. 'The first and only time I ever got on a horse, I thought I was sitting on a sideboard.'

'Where was that?'

'Some farmer Daddy knew.'

One of the horses in front of them was a chestnut, the other a spotted grey. They stood together silently. The air coming from their nostrils was visible. A pile of horse dung, still steaming, had gathered in a small pyramid behind the chestnut horse.

'Horse dumps,' said Gerry.

'Horse apples. We were much more refined in our house.'

Gerry reached out and held Stella away from the horses.

'Easy. Don't get behind them. Keep out of kicking distance.'

'I know, I know. They look so calm, so resigned.'

156

'Mysterious, even.'

Gerry and Stella stared up at them. The grey moved its head up and down.

'Can you tell if it's a stallion?'

Gerry ducked down and had a look underneath.

'I can tell you one thing,' he said.

'What?'

'It's not a cow. How would I know?'

The horses were not tethered to anything but were covered in paraphernalia and trumpery. Saddles, stirrups, reins – other bits of harness she couldn't name except for a crossword. Words she would recognise as something to do with horses – 'crupper', 'throatlatch', 'girth', 'bridle'. There was a sheath with what looked like a baton in it. Indentations in the handle for a better grip, sitting proud of the holster. The chestnut adjusted the position of its back hoof, its shoe making a clopping sound against the stones of the lane.

'This is magic,' said Stella. 'There's something so saintly about them. Aloof, even. Look at the veins, Gerry. Like so many rivers.'

The grey shook its head and engaged in a little eye rolling. Stella was conscious of the whites. Small sounds came from its harness.

'Easy, boy.'

'They belong to the police. Easy now. That word, that logo.' She pointed to the blanket beneath the saddle.

'*Pol-it-ie*,' said Gerry. 'Why don't you pat it?' The chestnut horse had a white flash on its forehead. Stella reached out and when its head came down to her level she said, 'You're a good boy,' and laid her hand on it. 'Feel, Gerry. Broad as an ironing board. I thought it'd be soft – like sheepskin. It's more like a man's chin.' Her hand continued to pat the white flash. The horse seemed to be enjoying it.

157

'They smell amazing,' said Gerry. 'Not like anything we know.'

'Leather and milk and horse apples.'

'There's a tang, a sort of a tang off them.'

'Do you think the cops are in somewhere for a bit of . . .?' said Stella.

'Never have it off when I'm on duty, ma'am.' They smiled at this and both simultaneously turned to go.

'In the future,' said Stella, 'when I think of the red-light district in Amsterdam, I'll remember these two beauties. And their silent standing.'

It was still early enough in the evening and it was Stella's suggestion that they go back to the hotel. Make an early night of it. In the room they made love again.

'Those horses have got me going,' she said afterwards.

They lay side by side staring at the ceiling.

'Why do I take the notion more often when we're away?' said Stella. 'Can you guess?'

'No.'

'Because I don't have to think of dinners. *The* dinner. On a daily basis. It's the bane of my life. Remember Mister and Missus Sheep?'

'No?'

'Mister Sheep says *I'm fed up eating the same grass, day in, day out.*'

'And?'

'And Missus Sheep says *At least I don't have to cook it.*' She smiled. 'We were driving to Edinburgh.'

'I remember.'

They were both silent for a while.

'Sometimes I wonder if that was the last time.'

'Wonder or hope?' asked Gerry. Stella cooried in between his arm and his chest. He kissed the hair on the top of her head, where her fontanelle would have been.

'I would have loved to have known you when you were younger,' he said. 'Maybe me and you at the same primary school – your wee white socks. The bows in your hair. I feel I've missed a lot of you.' She began to tap his chest rhythmically with her finger and croon the skipping song.

'Fair Rosa was a lovely girl,
A lovely girl, a lovely girl
Fair Rosa was a lovely girl
A long time ago.'

In the morning the first thing Gerry was aware of was the wind blustering at the window. The bed was empty beside him. Noises were coming from the shower. He turned on his back and put his hands behind his head. Stella came out of the bathroom, wearing a white towel tucked in high on her chest. She skooshed some foam from a spray can onto her hand and applied it to her hair.

'What's that?' said Gerry.

'Styling mousse.'

'And what's that supposed to do?'

'It adds body to my – sadly – limp hair.'

'I wonder would it do anything for me,' Gerry said.

'*Volumising hold*, as the can says. Have you never seen me do this before?'

'Not that I remember.'

'At home I do all this in the bathroom.' She shook the container and blew another plume of white froth onto her hand and patted it into her hair. It clung there in blobs.

'It's like egg white,' said Gerry.

She combed her hair, putting her head back, sweeping with strokes of first a comb, then a brush.

'What are you getting all dolled up for at this time of the morning?'

160

'Mass. It's Sunday morning.'

'Do you want me to come with you?'

'Not really.' She gave one last skoosh and worked it in.

'Do you believe what the tin says?'

'Yes, I do. It certainly makes my hair feel better.' She stopped her brushing and wet her finger in her mouth then smoothed her eyebrows.

'Do you believe what the girls tell you in the chemist's?' he asked.

'It depends.'

'It's all pseudo science. Those girls in white coats wearing lip gloss.'

'Sometimes I think you're the worst misogynist I've ever met.'

There was a long silence in the room which was broken by the noise of the brush beginning to move again through Stella's hair.

At the front desk while Stella talked to the clerk Gerry browsed the tourist rack of pamphlets. He took some to read later and put them in his shoulder bag. Stella was telling the clerk that there was a Catholic church in the heart of the red-light district called 'Our Dear Lord in the Attic'.

'Remember, Gerry, where we saw the horses.'

'And a few other things.'

'Would there be Mass there?'

'No. I do not think so.' The clerk shook his head. 'It is now a museum.'

'All religion should be in museums,' Gerry said.

The clerk tore off an area map and marked an X on the nearest Catholic church.

'A Christian symbol as well as a direction,' said Stella. The clerk said he did not know the times of the services.

'*Dank ya*,' said Stella and smiled at the clerk.

Gerry led her towards the revolving doors.

'I'd forgotten all about your PhD in Dutch,' he said.

'It's about making an effort – however small.'

When they were going out a gust of wind caught the revolving doors with such force that they were nipped one from the other. Stella stood until Gerry came catapulting out. She was holding the map flat against the wind.

'I think this is the church we've already been to.' Gerry looked over her shoulder.

'The vomiting miracle one?'

Stella nodded. In the daylight the block of ice looked mournful and a little dirtier than the day before. Gerry stooped to look at it more closely. There were silver streaks of air within it, like rising bubbles.

'D'you think it looks blue?'

'No.'

'I have a theory it's frozen piss from an aeroplane.'

'Gerry, don't be so . . .' Stella said. 'At least it's not raining. How did we get to be this lucky?'

'Luck?' Gerry said. 'I prayed for it.' He looked up. The grey and white clouds were racing. There was blue sky in between.

'If there's a Mass I'll go,' Stella said. 'But if not . . . I'm not so hidebound by rules . . . I'm a traveller – I'm exempt.'

'A pilgrim.'

Gerry walked with her as far as the dark passageway into the Beguine place. They went through in single file. When they came out into the green it was welcoming – a place they knew. There were a few people going into the church which didn't look like a church.

'A good sign,' said Stella. 'Mass must be starting.' Gerry followed her into the doorway just to check. The candles were lit in the floodlit interior of the church. The robed priest was moving about at the altar. Stella arranged to meet Gerry outside in an hour.

'You might need this,' she said and pressed the street map into his hand. She finger-waved goodbye and walked to a seat. Gerry turned and left.

He walked back through the passage. Church bells had begun to ring on the hour above the main streets. Real bells with a metallic tang to their sound. How best to fill an hour? The pubs were sure to be closed. He came across a music shop that was open and browsed CDs for a while. He worked out the currency difference from the price of Naxos. It was so advantageous to the pound that he bought a disc he didn't have at home – one he had seen excellent reviews for. *Seven Last Words from the Cross.*

Outside again he walked so that the wind was behind him, quickening his step. On the other side of the street was a flower market. It backed onto a canal because he could see the gunmetal colour of the choppy water between the stalls. He looked both ways and crossed. There was a huge range of bulbs and corms, tray after tray of purples and browns. Other things were onion shaped, octopus-like, with rhizomes and roots like tentacles – the colour of earth and mud and umber. A sign said,

> Don't touch
> Non toccare
> Ne pas toucher

Nicht anfassen
Niet aankomen

Things he couldn't identify were like bunched knuckles, fists with hair on them, muddy starfish, white sprouting spears. They all looked so awful because their appearance played no part in their survival. These bits were underground. There was a Grow Your Own Cannabis starter kit. Everything seemed to be lying in wait for spring. Each wooden tray had a coloured picture of what its tubers would look like when they blossomed – petals of scarlet and yellow, cream and sepia. Optimism in action. Counting chickens. The canvas screens around him billowed and flapped in the wind. Stella would love some of these to plant in her perimeter garden. Gerry selected a red onion bag of mixed bulbs. Tulips and narcissi. Small enough to carry, big enough to be a present. The Dutch word for tulip was *tulp*. He approached a guy in a navy puffa jacket who wore an apron underneath. His English was okay. Good enough to tell Gerry that he was doing the right thing. There was no problem about taking the bulbs on a flight. They were much cheaper here than at the airport. At the airport they were all crooks.

Gerry paid and put the bulbs in his shoulder bag beside the CD. The canal water darkened here and there under the wind, like a finger across suede.

A coffee would go down well. The place he chose had a huge figure of Goliath with his helmet towering into the roof beams. A statue of David stood to one side, complete with slingshot, his head only reaching the hem of Goliath's battle kilt. His grandson Toby would love this place. He'd be looking up Goliath's skirt. On the menu he read in English that these wooden figures dated from the nineteenth century and had begun life as automata in park amusements. Internal machinery could make Goliath's eyes roll and his head turn.

The coffee was good and the first sip made him want a cigarette. His hand went to his pocket before he realised it was decades since he'd had a smoke. The desire came out of nowhere. He thought how foolish, how stuck in routine the body becomes. Would the same thing happen if he tried to give up the drinking? His shoulders went down. He stared at the Formica tabletop. Featureless, the colour of pale porridge. He found it difficult to break his gaze. He heard the sound of an ambulance in a Sunday Amsterdam street.

He remembered a flashing light reflecting off the painted hospital walls. His mouth was dry – probably from all the smoking. He went to the water fountain in the nearby toilet and pressed the lever, drank at the arc of water. Coming out of the Gents he saw Mavis, the Pink Lady, sitting in the seat he had left. She beckoned him. Again she apologised for having no word about his wife's condition. She told him that the hospital chaplain had been there when the ambulance brought Stella in. She'd had extreme unction given to her. Or was it holy viaticum? Mavis said that she was not Roman Catholic and begged to be forgiven for not being au fait with how to use the terms. Wasn't it also known as the last rites? That was much simpler. But a Roman Catholic friend had told her that you could receive the last rites many times. To have received the last rites did not necessarily mean that you were going to pass. Gerry said that 'anointed' was what he would say. 'She's been anointed.' He shrugged and told her that none of that mattered to him any more. He had ceased to practise, to believe. All that mattered was Stella. Mavis then asked him if he would like to see his son. He almost said that he didn't have a son – that she had the wrong person, there'd been some mistake.

He followed her in her pink overall down yet another corridor into another room – a temporary nursery, she called it. She said that the baby was perfect and they thought he would like to see it before they transferred him to the real nursery. The door squeaked when she opened it. The room was part office, part store. Black ring binders shared shelves with folded bed linen, a desk with a typewriter, grey filing cabinets and some deckchairs leaning against the far wall. The woman in pink pointed to a Moses basket beside the desk. Gerry approached it, had to look down into it because of its high woven sides. Jesus – there was a child in there. Not beautiful but so utterly and distinctly a boy. A face a bit like a bunched fist. Asleep. Eyes closed. Swaddled in a white sheet. What hair he had was wet. His visible tiny hand by his ear. Miraculous survivor. Gerry asked Mavis if he could touch him. Why not, he's yours, she said. He reached down and stroked the upturned baby's cheek with the back of his finger. It was warm. Then the tiny face, gently so's not to wake him, with fingertips. As if she was a mind reader Mavis said, 'Don't worry – you'll not wake him. He's been through a lot. Isn't he gorgeous? The chaplain baptised him. Just in case.' The baby's skin had a purity to it. Took after his mother. Gerry found himself making a vow. You are mine and I will love you till the day I die. He kissed his fingertips and conveyed the kiss to the baby's face slowly, as if it could be spilled on the way down.

Inside the Begijnhof church there was a smell of extinguished candles and a blue haze in the air. In the silence Gerry could hear himself panting. Nowadays even hurrying produced a certain amount of breathlessness. The bright lights had been switched off and the place was lit only by small windows. Then there she was – Stella – the top of her head highlighted as she looked down, reading. It never ceased to amaze him the thrill he got at seeing her. Catching her unawares.

'Hi,' he said.

'Hi . . .' She looked up from what she was doing.

'How was it?'

'An awful lot of singing.' She smiled and beckoned him. 'I have something to show you. A small miracle in the Miracle church.' She was being provocatively mysterious. She had the *Book for your Prayers* open in front of her. It seemed as if it had fattened since the last time they had browsed it.

'I was passing the time waiting for you,' she said.

'Sorry I'm late.'

'Look what I came across.'

Gerry followed her finger. It was pointing to the looped unmistakable handwriting of the sad American girl. He leaned forward and read.

Thank you, Lord. For your generosity in restoring my family. The father of my child and I are back together again. For how long only You know. He is not a believer but he is good and I am happy. Forgive me for doubting You.

'Isn't that great?' said Stella.

After breakfast on Monday morning Stella headed off to her meeting. Gerry went back up to the room. And he stood there for a long time, his hands in his trouser pockets. She had asked him to make a start on the packing. In his stare around the room he avoided the bottle in the bag on the sideboard. There was no point at this time. To feel bad about himself was the wrong way to start the day. His stomach felt taut. He threw the bedclothes back into the shape of a 'made' bed, then swung the big case onto the coverlet. The lid now yawned open. He gathered a polybag full of washing and stuffed it in. Pyjamas, no matter what colour they were, did not need folding. He threw them in, smoothed them flat with his hand. Her night things as well. At the bottom of the wardrobe was a scarf and a brightly coloured tie loosely parcelled in soft tissue paper – the kind of stuff that wrapped oranges in his childhood. There was a postcard with the items. A Rembrandt of *Old Woman Reading*. He turned the card over and read the back. '*In Amsterdam for a few days. Hope you like the wee gifts. This is me reading in decrepitude while your father is out at the pub. Hope all is well with the three of you.*' Stella's signature. He was surprised to see he had signed it too. *Love Granda*. He had no recollection of it but it certainly looked like his writing. There was a pen marked Hotel Theo on the desk. At first it wouldn't work. To get it started he scribbled violently on a brochure. Then he wrote beside his greeting – *Give my love to Toby*.

He folded and packed what he could find. A spare pair of shoes stuffed tight with socks and underpants. A maroon waistcoat he hadn't worn. Stella's clothes hung on hotel hangers – she could pack them to her own satisfaction. He would not be accused of causing creases. In the bathroom he lifted his medication, shaving kit and washbag and put them in his shoulder bag. One of the towelling dressing gowns was sprawled on a chair. He took it and hung it on the back of the bathroom door. Once he had stayed in a hotel in Zurich which had prominently displayed a note that the price of any items removed from the room would be deducted from the chambermaid's wages. What bastards. He had actually complained before he left. Not verbally, but like a coward, on a piece of hotel notepaper dropped into their suggestion box.

He filled the kettle and made himself a coffee – 'a pour-over' as the Americans call it – then gathered up newspapers and flyers and brochures and dumped them in the bin. The empty coffee sachet he also dumped. Diversionary tactics. He sat sipping his coffee warily, it was so hot. And bitter – a brand he'd never heard of. Champion Coffee. Like the Tyrone Superior of whiskeys. He began remembering the day they'd left Ireland. Sailing to a different accent. Every stick of furniture they had was in a removal van below deck. They'd just endured the embarrassment of it being brought into the sunlight and realised that the feeling was to be repeated when they arrived at their new place in Scotland. That is, if the sun would shine the next day. They'd been warned that, where they were going, good days came in ones. But they were from the north and were used to such bad weather. Later their tired furniture would be briefly on show to new neighbours from behind mainland curtains. Embarrassments, both fore and aft.

The van driver and his strapping son were getting something to eat. They'd spent all morning packing the load. When they got to the other side they'd drive to the new place. Then sleep in the van and unload in the morning. It wasn't a big firm – just a guy with his son who owned a van. Or maybe he'd just hired it. When anything was asked of the son, be it lifting a tea chest one-third full of books or giving him directions to somewhere or asking if he took sugar in his tea, he'd say, 'Champion, sir.'

When they came back after eating, Stella asked the strapping son to take a photo. Of the family, the three of them on deck – her holding the toddler in her arms and Gerry beside her. Behind them the ferry's pale wake streaming out all the way to Belfast. A flock of seagulls trailing the boat, rising and falling against a blue sky.

'Champion,' the son said, handing back the camera.

It was mid-July and the bars and lounges were packed with Scottish bands and Orangemen making their way home to Scotland after the Twelfth. The floors were wet and the noise deafening. They had the drinking places to themselves. Ordinary travelling families crowded into the quiet lounges or sunned themselves up on deck. Children, unaware of the situation, ran here and there in corridors or up and down the stairs. The toilet floors were awash. There was evidence of many people having been sick. Stella, putting the camera in her bag, said that, if she could, she would hold on for the bathroom until they reached the terminal at the Scottish side.

Gerry stood looking back at the grey receding outline of the city. There was a column of black smoke rising into the air. Could be a fire or a bomb or a simple accident. The slight wind was from the south and it diluted the smoke until it formed a dark halo over the whole benighted, God-fearing place. A place which had been born in convulsions of sectarian hatred. One of the men in government – a prime minister, no less – said that he would *not* employ a Roman Catholic – and urged the rest of his cronies to follow suit. The country that came into being was ruled, or misruled, for fifty years by a right-wing, unchanging Protestant majority under the noses of the British. And when the time came for the Brits to sort things out, to unpick the knot they had tied so tightly over the centuries, they made a fearful bollocks of it. Bloody Sunday in Derry was an echo of previous British massacres committed to maintaining the Empire which had turned the maps of the world red.

He tore a paper tube of sugar and spilled a little of it into his coffee to make it less acrid. Of course the nightmare of the whole thing – the thirty years war – could be shared equally.

Which wing of the IRA, which loyalist branch of murderers, which politician or preacher – in some cases both under the same hat – was to blame? He imagined a deathbed scene with an old man surrounded by his family. 'I leave you my hatred for the other side. Don't ever give it up. Keep it close to you like a knife all your days and pass it on when your time comes.'

After the photograph on the boat he wondered how they would be received in Scotland. It didn't seem all that long ago that the three Scottish soldiers, all of them in their teens, had been brutally murdered. Two were brothers. Young fellas, off duty, having a drink in a Belfast pub when they'd been enticed by girls to a non-existent party. They were driven out of town to some remote place and shot dead. If the end of human decency is the price of a United Ireland, Gerry wanted nothing to do with it. Bloody Friday was even worse. Killing people left, right and centre. Whatever their politics, whatever their persuasion.

That lunchtime Gerry and an architect friend had been at a topping-out ceremony on the Lisburn Road, a building which was part of the City Hospital complex. It had been a balmy day and most people were glad to be out on the roof. It was a strange mixture of hard hats, yellow safety waistcoats and collars and ties. As always on these occasions, there were some women who were overdressed. Journalists and cameramen moved among them. There was laughter going on all the time. The kind of banter which happens when workers meet management and have to be polite to them. A table with a white damask tablecloth was loaded with drinks and dishes of nuts and crisps. The skyline was the Belfast hills – Black Mountain, Divis, Cave Hill. It was late July and the hills were green, almost emerald. There was a flock of birds doing the rounds. Gerry didn't know what they were but anything

171

could come in off the sea or from Iceland or Norway on a visitation, fly around – look and leave. Were they lapwings? His friend said he didn't know. During the speeches Gerry watched them fly then turn in the distance, their wings black, their underneaths flashing white. They created a sense of space as they circled from horizon to horizon. Just as it created a sense of height to look down on flying birds. The sky was blue and the lough, where it could be seen, reflected the blue. Gerry said to his friend that the birds were like venetian blinds. They went thin when they turned.

Some of the construction workers and architects involved in the building were just signing their names with fat felt-tip pens on an area of white-painted wood when the first bomb went off. A thump. It was near enough to make some of the people in hard hats duck. Yet when people looked around nothing of any significance could be seen. The cameramen looked about them but did not photograph anything. Not knowing what else to do, the workers continued their signing. But there was no doubt in people's minds that a bomb had gone off. This was something Belfast people knew about. After so many years. A big bomb vibrates your diaphragm, makes your chest full, churns your stomach – your ears become strange. But everyone was out in the air, above the explosion, so it was slightly different. It had been preceded by no fire brigade or ambulance sirens – a no-warning bomb – so there would almost certainly be deaths and injuries. Then another one went off. It was hard to tell where – because the shock waves seemed to have no direction – they just focus in the chest, pump the lungs full. After a minute or two a third bomb exploded, this one further away. By this time all pretence at partying had stopped. Everyone on the roof stood looking this way and that. Then Gerry saw a white puff of smoke appear at the foot of the Cave Hill. He pointed to show his friend. They both looked. Then the thud of sound came. Not so much in the chest, because of the distance, but audible. Oh my God, somebody said. People had gone pale. A woman who had decided to wear white gloves for the occasion covered her mouth, staring around waiting for the next explosion. Who's doing this? What is it? What's happening?

What was happening that day, they were later to find out, was that the Provisional IRA exploded more than twenty bombs, killing nine people and injuring one hundred and thirty. On the roof Gerry immediately thought of Stella. Because it was still the school holidays she had gone home on the bus to Dungiven for the weekend. At least she was out of range. But maybe the bombs were everywhere. Another one went off. Black smoke rose into the air. The people on the roof did not know what to do. They stood around the perimeter of the building and stared down at the city laid out before them in the sunshine, afraid to return to ground level. Voices asked where the last bomb had been. The bus station? The Ormeau Road? Somebody else said it was the Albert Clock. Gerry thought of Stella's friend, the Casualty nurse, who had made the remark about the big scissors. Would she be on duty?

Now ambulances had begun. Wailing sounds at different distances, their sirens interfering with each other. Later Gerry heard about people crying in the street with fear. Men, women and children herded into public parks – for safety. Away from buildings, away from cars. Away from the traps and atrocities which had been set for them.

Stella walked the now familiar route from the hotel. Into the passageway, into the Begijnhof garden, into the office. The woman with the glasses was on the telephone speaking in Dutch. Stella stood waiting. She put her hand in her pocket to check she still had the business card she'd been given on her last visit. She had another look at the name on it, tried in her mind to pronounce it.

Although she could not understand the language she could recognise when the conversation was coming to an end. The repetitions, the nodding. The woman put down the phone and looked up at her – her smile was bleak and without warmth. Stella knew the woman spoke little or no English. She smiled and said without thinking, 'Good morning.'

Stella placed the business card on the desk with the name of the person she was to see facing away from herself. The woman looked down at it. Then began to shake her head.

'No – not – no.' She pointed to a row of red plastic chairs against the wall. '*Asseyez-vous.*' Stella hesitated, then backed towards the chairs and sat down. This seemed to please the woman, who returned to her papers. There was a smell of polish. Stella looked down at her feet and saw that the boards were the originals – very old, at least. Each one a hand span in width. Polished to a sheen, beautiful in colour.

There were some framed diplomas with red seals on the wall behind where the woman was working. Too far away even to attempt to read the wording. Which would be meaningless to her anyway.

Stella was the only girl in Master Ryan's school to have gone to university. There was a time when she would have been proud of that but now it meant little to her. The green lawns on the day of graduation, the gowns, the red cardboard tube full of certificate. Her father's pride that day was what she remembered most and his shyness in front of her – trying to avoid being in photographs yet not knowing his way around a camera sufficiently to be the photographer. 'What do I press?' He was a farm labourer whose hands were hard with work, whose nails were like horn. How little it all meant now. A thing of the past. Her father in his grave. She included a prayer for him every time she prayed.

Not knowing a language was such a barrier. You appeared foolish if you couldn't understand. Not foolish – stupid. You just stood there looking stupid. Such an embarrassment. And she knew she wasn't stupid. She was proud of the fact that, even to this day, she could say the Hail Mary in any of four different languages. Latin and French and Irish and, of course, English.

'*Excusez-moi*,' Stella said. She pointed to the business card and made a universal gesture of not understanding – hands out, mouth turned down, shoulders raised.

'*Parlez-vous français?*' said the woman.

'*Un peu.*'

175

'*Madame est très tard.*' The woman indicated the telephone, mimed making a phone call.

'*A quelle heure?*' Stella pointed to her watch. The woman behind the desk raised her shoulders, spread her hands, then went back to her work. Stella had no confidence in her French. She had been taught what little she knew by a nun from Omagh who, by the sound of her, had never been to France in her life. 'Window' was pronounced fen-etter. 'Perhaps' was poo-tetter.

She wanted to ask, how long will this woman be? Should I go and do some shopping in the meantime? Will she be here today? What did she say when she phoned?

The door opened and a woman came in. She was not dressed for outdoors but had a green woollen scarf lapped around her neck and an envelope in her hand. She was dark-haired, in her fifties, wearing a stylish trouser suit. She walked up to the woman at the desk and handed over the envelope. They greeted and smiled and talked in Dutch. Both of them began looking at Stella. The woman with the green scarf smiled over at her. The conversation, half whispered, half spoken, went on in the silence of the office. Then the woman with the scarf walked across.

'Hello – how are you?' she said.

'You're Irish?'

'Indeed I am,' said the woman.

'Where from?'

'Waterford, originally.' The woman slid onto the vacant seat beside Stella. She looked over to the desk and smiled. 'Hennie's English is not so good. Is there anything I can do to help?'

'I don't know where to begin,' said Stella.

'Hennie says to tell you that the woman you want to see has been delayed – I don't know why – and she'll not be in

176

for some time.' There was silence between them. 'My name is Kathleen Walsh and I'm a resident here.'

'I wanted to make an enquiry . . . How would someone go about applying to become . . . a part of this. To live here?'

'You've said a mouthful there.' Kathleen stood and went back to the woman at the desk. They talked quietly. Kathleen returned.

'The best idea is to come with me and I'll give you a cup of tea – or coffee, if that's your thing. And you can see where I live. Maybe by that time herself will be here.'

Stella stood.

'Are you sure? That's very kind of you.'

They shook hands. Kathleen spoke over her shoulder in Dutch to Hennie as she guided Stella out of the door.

'And where are you from yourself? I can hear the North in you.'

'County Derry. From a townland nobody's heard of. From a place nobody knows. Dungiven.'

They walked slowly along the path.

'This is such a beautiful garden,' said Stella. 'So quiet.'

'It's a metre lower than the outside world. The noise goes over its head somehow. Anywhere'd be quiet after the North.'

'Oh I don't live in Ireland any more.'

'Where are you now?'

'Glasgow.'

Kathleen pointed out the English Reformed Church and the Catholic Church which was camouflaged in the line of buildings.

'I take it you're Catholic?' said Kathleen.

'Yes, I am. I was in there for Mass yesterday.'

'Isn't it great we can ask questions like that once we're out of Ireland.' Stella nodded and smiled.

177

'Around 1600 Catholicism was banned by the City Fathers.'
Kathleen reached out and touched Stella's elbow. 'It's very
hard to be a guide and have a reasonable conversation at the
same time.'

'Don't worry – you're doing great.'

'Catholics were allowed to attend Mass but not in public.
To get around it they went to each other's houses.'

'I like the intimacy of that. It was very popular in the sixties
to have a priest say Mass in your home. Even in the North.'

'I wasn't born till the seventies.'

'Oh, I'm sorry. Sometimes I forget myself.'

'This place has been here since medieval times. It was an
island – a woman's island – "manned" by Beguines.'

Stella laughed and nodded her head elaborately. Kathleen
went on.

'It all began with women who wanted to live alone – to
devote themselves to prayer and . . . this, that and the other.
Good works – without taking vows. Thus the first Beguinages.
They could hardly be called nuns, because they could go back
to the world if they wanted. And marry. There wasn't a vow
of poverty either – no woman renounced her property. If
she became broke she neither asked for nor accepted charity
but supported herself by getting a job. A lot of them became
teachers.'

Stella stopped and looked over a wrought-iron fence.

'The gardens are so beautifully kept,' she said. 'Aww –
snowdrops. I thought they were late this year. Then I saw
some in Scotland, the day we were leaving for here.' Stella put
her head back and sniffed the air. 'What's that divine smell?'

Then she spotted a pink bush, flowers but no leaves, the
flowers growing straight from the bare branch.

'Isn't that viburnum?'

Stella pulled a branch towards herself and inhaled, then closed her eyes with pleasure.

'Such a smell in the depths of winter.'

'In the summer this place is beyond belief – especially in the evenings – with the night-scented stock.'

'The garden I have at home is only a street garden. A couple of feet by the length of the building.'

Kathleen guided Stella into a doorway.

'This is me, here.'

The entrance hall was small and the staircase resembled a ladder more than anything else. It was immensely high, funnelling upwards.

'A Stairway to Heaven,' said Stella as she began to climb using, instead of a banister, the white hand-rope which looped upwards. There was no carpet and she heard her own footsteps creak and squeak as she put her weight on each tread. It seemed to go on for ever.

'Can you manage?' said Kathleen.

'You must be fit – living in such an eyrie.'

'You get used to it. The only disadvantage is when you want a grand piano. Then you have to take it up by sling – on the outside.'

'If it was me I'd learn the violin.'

Eventually Stella's hand reached the end of the rope banister. It was tied into an ornate knot.

'Oh, I like that. Very secure. Very decorative.'

'A monkey's fist, it's called,' said Kathleen. Stella was panting, still holding onto the rope.

'The Franciscans have three knots in their cincture. Poverty, Chastity and Obedience.' She took a breath between each word. Kathleen patted her on the back.

'Are you okay?'

'Yes. Fine.'

She edged past Stella, opened the front door and glided in. The door was not locked. She made a little gesture with her hand to invite Stella in.

'This is lovely.'

'Minimalist,' said Kathleen. It was a bright space of varnished floorboards and white walls. A small dark cross hung in an alcove. There was an infinitesimal smell of flowers. At one end of a sideboard a stone vase of daffodils and at the other end by the window a clear glass container with yellow tulips.

'We have climbed to the light,' Stella said. 'Where did you get the flowers?'

'In the supermarket.'

'In January?'

'In Amsterdam.'

'Of course. The tulips are assembly-line perfect.'

Stella walked to the window and touched one of the flowers as if she did not believe it. She looked down onto the green space, onto the bare tops of trees, the surround of houses with their terracotta roofs.

'How wonderful. Another world.' There was a bird feeder outside hanging from the lintel, full of nuts and seeds. Stella turned apologetically. 'When I come into a new place I'm like a dog. I nosy about. Sniff in the corners.'

'Feel free. There is not much to see but at least it's mine.'

'An ill-favoured thing, sir, but mine own,' said Stella.

'Take the weight off your feet first. Get your breath back.'

'I'm not out of breath,' she panted. 'Out of sorts, maybe.' And they both laughed as she half fell, half slumped onto a cream linen sofa. Kathleen stood over her.

'Tea or coffee?'

'Tea would be nice at this time of day.' Kathleen turned and left the room. Stella looked around. The place reminded her of a caravan – it had that mixture of utility and economy of space. But it was stylish too. Like something out of a brochure.

There was knitting in progress at the end of the sofa, part of a white Aran sweater, a mixture of cable and blackberry stitch, with knitting needles plunged into the wool. There was a framed picture on each wall, the frames black and severe against the white. A single shelf of books – she could make out a Bible and a Mass missal. And a fat dictionary. An atlas, judging by its height. She leaned forward and made out several books of prayer-poems by Michel Quoist – she had a translation of *Prayers of Life* in her own bookcase at home. Stella stood and looked at the pictures. All except one were poster-sized reproductions. Miró, Morandi, Mondrian – all the Ms, but maybe Kathleen hadn't noticed this. It was the kind of thing somebody who did crosswords noticed. The exception was a small icon of Christ Pantocrator. It was an original, not a reproduction. From the darkness within the frame, the gold of the halo glowed in the light from the window.

She turned and wandered into the kitchen.

'I'm doing my dog trick,' she said.

Kathleen was putting biscuits on a plate. A kettle was coming to the boil. 'It's more a galley than a kitchen.' On the wall above the sink was a board, with tools clipped to it. A hammer, screwdrivers – a pair of pliers, a hacksaw. And other stuff. Each item was outlined carefully in red paint.

'I like your board arrangement,' said Stella.

'It's to remind me to put things back. If I don't, the empty ghost yells at me. So I put things back. And there's plenty to do – these houses are really old. And odd. If you drop a ball

181

of wool it'll go on rolling until it hits the next wall. Virtually nothing is eye-sweet.'

'Can I do anything to help?'

'You could level all the floors.'

Kathleen laughed, lifted the tray and headed for the other room. There was a movement from outside the window – a flash, almost.

'Oh, would you look.' She set the tray down and stepped to the window.

'What?'

'Waxwings.' Kathleen pointed. 'Aren't they lovely?'

Stella stood almost on tiptoe with her hands joined behind her back and saw a flock of colourful birds traversing the green space below.

'They came yesterday. Some years they don't come at all. Bright visitors.'

'I like their Mohican haircuts.'

'And the little bit of yellow. They're after the berries. It's the cotoneaster's attracting them. Oh, I so love birds.' She turned, a little reluctantly, from the window and began to pour the tea. 'The Dutch have an unfortunate name for them. *Pestvogel*. In medieval times they thought they brought the plague with them.'

'Your neighbours wouldn't be too happy about putting out the bird feeders, then.'

'No indeed.' Kathleen handed her a china mug of tea. 'Milk and sugar are there.'

'Thank you. This is very kind of you. To be taking in waifs and strays.'

'Don't mention it.' Kathleen doctored her own tea.

'I love that image of the sparrow flying through the barn,' said Stella.

'Which?'

'I think it's the Viking version of waifs and strays – the sparrow who flies in out of the storm through the banqueting hall. In one door and out the other.'

'And that's it?'

'An image of life.'

'There's more to it than that, surely.'

'It's just such an elegant summary. The fire, the food, the finite . . . And the older you get the quicker it goes.'

They both busied themselves with their tea.

'So what can I do for you? How can I help?' said Kathleen.

'I just wanted to investigate this place, this order. Maybe enquire about the life. I said as much to the woman in the office . . .'

'Hennie.'

'Yes, Hennie. I'm not sure she understood.'

'Milk?'

'No thanks. Just as it is.' Stella raised the china cup to her lips and blew on its surface. She sipped, half closing her eyes. 'How difficult is it to join such an organisation?'

'Why would you want to?'

'I was here about thirty years ago – at a teacher conference and somebody told me of the set-up, the Beguines. I was intrigued . . . but at that time there was no urgency.'

'And what's the urgency now?'

'Time.'

'But for what?'

'A more valuable life. Which is spiritual *and* useful.' Stella shrugged her shoulders. 'How can we make the world a better place? To make a contribution, however small. Despite what the Church thinks about women.'

'I once knew a wonderful nun who said that the last Vatican Council was attended solely by the Bishops of the Church. But at the next the Bishops would be there with their wives. And the one after that, the Bishops would be there with their husbands.' Stella laughed. Kathleen sat back in her chair and clapped her hands. 'We have that to look forward to.' She offered the plate of biscuits. Stella took a digestive.

'I used to love making butter sandwiches. Squeezing them and watching the butter come up through the wee holes.'

'I wish I'd known to do that.' Their laughter slowly ebbed away.

Kathleen crunched her biscuit then wiped her mouth and said, 'I know you didn't come for flippancy. How much do you know about us?'

'Not a lot. I've heard some things, seen some things on the internet.'

'Well, we go back as far as the twelfth century, a time when everybody was Catholic – *including* the Protestants. The whole thing started off as a group of women who prayed and looked after the sick. Later they decided to live together in a community. They weren't exactly nuns – they didn't take vows and were a lot less strict than other orders – although the "no men" rule was sacrosanct – they had to be prepared to live by themselves. Not as anchorites, not in the desert – but in the everyday.'

'And now?'

'That's all gone. There's no religious order now. But there's still about a hundred or so apartments and very occasionally one comes up. Everybody has to pop their clogs eventually. And that leaves vacancies.'

'What happened to the nuns?'

'The last nun in the Begijnhof died in 1971.'

'So I've got this all wrong?'

'I'm not sure,' said Kathleen. 'I don't know where you're coming from.' There was a moment of hesitation before Kathleen went on, 'I was a nun in Ireland – the Sisters of Mercy – but I left and ended up here. This halfway house suits me better.'

Stella didn't know what to say. The silence seemed long. It reached a point of embarrassment – so she said, 'And why did you leave?'

'Oh, it's a long story.' Kathleen smiled. Stella knew to go no further.

'And is your woman – the one I'm going to see – is she . . .'

'She's more of an estate agent.'

'What kind of women live here now?'

'Anyone single who can afford it. A well-heeled cross section, really. A well-*high-heeled* cross section. Although there's precious few of those to be seen in here.'

'And you – what do you do?'

'I'm a teacher.'

'And so was I. An Irishwoman in Scotland teaching English.'

'I'm an Irishwoman in the Netherlands teaching Comparative Religion and Maths.' They laughed aloud. 'The school is ten minutes away. Mondays I work from home. So we were lucky to meet.'

'Can I ask?' Stella hesitated. 'Do you still practise?'

'Oh yes. My religion is very important to me. It's what made me want to come here in the first place. I was taught by nuns in Waterford and liked the most of them. But nowadays the spiritual side of things is up to yourself. Having a chapel on site makes things easier.'

'And what about prayer?'

185

'That's entirely your decision,' said Kathleen. She smiled. 'The volume, duration and intensity.'

'But the sisterhood is a figment of my imagination?'

'No, the sisterhood is very real – a lot of great people. But the religious thing has largely disappeared.'

'My crest has just fallen.' She smiled. 'Like an old waxwing.'

'Oh, you poor thing. But it's still possible for women to live here. Although the waiting list is very long.'

'How long is long?'

'Years, I'm afraid. Maybe five or more. Worse than any golf club. The only criteria are that you must be a woman who is prepared to live by herself. And you must be anywhere between thirty and sixty-five. And you have got to be able to afford it.'

Stella sat for a long time digesting this. She tightened her lips and her whole face sagged.

'Well, that's that. I'm too old.'

'You're not over sixty-five, are you? You look ten years younger.'

'I certainly don't feel like it at the moment.' Stella couldn't think of anything to say for a long time. Then she asked, 'Is there anywhere else? That has a similar set-up?'

'In Belgium there are some places. In Bruges. But there are no sisters. Just buildings. The Benedictines took them over, I think. Kind of spiritual squatters.'

'Are there any in Britain?'

'Not that I know of.'

'English-speaking Beguines would be good. Like you.'

'Prayers don't need translation.'

Stella smiled. 'The other hitch is that I'm married.'

'Any children?'

'A boy, Michael – a man now. And a grandson called Toby. But they live in Canada.'

'And do you go out to see them?'

'Oh yes – we went to see Toby when he was a year old.'

'I'll bet that was lovely.'

Stella nodded. 'If there'd been a place here,' she said, 'I'd have found a way around the husband issue. There's not that much marriage left in us.'

'Are you sure?'

'I was just reading the other day that older couples are more prone to war with each other – when the children have flown the coop. They've too much time on their hands.'

'Don't take what I say as official. There may be ways around things. Hurdles turned sideways, if you like. Talk to herself when she comes in. This is obviously something you have thought about.'

'Yes. These things that are on the back burner of your life, nobody sees them – when you pray or go to Mass, you take them out and give them a polish. Nobody knows. That first time after I came back from Amsterdam we went for a Sunday run in the car – somewhere just outside Glasgow – the Campsies. It was an accident in a way because the weather was beautiful and that doesn't happen too often in Scotland. My husband fell asleep on the grass and I went for a walk. I'd seen a little white church down the road. It turned out to be a German order of nuns and I got into conversation with one of them – she was changing the flowers on the altar. She said that their movement – Schoenstatt, I think she called it – was made up of ordinary people seeking to live their faith in the modern world.'

'Yes, yes. I know of them.'

'I told her I was just back from Amsterdam and talked about *this* place. She knew all about it. She had the loveliest face and a disposition to match. I must have talked to her for the best part of an hour. I'll never forget her. Gerry was still asleep when I got back. That night he was badly sunburned. The side of his face and the tops of his feet – he'd stupidly taken off his shoes and socks. I felt very like Mary Magdalene – putting cream on his feet.'

Kathleen lifted the teapot and gestured towards Stella's cup.

'No, thank you. I'm sure you've plenty to do which doesn't include listening to the likes of me.'

A phone rang and Kathleen picked her mobile from the sideboard.

'*Hallo met Kathleen.*' She nodded, listening. Then switched off. 'That's Astrid now.' Stella looked at her, not understanding. 'Astrid Hoogendorp. In her office.'

'Her ladyship.' Stella nodded and stood to shake her hand. 'No matter what the outcome of all this is, it was great to meet you.'

'And you too.'

Stella held onto her hand.

'I've been asking all the questions but . . .' Then she let go of her hand. 'You are very easy to talk to. And I want to tell you something about myself before I go. Something I've left out.' Kathleen gestured that Stella should sit down again.

'Thank you.'

Stella began, and she did not begin. The words were inside her head but she could not translate them onto her tongue. Her mouth opened and closed. She met Kathleen's eyes, now smiling in anticipation.

'What is it?' said Kathleen.

The breath Stella took in was shallow, insufficient for what she knew was coming.

188

'You're a stranger . . . I was involved in something a long time ago, an accident. And I made a vow . . .' Stella let her eyes fall to her hands. 'You know how vivid things are *in extremis*. There's something going on in the brain. Chemicals. They make the moment indelible. But I have never been able to keep it. The vow.' The pause lengthened until Kathleen tried to help her.

'What kind of accident?'

'I was pregnant.' Kathleen continued to gaze at her but there was an aura of surprise on her face. Stella smiled. 'No, not that kind of accident.' The older woman's face straightened. 'I was married. It was our first summer together. I was very, very pregnant.' Kathleen stared, waiting. 'I was shot. In the stomach. I lay there on the street and I said a prayer. Spare the child in my womb and I will devote the rest of my life to You. But I failed. Here I am, at my age, looking to pay a debt. But . . .'

'What happened?' Kathleen's eyes were wide and her mouth open.

'It was Belfast. In the early seventies. That's what happened. Somebody was ambushing somebody else. Anyway I was left lying on the pavement. And the only prayer I could remember was an Act of Contrition. But that was not what I wanted. That's to save yourself. I wanted to save my baby. How could it not be dead? I needed some kind of a miracle.'

Kathleen shook her head, seemed lost for words.

'I didn't know whether I'd wet myself, or my waters had broken or I was just bleeding. But it wasn't the physical things. It was what I was saying to myself. The prayer. The bargain I was striking. Lord, let my baby live and I will be in your debt for the rest of my life. And that's the way it turned out.'

Kathleen reached over and took both of Stella's hands in her

189

own. 'I've never breathed a word of this . . . this pledge to anybody. Not even to my husband. Nobody. It seemed the bullet had passed through me. In one side and out the other.'

'Oh, you poor thing. How awful.'

'It was a miracle or else the wee one must have ducked. The only damage, the doctors said, was that I would not be able to have any more children. My son Michael's an only child.' Instead of saying something Kathleen squeezed Stella's hands. 'It was in all the Irish papers. Not my name, just the incident. *Pregnant woman shot* – blah-blah-blah, that kinda stuff. But when we moved to Scotland nobody seemed to know. And I didn't bother to announce it because, if I did, it was all people wanted to talk about. So it became, if not a secret, then something which wasn't mentioned.'

'If you're upset . . . if you want me to come down with you . . .'

Stella sighed and gathered herself.

'No. I'm all right. What I'm talking about happened a long time ago. I'm a different person now.'

Kathleen helped Stella to her feet and put her arms around her. She patted the older woman's stooped back. They extended their arms to look at each other again, hugged once more and then Stella left.

It was Stella who'd noticed the first snowflakes outside the hotel before reaching the taxi. Large wet ones landing on her face and overcoat out of the darkness. She had to step around the abandoned block of ice still sitting there like a lump in the throat of the street. Some snow lay on top of it. Gerry shoved it with the sole of his shoe and it slid to one side, allowing them access to the door of the taxi.

'That wind would cut you in two,' she said.

'In three,' Gerry said. 'It would cut you in three.'

As the train moved on the exposed parts of the track the snow streaked horizontally past the windows. Then the train stopped. The snowflakes melted and slid down, leaving wet trails. Once or twice she caught Gerry looking at her. He seemed afraid to ask how things had gone. When the train started again it passed slowly over a road. They saw, under the street lights, that the roofs of cars had become white. All the way to the airport the snow kept falling.

Gerry pulled their big case. It rattled or purred according to the type of Lego pattern on the station flooring. He had his shoulder bag slung halfway round his back and was stooped forward to counteract its weight. Stella followed him at a little distance. There were very few people about.

He waited and let Stella onto the escalator first and stood behind her as they ascended to the airport. She seemed in a dwam as she was being carried upwards, one hand resting on the black rubber banister. She wasn't good at these things – her hand–eye co-ordination was a lot poorer than his, so generally he travelled behind her in case she stumbled. If they were descending he would go in front. When she reached the top she stepped off and Gerry passed her. Her gaze remained on the escalator as it went on and on rising, continuing to bring nobody. It had a dream-like rhythm, hypnotic, lulling like a pendulum. But Gerry was away like a greyhound towards check-in. He looked over his shoulder to see what was keeping her.

The queues were short and they began to hear familiar words and accents, see styles of clothing they knew. They looked at one another, raised eyebrows enough to know they were among their own again. Once they had checked in and deposited their large bag, Gerry said, 'Wouldn't mind a drink.'

At the next opportunity she steered left into what looked like a British pub and sat down. Gerry set his shoulder bag on the bench seat beside her.

'Fizzy water,' she said. He went to the bar and ordered. Stella sat still, listening to the muzak without being aware of it. 'Blowin' in the Wind' segued into 'All Shook Up'.

He came back to the table and pushed her bottle of water and a glass across to her and set down his whiskey.

'Where do they dig up these ancient songs?' he said. 'It's the kinda thing we used to dance to in Fruithill fifty years ago.'

Stella agreed. Gerry sat down.

'So. How did your meeting go?'

'I don't want to talk about it.'

'Why not?'

'Because it was a complete failure.'

'How so?'

'I'm too old,' she said. 'If I want to be a religious I'll have to do it on my own.'

'You planned this whole thing.'

'It was a notion I had,' Stella said quietly. 'I had to look into it.' She cleared her throat and began, her voice on edge. She said that a religious order in that place was a thing of the past. She'd missed the boat. The last Beguine died in the 1970s. But women still did come to live special lives there although she herself was too old. And that was it.

Another song came on. 'I saw Mommy kissing Santa Claus.' Even though it was well after Christmas nobody seemed to care. Maybe it was something to do with it being in a foreign language – it meant nothing. Maybe it was the barman's own tape. The voice was a nasal American kid.

'D'you think we'll get away?' she said. She looked all around for a window but couldn't see one.

'It's not too bad,' he said. 'It's only been going about an hour.'

'I think they've heated runways here,' said Stella. 'The bruise on your chin is changing colour.'

'From what to what?'

'Purple to black?'

'No green?'

'That comes much later.'

'Thanks. Who needs a mirror?'

Gerry's hand came up and he fingered the bruise as if it was a beard.

'Can you remember the day you twigged what that song was all about?'

'No,' she said, 'although I must say, it created a certain amount of eye-rolling in our house.' She screwed up her face. 'Mammy always shouted, "*Turn that thing off!*" Even though we hadn't a clue what adultery was.'

'But that's the whole point,' Gerry said.

'What?'

'It's not adultery. It's her husband.'

'Santa Claus is her husband?'

'Yes. Dressed up on Christmas Eve. Like an American magazine cover. Putting the presents round the tree. And a little touching love scene ensues between husband and wife. And they kiss. And the child sees them.'

'I can feel my face going red. I never even thought about it. I so believed in Santa Claus.'

Gerry laughed. 'Seriously?'

'Yes. And there was me thinking it was the real Santa Claus.' She sipped her glass of water. 'What age would we have been?'

'God knows.' He drank off what remained of his drink. 'The early fifties.'

Gerry went to the bar and got another large one. He complained to Stella about how expensive it was here at the airport. He picked up his shoulder bag.

'Listen,' he said. He rocked the bag to and fro. There was a liquid noise. Stella shook her head.

'I can't hear a thing.'

'It's the Traveller's Friend. I miscalculated. Over-provided.'

'They'll not let you take that through security,' said Stella. Gerry shrugged. 'You should have packed it in the case. Wrapped it in your *noir* pyjamas. They'll confiscate it.'

'They'll not get the chance.' Gerry checked where the barman was. He was serving a family who had just come in. Gerry produced the duty-free bag and, without removing the bottle, poured himself a substantial dram. 'There's no way I'm going to let somebody in uniform pour this down the plughole.'

'So you're going to pour it down you?'

'Exactly. I was behind a guy once – a full bottle of vodka down the sink. And a pot of jam straight after it. Glug.'

'Shame about the jam.' She nodded to Gerry's bag. 'How much is left?'

'The heel of the bottle.' She pursed her lips. Not good. He looked towards the bar. The waistcoated barman had served the family and was arranging glasses on a shelf with his back to them. Gerry heaved himself to his feet, went to the bar and asked for a glass of 'aqua'. He said it twice and the barman asked if he wanted water. Gerry nodded. Automatically the barman put ice in the glass then filled it from the tap. Gerry would have preferred it without ice but because it was free and a favour he said nothing. He came back with the glass rattling. Beneath the level of the table and out of sight of the barman he diluted his whiskey.

Stella tapped her fingers to Dylan's 'Mr Tambourine Man' until it changed to ABBA's 'I Believe in Angels'. Gerry closed the bag tighter round the neck of the bottle.

'What's wrong with my water?' said Stella. 'I'll not drink all of this.'

'I hate fizzy. Makes it feel like poor man's champagne. Or bin juice.' The barman looked at him and Gerry put his hand around the whiskey glass. 'They play that stuff all over Europe,' he said. 'Especially ex-communist places.'

'They're just catching up,' said Stella. 'They missed the good ones the first time around. Those songs are just part of the lining of your brain. That barman has his eye on you.'

'He doesn't like self-service. Let's go.' Gerry drank the glass off then lowered the bag between his knees and uncapped the bottle. He began attempting to pour water into it. Some of the ice cubes clinked off the bottle mouth and clattered into the polybag.

In an effort to get up Stella leaned on the table and glanced down into the polythene bag.

'The heel of the bottle?' she said. 'Since when did the heel of the bottle become the knee?'

'Are you nosying into my bag?'

'Gerry, gimme peace.'

'I was very abstemious in the hotel. You should be proud of me.'

'Why are you doing all this, anyway?'

'Because I don't like straight whiskey.' His voice was full of exasperation and he turned away from her to complete his task. 'The water takes the fuckin' burn off it.'

Stella stood, put her bottle of water into her bag and walked out. Given the mood Gerry was in she didn't want to go to the gate – to be isolated with him or to sit in ranks with other people. Here they could wander away from each other.

'First let's find a base,' she said.

They walked until they came across half a dozen empty seats in a corridor – all black leather and stainless steel – looking out into the night. She walked around the line of chairs to the window side and sat down.

'This is perfect,' she said.

The blizzard outside continued slanting across the airport. Stella sat mesmerised watching the relentlessness of it. It was visible mostly in the haloes of lights, the nearer the more defined. Some sodium lights made yellow of it, ordinary ones made it blue-white. Always agitated, streaking and swirling. Away from the light there seemed to be no snow. Scored velvet-black darkness. Except directly outside the window overlooking the apron. Tail fins and bodies and swept-back wings becoming more and more indistinct the further away they were. Then the storm would take a breath, the wind would stall and large flakes would climb back up the dark in the lee of the window. Stella found herself isolating one particular snowflake – a small one – and watching its progress. Lifting, floating, eddying upwards, sinking among the others. Dithering. Then when it went off her radar she would choose another and watch it and will it to survive for as long as possible. Gerry set his shoulder bag on the ground and sat down several feet away from her.

'I love the Hardy poem,' she said. '*Every branch big with it, bent every twig with it.*'

'You'd have to be hardy to be out there at the minute.'

'But it's so lovely,' she said. 'Snow on snow. Like in the carol.' She heard the little scissoring noise of Gerry unscrewing the metal cap, followed by the liquid tilt as he drank. He made a noise with his lips – then the scissoring sound again as he screwed the top back on. She had no need to turn and look at him because she could see his reflection in the window straight in front of her. There was a sense of her prying like a detective, watching events through a two-way mirror. She saw through it to the movement of snow outside – the speed

197

of its different layers. Gerry didn't bother putting the bottle back in the shoulder bag. It was now naked in his hand, out of the duty-free bag.

'I've stripped the stockings off her,' he said.

'You're dribbling.' Gerry looked at the puddle at his feet. It was coming from the duty-free bag.

'It's just melting ice.'

'Careful, Gerry,' she said, 'sometimes they bar drunks.'

'Who do?'

'The airlines. They have the power to stop you at the gate.'

'Who's drunk? I just hate to see waste.'

'Maybe we should go through security now?' she said. 'Get it over with?'

'Why do you think I'm sitting here finishing the heel of the bottle?'

'It's getting bigger.'

'That's because I put water in it. I'm determined to drink the security man's share. We'll go through when they can't take it off me.'

'You'll do yourself damage.'

'As if you would care.'

'Pardon?'

'You heard me.'

Stella stared at him for a long time.

'What if I took myself off by the hand and left you?' she said. 'Would you blame me?'

Gerry shook his head. 'No.'

'If you could only see yourself. You used to be so kind and considerate. What's happened to you? You're nothing but appetite.'

'Waste not, want not.' He clumsily moved along the seats closer to her. He tried to take her hand in his but she snatched it away and stood.

'I'm going for a walk,' she said.

'This kind of talk . . .' he said, 'it scares me.'

Stella threaded her arm through the handle of her leather bag and walked like a woman late for work. Sometimes Gerry was beyond the beyonds. In the distance she saw the warning light of an airport shuttle cart flashing. It had an alarm which made a noise like a corncrake. This grew in volume as the cart approached, its tyres silent on the flooring. It was driven by a turbaned Sikh in a navy blue uniform. Stella looked at the passengers. Four old folk with walking sticks – two bald men, two women with their white hair freshly done for going away. They seemed shy of the publicity their cart journey was bringing them. We're not that bad yet, thought Stella, we can still self-propel – get about on our own two pegs. She looked at the signs and followed the one for WC.

In the Ladies she was amazed to find a cubicle empty. Inside, she slid the bolt across. She spooled out a length of toilet roll from the enormous dispenser, wiped the seat, prepared herself and sat down. Her elbows on her knees, her head in her hands. After a while she began to weep. Her inferior tears spilled onto her cheeks. She did it quietly for fear the women on either side would hear and then come to see if they could help. They couldn't. How utterly foolish she had been to concoct such a dream. And a dream is definitely what it was. She should have had more sense. At her age. The attempt to repay a spiritual debt had failed. She knew that the only way to improve the world, without patronising anyone, was to improve herself. To be the receptacle for love, yet not to feel herself worthy of it. There was a poem by Raymond Carver called 'Late Fragment'. He had a problem with drink too. But he beat it in the end before he died. The short poem began with a question – '*And did you get what you wanted from this life, even so?*' A nod of the head, yes. And what was that? '*To call myself beloved, to feel myself beloved on the earth.*' But Stella wanted not so much to be loved by another person as by something altogether greater. And at the same time to be self-effacing – even when putting on her wee bit of make-up in the morning. She would have hated to give that up, it was such a small habit. Mere watercolour. Her dream had crumbled. The woman she had seen that morning – the woman in charge, Astrid Hoogendorp – had been straightforward and spoke serviceable English. Everything she'd said had backed up Kathleen's version of events. There was no religious order now, it seemed. There was a community of women who lived useful and happy independent lives. Except. Except. Except for Stella's age. She was too old. Not too old to be religious but too old to take part in their organisation. Stella had bitten her lip. She hadn't said a word about what had happened to her in Belfast. It was all too complicated and this woman did not possess Kathleen's warmth. Astrid Hoogendorp had looked over her glasses and pulled a face of sympathy. We have rules for good reasons, was what she was saying. Stella had nodded. As for waiting for simple accommodation – not to put too fine a point on it – by that time she could well be dead. Indeed she felt she could have died right there at that moment. All hope had drained from her. Despite the look of sympathy, there was an element of a schoolgirl being given a dressing-down. You're wasting my time and you've worn a hole in the elbow of that cardigan. Besides nowadays, the woman went on, it was a real estate transaction rather than a spiritual one. Supply and demand. Stella flinched a little at the 'real estate' phrase. Can there be so many women in a similar position? Widows, the brutalised, women in need of a room of their own, women with leanings to a life of seriousness, women who wished to practise a life of devotion, a move away from the world towards sanctity. She wanted to live the life of her Catholicism. This was where her kindness, if she had any, her generosity, her sense of justice had all come from. And her humility, she must not forget humility. Catholicism was her source of spiritual stem cells. They could turn into anything her spiritual being required. Like coping with difficulties, like a priesthood which had thrown up frequent monsters, right-wing control freaks, sexual deviants. Indeed there was a time when everyone in charge of children in institutions seemed to be a paedophile with a thin collar. And those in charge of the paedophiles had thicker collars and were covering up to help Holy Mother Church save face. Because she thought it a great and good organisation. She had learned it from birth – from her mother and father – her sense of calm resignation, her ability to absorb and to distribute love. She wanted a Church which was rational, kind, loving, ritualistic, Christ centred. One that would eventually involve women. Although she knew there was no hope of that in her lifetime. A Church with no emphasis on sexual prying or interference – anything consensual had to be without sin. A religion which prays, which has satisfying and beautiful rituals – like Easter. A faith which shows concern and benefits others, a religion of values, always on its toes to help, which in a thousand acts a day looks out for others and their needs. Her faith came from her humane heart rather than her head. And now the substance of the things she had hoped for had come to nothing.

*   *   *

201

To leave Gerry seemed such an impossibility. Things would be as they had always been. How could lives be changed at their age? She'd known many people who'd split up – people she'd believed were perfectly suited to each other. But that was just sloppy thinking – nobody could peer into a relationship – even for a day or two – and come away with the truth. She had even attended – out of loyalty to both partners – a separation party – the now adult children going round offering crisps and peanuts and refilling drinks, everybody chatting nervously. The only people who were comfortable were the couple splitting up – everybody else was in a state of dread, terrified of saying the wrong thing. Until the drink took over.

Where would she live? Where would Gerry live? How could she tell her son? Although at one time these things seemed insurmountable now, with drinking on this scale, they seemed possible. She might not be able to join an organisation but she could still live on her own. They could sell the tenement flat and buy two bijou flats. Hers would have to have a garden. And Gerry would have to get rid of all those books and CDs. Make his own dinners. Maybe he should look for a flat near a Marks & Spencer. But there she was – doing it again – organising him. Trying to look after him.

She sniffed and realised she was no longer crying. She might as well use the toilet while she was there. She rumbled off another length of toilet paper and blew her nose. She feared she might dehydrate herself – peeing and weeping at the same time. And the thought started her smiling. Maybe the nose blowing would also have to be taken into account. Another form of leakage. The last time she'd cried was at Christmas night Mass, in the church with Gerry. Any more and she'd have to move on to the reserve tank. Having dry eye syndrome didn't stop tears but they were of little help – being made of the wrong stuff. Not enough lubrication, said the eye doctor – wrong amounts of water, oil and mucus. Too watery by half.

When she looked down, there were two round red marks, one on each of her thighs. The marks reminded her of the cheeks of her Raggedy Anne doll. Perfectly round, perfectly red. For a moment she wondered what nature of a disease she had contracted. In a foreign place. It also occurred to her how thin her thighs were. Then she realised what the marks were – elbow prints, where she had leaned as she held her head in the act of weeping.

It was amazing. Here she was weeping about being too old and she was remembering the things of her childhood. She had a cardboard tube at home with her Junior Certificate in it. The section marked 'Passed with distinction' was filled to overflowing with subjects. She was a pensioner, for God's sake. Why was the stuff of her life compacted like this? Also she had kept a card in a photo album for Baby Gilmore with his weight in pounds and ounces – and a wrist tag to go with it. A single thought could whizz her through sixty years. And yet there were such gaps, periods where no memory surfaced. Where had *they* flown? She prayed that, like the pigeons in the square, they would not all take off at once. Leaving her empty, doting. Hoping that the handclap of her accumulated years would not scare every thought she ever had into the air. She had seen what had happened to both her mother and grandmother in their dotage. It was part of the reason she kept up her regime of crosswords. The keep-fit brain. These things seemed to be hereditary. What would it be like to avoid all the serious diseases throughout life only to end up staring at the wall, not knowing who you were. To have slalomed all obstacles only to arrive at a white-out. Then a black-out. Then nothing. Sans everything. Gerry was doing it too, not just with wrong words, but with whole conversations. Time and again he'd ask, 'What are we eating this evening?' and time and again she would tell him. And still he would forget. He would become absorbed in what he was doing and forget that they were going out to a reception at the City Hall or somewhere. Stella would appear at the study door all glammed up in her best coat and he would look up from his reading like a startled animal caught drinking at a watering hole. With the result that he would appear among fellow architects unshaven and grubbily dressed, the collar of his navy overcoat sprinkled with dandruff. 'Lucky for you, grey stubble is the current style,' she would whisper. 'Although I'm not fond of it myself.' At such receptions she would never keep an eye on his drinking. He was always responsible enough. Knew that he could not disgrace himself to the point of slurring words or staggering. Indeed, over the years, she had rarely seen him drunk. But he had spent a lifetime of such socialising – so he knew how to do it. Eat as many of the canapés as he could to absorb any alcohol. Drink a glass of water now and again to wash it all down. Go easy on the red wine, unless it was a really good one. She didn't drink much but she *did* know a good wine when she encountered it. Although they never served a good red wine at civic bashes. After such a do she hated the navy spit she produced cleaning her teeth before bed. Gerry'd admitted once in his cups that as long as he knew there was a bottle of Jameson at home he was all right. 'Just if I take the notion.' He needed that sense of security. When away from home, the Traveller's Friend had to be in place.

What was she doing? Sitting on a toilet reviewing her life? The vocation she imagined for herself had begun as no more than a possibility. Something she should investigate. And in the meantime she had taken shortcuts, made assumptions, said

204

prayers, daydreamed only to find her ambition to become a person with a purpose had failed. She was still where she had started out from her home three days ago. Or was it four? With today's meeting, her plans had evaporated. She would have to find another place to go. Another place of sanctuary. If life with Gerry continued in the same bibulous way. She rumbled some more toilet roll off the spool and blew her nose again. Then flung the paper behind her into the bowl. She sighed and stood, making sure she was decent, checking all around herself. With a wave of her hand she flushed the toilet. The world began to impinge upon her again. The place full of the noise of falling water, doors being banged and bolted, taps running, hand driers roaring.

When Stella had walked out of sight Gerry put his head back and looked up into the cavernous ceiling. She'd seemed annoyed and that wasn't like her at all. This was just one more waiting room. But the circumstances were very different. How long ago was it? Michael's age would provide an answer to that. So forty-two years ago Gerry had spent most of the day and a night in a Belfast waiting room. With his stomach clenched. How many cigarettes did he need to smoke to loosen the tightness? He'd lit another with tremulous hands and crumpled the packet. He walked to the waste bin, dropped it in and went back to his seat. He told the Pink Lady, Mavis, he was going to the hospital shop. She said she would go for him – what was it he wanted? And just as they were talking word came through from the sister in charge that he could visit his wife in Intensive Care in an hour's time. The visit would have to be very brief – no more than a few minutes. Sister indicated to Mavis that she should show Mr Gilmore where to go when the time came.

Mavis said she would take him to the shop. He bought twenty Benson & Hedges. His personal Pink Lady remained discreetly outside, pacing the corridor with her hands behind her back. Gerry thought her so attentive and considerate. He stripped the cellophane off the packet and lit a cigarette. His instinct was to smile at the girl serving him but his face wouldn't do it. The headlines on the papers had nothing to do with him or his life. There were public happenings and there were disasters which were private. He stood staring down at the selection of flowers. Such an array in the height of summer – such a splash of colour. Carnations. Stella was very fond of carnations. There were red ones and white ones. Given the circumstances, he bought a bunch of white ones and had the girl wrap them. There were droplets of water on the counter when the parcelling operation was finished. The wrapping paper was plain, brown. It darkened with the moisture. He paid. The girl handed them over saying that she loved the smell of them. He stared at the flowers, their intricate crenellations, their whiteness. He looked at his watch. The time was going so slowly. He supposed there were many things to do before she got settled into Intensive Care. Since coming into the hospital his knees had begun to shake – not a shiver but an infinitesimal trembling – the frequency of a tuning fork. It depended which leg he put pressure on. A kind of shudder. As if there was an intense cold in him. As if they would suddenly buckle beneath him and he would be taken into hospital without the bother of going. The white of the carnations was not an absence of colour, a colour drained, but an intense colour itself, vivid and pure. Gleaming white – reflecting. He heard what the girl had said and raised the bunch to his face and inhaled the smell. He barely knew what he was doing. Yes, they are

206

lovely, he said – or something like it. They reminded him of buttonholes at his wedding.

Mavis pulled a sad face when he came into the corridor. They're not happy about having flowers in Intensive Care, she said. He discarded his cigarette in the next ashtray. Mavis looked at her watch and said they might as well return to the waiting area. It was an upside-down lapel watch but he couldn't be bothered to ask her about it. Later she told him she was a retired nurse. Maybe that would explain the odd timepiece. He offered the flowers to her and she accepted and for a long time sat with the flowers cradled in her arms. She said she would find a good home for them. Some soul would be glad of them. He wished she would go away, not least because of the smell of the carnations. He felt the place bulge with their sweetness. And, as if reading his mind, she asked him would he object if she went off for a while and dealt with another matter which had come up. She would be back in good time to show him where to go. He sat looking down at his feet. He couldn't *not* listen to what was going on around him. He looked at his watch far too often but could not help himself.

Eventually Mavis arrived back, thankfully minus the flowers. She walked with him towards the lift and pressed the button. It took ages to come. Inside, Mavis pressed the button for the floor number. There were two other people in the lift. Someone had managed to scrawl graffiti on the back of the door. Although the two people were together they did not speak. They both got out on the third floor. There was an absence of mirrors. No hotel, this. He wanted to pray but couldn't because he no longer believed. Prayer was just an intense wishing. For Stella to survive. For her not to be damaged. The doors opened and, outside, he felt less claustrophobic, was able to breathe again. What was he going to see? In the Intensive Care Unit they washed their hands when they entered. Soapy stuff which cooled when it evaporated. Gerry stood with his hands behind him, his right hand holding his left wrist. The sister stressed that his visit should be short. At the risk of sounding brusque – a minute or two. And he must remember that she was only coming round from the anaesthetic. He could talk to the doctors afterwards.

The bed seemed large and high off the floor. Like a kind of draped altar. There were tubes and monitors, drip stands and catheters everywhere. But in the middle of it all, her face. With eyes closed. He said her name. Then his name, in case she didn't recognise his voice. He went to the side of the bed and took her hand. There was something like a clothes peg clipped to her fingers. He squeezed her hand as best he could.

'I love you,' he said.

He stood and looked at the snow beyond his reflection in the window glass. It must have been double glazed because there were two images overlapping. Seeing double. It was only in movie cartoons that drunks saw double. He tried to look at the reflection of the bruise on his chin but the moving images of the snow and flashing lights from aircraft made it difficult. The bruise was too small and the wrong colour. They had passed a chemist's shop on their way to this row of seats. There was bound to be a mirror there. He had looked at himself in the hotel lobby before leaving – but hadn't noticed the colour. But damned if he was going to trail back to the chemist's just to see a bit of purple and black. Trailing two sets of hand luggage. His shoulder bag and Stella's cabin case. If he left them unattended, there would be an announcement over the tannoy and before they knew it, their stuff would be blown to smithereens. So he sat down again. The whiskey was talking to him – murmuring pleasantly in his ear. He felt good and spread out his hands on either side of him. These chairs were a poor man's version of one of Marcel Breuer's creations. Steel tubing and black leather. He scored the black covering with his thumbnail and looked closely at the mark. It quickly disappeared. Synthetic. Not leather at all. Like old human skin – leather would hold the mark of his nail for longer.

There was still some left in the bottle. It looked like a last mouthful. He denied himself the pleasure a little longer. Then he remembered he had bought a CD. He dug into his shoulder bag and produced it. *Seven Last Words from the Cross.* The shining disc sat looking up at him. He levered it out, turned it over and held it up to look at his chin. Bad enough – and getting uglier. She was right about the colour. The blood darkness he could see for himself. What a dish that would be – aubergine and strawberry. But what about the custard? When did the yellow come into a bruise? Later. Custard was for afters. Staring at himself he realised that there was a hole at the centre of his reflection. No soul. No such thing. Didn't exist. He snapped the CD back into its case and slid it into his bag. 'Seven Cross Words from the Last'. Fucking hell – he *was* getting drunk – mixing up words. Or maybe it was age? Beginning to dote. Getting to be an oul boy. He tried to imagine it, if those words were correct. If Stella was going to die soon – and she had only a week's crosswords left to do *before* the last one in her life. Seven Crosswords from the Last. He should try and remember this. Tell her and she might laugh. Placate her, mollify her. That had been a terrible stare she'd given him just before she bolted.

209

'Cross words' might mean 'Angry words'. Seven of them required. As a child, on his way to school, there'd been a plugged-in puppet in a shoe repairer's window which hammered his last constantly all day, every day. Gerry grew to hate him. Slow tap – slow tap – slow tap. 'Go and fuck your self, ya bastard.' He couldn't stop laughing. This was what he meant about wit and drink. Oh boy, did he feel good. He counted the words on his fingers. 'Go and fuck your self, ya bastard.' That was seven. Yet there was some difficulty. Was 'yourself' one or two words? He closed over his hand and began releasing and straightening his fingers one by one. Definitely seven words. He began to laugh and pretended to hammer nails into boots. Tap – tap – tap. He laughed so much he had to wipe the tears from his face with a hanky.

It had been a really good break. Just the two of them. Stella had been very quiet, hadn't opened her cheeper all that much – yesterday and today. And that wasn't like her. He should ask her. If anyone knew what was wrong with her – it would be her. She knew everything. Every last fucking thing. And he admired her for it. He had always found admiration part and parcel of love – even though he said she could have been prime minister or pope except that one of those jobs was not open to her. She had a Quality Street tin at home – full to the brim – labelled in her distinctive handwriting 'keys of unknown origin'. He loved her optimism. Keys kept just in case locks should ever be found to fit them. As well as ornamental dishes full of things whose use he'd long forgotten – black plastic goes-inteys, small bent screws, nail clippers, unsharpened pencil stubs, dice, tweezers, tokens from Christmas crackers, small round tins of lip balm, nail files, a table tennis ball, a half-stick of white chalk, countless kirby grips. God knows what else. What kind of things did she know? There was no end to the categories. No end to the degrees he attributed to her in Gerontology and Dentistry and Philosophy and History and the PhDs she had in Theology and Embryology and William Morris wallpaper designs. She knew that the full name of the Litany recited after the rosary at benediction was the Litany of the Blessed Virgin Mary. She knew that Albert Pierrepoint's father was also a hangman, that farinaceous meant floury when applied to potatoes but that flowery language could not be described as such, as farinaceous. Even though she had never suffered labyrinthitis herself she knew it was something that brought a middle-aged woman to her hands and knees suffering from dizziness and nausea. If she ever got such an attack she knew all the bus routes in the city of Glasgow that would bring her home or near home – the 66, the 20, the 11, the 59, the 18, the 44 and the 44A. That was until the City Fathers decided to change the bus route numbers, all on the same day, and then – like everybody else – she knew nothing about where she was going. And for months on end Glasgow folk were seen wandering round the city of Barcelona looking for Drumchapel. She knew what school Seamus Heaney's sisters went to. She knew the Memorare off by heart. 'Remember, O most gracious Virgin Mary, that never was it known that anyone who fled to thy protection, implored thy help, or' – what was it now? He was forgetting the Memorare. No great loss to the memory bank.

She knew the recipes for mushroom stroganoff and spaghetti carbonara and about forty-two other dishes without looking at a cookery book. She knew that a bonspiel was a major gathering of curlers on ice, that curling stones were quarried on Ailsa Craig, that Ailsa Craig was also known as Paddy's Milestone. This and much, much more. Oh – and that a Sitzprobe was nothing medical but the rehearsal for an opera.

211

She knew that another name for chambermaid was abigail. That jeggings were a cross between jeans and leggings. She knew the times of day when the News was on BBC1, ITV, BBC2, Channel 4 – even on holiday weekends when the schedules were upset. She knew that the make of a bin lorry was a Vulture. After a crawl of charity shops she was amazed at the number of people who had given up calligraphy. And those who had ceased to read the fictions of Cecelia Ahern and Maeve Binchy. She knew the questions to ask the wee ones who had just started at school. Questions they knew the answer to, like, who do you sit beside? She knew what stump work was, but was unable to do any of it. She had to content herself with knitting. She knew from her own primary school that Cambridge was on the river Cam and that Oxford was on the Cherwell. She knew that wedding invitations were issued only by the bride's parents. She knew the novels of Graham Greene – not so much the thrillers but the big ones about faith. *The Heart of the Matter, A Burnt-Out Case, The Power and the Glory.* She knew that dances in the country districts of Northern Ireland were known as 'fifty fifties' – half ceilidh, half ballroom – that CODA stood for the Carnival of Dance, Andersonstown – a huge marquee with showbands playing in the 1960s which involved moving to music, licensed touching for all to see, hand holding with strangers. She knew that Vicky Coren, who wrote a column in the *Observer* on Sundays, was also a world-class poker player and that she was the daughter of Alan Coren, the humorist who wrote for *Punch* but was now, sadly, no longer with us. She knew that Claire Rayner, the agony aunt, was mother to Jay Rayner, the restaurant critic. She knew how to spell almost every word in the English language except 'carrots' – which she always misspelled with a double 't'. Carrotts. Chrysanthemum, hieroglyphic, miscellaneous, kaleidoscope, toucan – all these she got right. Carrotts she got wrong. She knew, despite her scant encounter with drink, that a few drops of vodka would remove red wine stains from a white linen tablecloth. That a Madrileño was a man from Madrid and his female counterpart could be referred to as Madrileña. She knew how to convert kilometres to miles by multiplying by five and dividing by eight and could do such sums in her head in a trice. 'The town of Baltimore is 32 kilometres away,' she would say with the map on her knee. 'Twenty miles.' She knew that it was Glen Campbell who sang 'The Wichita Lineman'. She was of the opinion that if you were lying down you did not experience the wind as badly as when you were standing up. The breeze, not the belching. She knew that a routine eye test took three-quarters of an hour and not, as her husband suggested, thirty minutes. She knew something but not everything about Hopi ear candles. She knew that TMJ was an acronym for Temporomandibular joint disorder. She knew that Tony Blair's son went to university in Bristol and that St Pauls was a dodgy district of that same city. She knew that Diego Forlán used to play for Manchester United but had moved on to play for Villareal, then Atletico Madrid. She knew that the Americans always elected their president in November and that British general elections were always on a Thursday. When it came to bullets she knew the difference between roll, yaw and pitch – knew when yaw became tumble. From the nuns at school she knew the different techniques for darning a hole and darning a thin place to strengthen it. She knew that there was a single word in Irish for a cow that sucks the tail of another cow. *Bradáan.* She knew that Cecil Frances Alexander was a woman from Derry, not a man, and that she was a writer of such well-loved hymns as 'All Things Bright and Beautiful',

'There is a Green Hill Far Away' and 'Once in Royal David's City'. Indeed, he thought, if he thought anything, that this was developing into a hymn to her. To Stella. Star of the Sea. Maybe even a him to her. Man to woman. Her ladyship. Although to set his thoughts to music would take a bit of time. She knew that Valencia oranges were very juicy and did not have a lot of pips in them and therefore were better for making an orange drink. That Seville oranges straight from the tree were as bitter as soot and fit only for the making of marmalade. That, to produce red berries, there have to be both male and female holly trees in the vicinity. And she knew about love – how to make it and how to mend it. She knew every step of the St Patrick's Day Hornpipe and could have danced it – with or without him – had it not been for the present inflexibility of her limbs. She only knew two jokes but could tell neither of them. At any time, she knew where everything in the flat was – the double-sided mirror, the mustard – both the powdered variety and the stuff straight from the jar, the red-handled nail scissors, the tube of UHU glue, the black drinking straws, the ball of string, the Scrabble and Monopoly sets, a brass drawing pin or as she called it a thumb tack, paper clips, new toilet rolls, candles, paint scrapers, and where to find Radio 4 on the dial. She knew Ashby de la Zouch was not in the flat but in Leicestershire.

So she was no dozer. Except for spelling carrots with two 't's. He finished the bottle.

A flashing orange light reflected from the window. Gerry looked up, heard the alarm of the shuttle cart. It stopped beside the row of seats but still its warning noise grated on and on. He turned. Stella was the only passenger behind the Sikh and she was gingerly climbing down onto terra firma.

'Thank you. I'm much obliged,' she said. The driver nodded. 'He thought I could do with a lift,' she said to Gerry. She was like a shy child. 'He insisted.'

'I thought I told you not to take lifts from strange men,' said Gerry. 'He probably thought you were old.' The shuttle cart pulled away. 'The sound of a corncrake. That suits you down to the ground. A species in danger of extinction.'

'What do you mean?'

'Believers. I mean, where have they all gone? Apart from yourself.' He was gesturing too much, waving his hands, trying to focus, swaying slightly. 'You only find corncrakes in the outer bloody isles. Them and religious fanatics. Women who never get their hair cut. Places where the modern world – and its method . . . methodology have not reached.'

'You *are* drunk,' she said. 'I know you're drunk when you mock me.'

'I do not.'

'You don't remember the mockery because you're drunk.'

215

'What *is* wrong with you?'

'It's not what's wrong with *me*,' said Stella. 'If they don't let you on this plane, I'd be delighted to go home on my own.'

He heaved himself to his feet and stood facing her, staring.

'Have you been crying?' he said. She didn't answer. 'What about?'

Stella sat down. She did not want to look at him but even when she stared ahead she could see his reflection. She made a visor of her hand, shaded her eyes and looked down.

'Gerry . . .'

'What?' There was a long silence. 'I always know it's something bad when you start with my name.'

'I want to leave you,' she said, 'but I don't know how to go about it.'

Gerry stood in the same position for a long time.

'Is there somebody else?'

She laughed out loud.

'Catch yourself on.'

He tried to drink from the bottle but failed to get anything out of it.

'That's it. *Feeneeto.*'

'Us or the bottle?' He turned to look around him but lurched a little. 'Now if I could find a bin I could dispose of this fellow.' He wandered off, both hands behind his back clutching the bottle. 'You're probably thinking exactly the same thing about me,' he shouted over his shoulder. 'I'll not be long.'

Stella took out her washbag and unzipped it. Had he heard what she said? It was really foolish anyway, bringing it up at a time like this. He wouldn't remember a thing about it. She found her wristbands and slid them on, making sure the plastic studs were to the inside – against her skin. Next, her powder compact – she opened it and looked at herself in the mirror. Her eyes were a little red but they weren't *that* bad. She found her glasses and whatever way she unfolded them, the hinge nipped her finger. Like being bitten by a ladybird. Just one more indignity. She put on her specs and looked at the finger. She had not drawn blood. That summer in Toronto the ladybirds were everywhere. Millions and millions of them along the beach by the lake shore. And occasionally one nipped you. It was like the end of the world, being attacked by ladybirds. They were brown and yellow – not red and black like the British ones. It was impossible not to crush them underfoot – like walking on Rice Krispies. Coco Pops, even.

It was difficult to see her eyes, in this light. She took off her glasses and bent close to the mirror. How strange it was – eyes looking at eyes. Seeing eyes by using eyes. The wound was inside her. And it had no reflection. Gerry had once said to her in the middle of an argument that he didn't believe in souls but if, just perchance, they did exist hers would be like a razor. She had been made that way by the Catholic Church, he said. Inflexible, narrow, capable of doing terrible damage by her adherence to rules and systems. But she totally objected. She told him that if she was a good person at all, it had come from her religion. If she had any sense of justice and fairness, any concept of equality, then it had come from the Church. She'd been taught by the Church's representatives, her parents and schoolteachers, people she loved and trusted, people who had imbued her with a love of others and a love of Christ. It was so utterly simple a child could grasp it, so completely compelling because it came from her natural capacity to love. It had nothing to do with philosophy or intelligence. Her religion was the great equaliser. You could be at Mass in a pew with someone of a different colour or

217

race or brainpower – some woman professor, actress, farm labourer or unemployable dunce – and you knew absolutely that they were all the same in the sight of God. Also whatever kindness she had and whatever generosity she possessed came from those early sources. No room in it for snobbery or hatred of any kind. Except, Gerry would always say, for 'the treatment of your own fair sex'. Other things – her sense of resignation, her ability to absorb and to distribute love, her calmness, her stoicism, her humility. Her husband's reply was always to say who in their right mind could boast of humility? Such things, replied Stella, can be said between those who love each other. Her church was her everything. Like any human organisation it had its bad apples. The Garden of Eden was a metaphor for a place and a tribe but you could bet your bottom dollar it included a percentage of those who erotically loved their own gender. In the context, Gerry said, bottom dollar was good. Both male *and* female was Stella's answer. There was no gardener in Eden. Indeed, there was no Eden. But if you ran with the metaphor – one or other of Our First Parents had to be a gardener and the other one had to be the flower. To this inevitably Gerry added, 'And the apple was a bad apple.'

She became aware of a noise she knew well – a kind of snarl. She looked over her shoulder and there was Gerry weaving into view.

'There isn't a bin in the whole bloody place.'

'People put bombs in bins,' said Stella. 'That's why there are none. It's to do with security.'

'Unfortunately I don't have a bomb with me at the moment.'

'Go to departures, to security. There'll be a bin for empties there.'

Gerry shrugged and blundered off. Stella watched him, saw him wander past a bin, his eyes looking up for signs to departures.

Her washbag was still open in front of her. She took out her eye drops and unscrewed the top. Her glasses were set aside, her head went back and her elbows came up almost like a reflex action. This had to be done ten, twenty times a day – day in, day out. She stared into the high metallic rafters of the airport and squeezed the small plastic bottle. Nothing. Then the cold splash into her left eye when she least expected it. Involuntary blinking. The same with the right. Involuntary blinking. This time a tear overflow, spilling down her cheek. Watering her eyes, like they were flowers. Looking after them. After them looking. Gerry will be the cause of tears before the night's out the way he's blundering around. She'd just cried in the toilets and remembering crying brought back the airport in Glasgow, saying goodbye to their son and new grandson. And Danielle, of course. In the days before she'd had this dry eye condition she could cry like the best of them. That first summer when the Canadians visited Glasgow they'd had the luck of good weather – almost a heatwave – and the bridges felt warm under their forearms as they looked down at the diminished rivers. The air was hot in the evenings and people were in T-shirts on their tenement steps. Too early in the year for wasps so it was bliss to sit out at picnics. The baby cried a lot and she had a vision of Gerry behind the pushchair or the stroller, as they called it, in the Botanic Gardens as if he was mowing the lawn. Up and down, up and down till the baby was asleep and the grass full of tyre tracks. And when it came to the farewells at the airport, for Stella, it contained the possibility that it was the last time she would ever see them. Some accident or something unforeseen and tragic would happen before they could meet again. She and Gerry had once been to the Cliffs of Moher, the highest in Ireland, which overlooked the Atlantic. During the famine years families would come to that spot to catch a last glimpse of the sailing ship taking their loved ones to a better place for ever. Migrants. Exiles. The fact that Michael and his family were travelling back by plane didn't make it any easier to say farewells. She knew they could keep in touch by phone – the days of three-pounds-a-minute calls were long gone. And those were the days when pounds were worth something. None of these things made a difference. What Stella was missing was the rearing, the day-to-day grind of the rituals of love, the babysitting, the bathing, the book reading, the arms around, the cheek to cheek, the sheer physicality of it all. The first words. The first steps. The need to be involved and spoken of as Grandmother. Of course Stella and Gerry went to Canada in between times but it was not the same thing. On such visits politeness intervened. Danielle had to be respected. Lips had to be buttoned. She screwed on the top of the eyedropper and wiped her cheeks with a tissue. Now clear-eyed, she looked around for Gerry.

He eventually came back empty-handed and sat down on the seat beside her. For a long time he said nothing. She didn't look at him but fiddled with her wristbands.

'So?'

'So what?'

'What is it you're saying?'

'When we get home,' she said, 'we're putting the flat up for sale. Then I'm getting a place of my own.' Gerry's hands were empty. He threaded his fingers together, tightened them until his skin shone.

'You'd be better waiting till the summer,' he said. 'You'd get a better price.'

'The place I buy will be at summer prices too.'

Again there was silence. Gerry let his head go down. His chin rested on his chest and she wondered if he was asleep.

'You're a bit premature wearing those,' his voice said without his head moving.

'What do you mean?'

'The wrist things. The flight's delayed,' he said.

'Because of snow?'

'I'm not Sherlock Holmes but I'd say that was a fairly reasonable guess. There's no room for explanations on the screen.'

'We could be here all night,' Stella said. She began to take the wristbands off. Gerry straightened up, sat more like a man awake and said, 'There's lots of them delayed.'

She looked out at the falling snow.

'It's getting worse. Maybe we should go through security and wait at the gate. If we fall asleep here they might go without us.'

'Might? They'd *deffinately* go without us.'

Stella stood and waited for Gerry. He sighed and got to his feet.

'You know the way,' she said. 'The way of the empty bottle.'

They began to walk, he unsteadily, she with her eye on the signage of the distance they had yet to cover.

'Are you sure you're all right?' she said. 'Maybe we should hitch a ride with your Sikh in his wee cart.'

'You'll do no such thing.'

At security there were queues. Miles of them. It would take ages to get through. As they wove their way through the labyrinth which doubled back on itself again and again like a folded fire hose Gerry came level across the tapes with an attractive young woman. Several times. He tried to engage her in conversation about the blizzard but each time she looked away from him. Perhaps she does not speak English, Stella suggested. The next time the woman and he coincided Stella engaged Gerry, eye to eye, to prevent him speaking to her. Not because she's an attractive woman but because you're being a pest, she said.

Flat screens showed what was required of them – take off jackets, remove laptops, empty pockets, what to do with gels, creams, toothpastes. Eventually they made it to the X-ray machines.

They reassembled themselves at an aluminium bench and set off again for their numbered pier.

'That was ridiculously straightforward,' said Gerry. 'I was going to tell the guy I had hidden a half-bottle about my person.' He pointed into his mouth. 'But I thought better of it.'

At the gate there were plenty of people – but still some empty places to sit. They found a seat in a corner facing outwards into the night and Stella sat down. Gerry stood swaying.

'I want to stretch out,' he said.

'You can't take three seats.'

He put his shoulder bag on the ground for a pillow and lay down on the carpeted floor at Stella's feet. He began snoring almost immediately. A woman reading a German newspaper looked around to see where the noise was coming from. Stella smiled at her but got no response. After a while she reached out the toe of her shoe and gave Gerry a little nudge. It had no effect. She pushed him harder – then almost kicked him. He stopped the noise and turned without wakening. The German woman shook out her newspaper and looked at Stella again. Gradually the snoring returned.

The German woman produced an iPod and slipped earplugs into her ears.

Stella opened a compartment of her bag and took out one of the English crosswords she had torn from the paper in the Amstel place. It was the only one she had left. It took her about half an hour to finish it then she wanted to stretch her legs. But she was afraid of her bag disappearing or causing a fuss. She moved it closer to Gerry.

She walked to the nearest screen. Multiples of 'delayed' were stacked one upon the other. It was lucky they didn't have a connection to catch. They had no particular reason to be urgently at home. There was just the irksomeness of waiting, the disappointment of disruption.

By this time a crowd had accumulated. Almost all the seats were taken. People were sitting on the floor. Children slept on overcoats laid down as mattresses. Stella smiled at a little girl sucking her thumb who was staring up at her. She marvelled at the brashness of tiny children – the way they gave you the once-over. Unaware of politeness, of giving offence, of themselves. Beside this girl was her mother, whose hand had strayed down and was stroking the hair at the child's neck. And beside her, slightly sprawled on the seat, was a grandmother figure talking, talking, talking. Three generations.

She might as well get some information. There was a long queue at the desk. Stella joined it. The poor girls in uniform were run off their feet. When she asked her question about how long the delay would be the girl looked over her shoulder at the snow – as if to say your guess is as good as mine. Dozens of flights have been delayed or cancelled, she said, and to make matters worse there is a strike by Spanish

223

air traffic controllers. The snow is all over, in the UK and in Germany. Here in Schiphol the airport authorities are using snowploughs to try and keep the runways clear. More heavy snow and black ice are expected tonight. There was a pause. The blue-uniformed girl gave a little shrug. They both smiled at each other and Stella turned and walked away.

She wandered along the central corridor with its travelators going in opposite directions. She saw a sign pointing to a Meditation Centre but resisted the temptation. She had been to such places in other airports. Lowest Common Denominator Religion. Hire-a-prayer-mat. A picture of the Sacred Heart kept in a cupboard. A sign, 'Praying clothes for women are stored in this wardrobe.' And God knows what else. So she walked to the shops. Outside the wind hurled and flurried the snow at the building.

People stopped and listened to a long announcement in Dutch, which was followed by muttering and resentment. Some rolled their eyes, others shook heads. A translation into English stated that weather conditions were so adverse that all flights for the foreseeable future would be disrupted. Passengers would be informed of developments but there would be no more incoming or outgoing flights that evening. Now it was the turn of the English-speakers to grumble and pull faces. One woman began weeping aloud. Stella shrugged but continued to browse magazines. The announcement was repeated in other languages. She should tell Gerry – give him the bad news.

She made her way back to where he was lying. Of course she had lost her seat – to some old man in a red baseball cap who was sound asleep. In her absence Gerry had turned to face the wall. Stella knelt, opened her case and produced the novel she was reading. Before she went off again she crouched and shook his shoulder.

'Gerry.'

At the third call of his name he opened his eyes and looked up at her.

'We're not going to get away tonight,' she said. 'Everything is cancelled. So you can go back to sleep. Keep an eye on those bags.' She straightened up, leaning on the arm of the chair she'd forfeited to the old man in the red baseball cap. Then wandered off again.

She came to a gate which had reduced lighting and no destination displayed. There was a certain amount of overspill from other crowded gates but still there were empty seats and the area seemed much quieter. It was dark and warm. Whether the light had been reduced to indicate the gate was not functioning or whether something had fused and the gate had been withdrawn from use, she didn't know. She sat down. There were empty seats on either side of her. One or two people stretched across other seats, sleeping. She couldn't make out if they were men or women because they had removed their shoes and their heads were half hidden – either by elbows or hijabs. She extended her legs, crossed her feet and sensed the seat comfortable, hugging her back. This was a better place than any Meditation Centre. She tried to read but the low light was a problem. Eventually she gave up. The partial darkness made the world outside more visible. Still the snow slanted silently down.

She tried closing her eyes, folding her arms for ballast. Sleeping upright was a skill her mother had developed late in life because of a hiatus hernia. It was a skill Stella did not have. She could doze, and frequently did, during sermons but it was more sleep-interrupted than sleep. That slow sinking of the head and then the sudden jerk into consciousness when

225

the head went too far forward. The inability to guess what the priest was talking about when she came to. Without opening her eyes she said a prayer for both her parents – that they would both be at peace. That was another phrase of her father's when, as a child, she'd climb into his bed. If she so much as moved an eyebrow he'd say, 'Lie at peace.' Was she asleep? Had she dreamt the whole nightmare of the Beguinage? She tilted herself and leaned her elbow on the arm of the seat, then rested her head on her hand. Eyes still closed. Drifting. Today had been a cul-de-sac. The whole holiday had been a cul-de-sac. The substance of things hoped for had melted away – a snowflake touching her tongue. Relying on the evidence of things not seen. How different the setting out and the going home. In primary, Master Ryan had furnished them all with stock phrases to be used in their compositions. First he would clean the board. If the sun was shining everyone saw the chalk dust turning in the air. He would write 'Words and Phrases' in his flawless hand. She especially remembered 'A Walk in the Country'. As he wrote the chalk would hiss and when it came to full stops and commas it would smack and click against the blackboard. He would raise his voice above the noise he was making. 'I'm writing these phrases to help you. I want to see them used. But there are some people in this class who think they can do better. Isn't that right, Geraldine Kearney?' This meant that many of the compositions were similar. Children 'rose early' and 'set off in high spirits for the mountain or woods', their mothers 'packed their egg sandwiches'. On the way, they all met the same shepherd who warned them not to ignore 'the donkey braying from afar'. Such a thing 'was a sure sign of rain'. But just when they were about to 'tuck into our outdoor feast', 'the first roll of thunder was heard', which meant that 'we returned home under a different sky than witnessed our commencement'. Such phrases identified the teacher and *where* the child had gone to school. Sister Marie-Thérese who taught English in the first year of grammar school would return corrected essays and say, 'And how is Master Ryan getting on these days?'

The noise of the terminal began to diminish. It came and went like a radio not quite on the station. Like they did in the old days – before this digital stuff. But she found little difference. She liked to get on the station and stay there but Gerry liked to fiddle, change it to Radio 3 and be selfish enough not to return it to where he found it. Like the kettle. When she emptied the kettle she always filled it for the benefit of the next person. Which inevitably was Gerry. Maybe it was her hearing, coming and going. Cave echoes, a child crying, chimes, announcements on the tannoy – although it was difficult to tell if they were in Dutch or English. Just as it was difficult to tell a dream from the reality. Angst crept into her. Her head was too heavy for sleep. She was tired – deeply, deeply tired. It felt like a lifetime's tiredness. Apart from the exhaustion of teaching there was every nappy she had ever washed, every meal she had ever made, every shirt she had ever ironed, every floor she had vacuumed. It all seemed registered in her bones at that very moment. When Gerry started into the heavy drinking it affected her, put her on edge, made her think thoughts she was not proud of. And as well as that, going back to the shooting. Telling it all to that woman, Kathleen. It was too much in such a short time. She clenched her eyes, hoping to sleep, but that was useless. Sleep was about relaxation, not tension. She switched her visions to something else but each time she gradually returned to the day in Belfast. It was the kind of day which doesn't happen very often there – *As I Lay Dying*. Sunny and hot – the sky blue with white clouds waltzing around the horizon. This line of thought was edging too close to danger. She should think of other things. There had been days like it in her childhood – July days when the tar of the roads went soft in the sunshine. And the wonderful smell of it. She'd been warned not to play with it. This was a good deflection, a good shield. And she remembered her mother, and her yelling, 'That sort of black would never come out of clothes, no matter how many times you washed them.' Everything was boiled in the zinc bath on the range. The clothes swelling up, the wooden spoon pushing them down again. Bursting the air out of them. The warm kitchen soapy and perfumed. She had dug at the road stuff with a lollipop stick, moving it like stiff treacle. Squatting in the gutter. Seeing the shimmer of air above the black surface. Dark stuff. Dangerous. Too close. But she loved the dark smell. It got on her hands and, of course, she wiped her hands on what she was wearing, which was not very much, the day was such a scorcher. 'How dare you come in here in that state,' her mother had shouted, 'those things are going straight in the bin. That tar would get on everything else in the wash.' William Faulkner's *As I Lay Dying* – you couldn't make it up. A strange and great book, which she'd just reread. Not to be confused with Brian Faulkner – the prime minister of the time. The early seventies when the war was at its worst. Maybe she should go back to the black stuff again. The black stuff and the boiling of clothes was safe. One of the things that amazed her was the sharpness of her recall of events just prior to the main event. How did the mind do that? Select and retain in detail without knowing the awfulness of what was to come. There must be some kind of fixative that washes the brain. She was wearing a white summer dress and open-toed sandals. A variation of the 'A line' was still around and it made her condition a little less noticeable. She disliked the idea of boasting – even about something as natural as having a baby. But it was now just too noticeable – carrying all in front of her. The day, too hot for tights. At the antenatal clinic they told her that some mothers were grateful for a winter pregnancy because in their condition the body temperature actually rose – like carrying a hot-water bottle round their waist. And she remembered even to this day that she was actually imagining how her life was going to change. I will become a mother and I will get up in the middle of the night and I will breast-feed and it will be a joy. And Gerry will turn oh so sympathetically in his sleep. Maybe bring me my breakfast-in-bed before he goes out to his work. It was a whole word – breakfast-in-bed – such a rare occurrence it required that completeness. Sheer fantasy, as it turned out. *As I Lay Dying* – when she'd read it the first time in her Senior Certificate year she'd been confused. Each chapter was called something odd like Darl or Jewel and it was all written from the 'I' point of view and she read it – stupidly, as she afterwards thought – as the thoughts of the same person, the same 'I', when it was actually the thoughts of different characters called Darl or Jewel. She kept flicking the pages backwards and forwards – what's going on here? – until she got what was happening. Could have kicked herself. She had just been to the library and left back *As I Lay Dying* along with two or three other books she couldn't now remember. Probably things on childbirth and mothering. Doctor Spock, maybe. 'You know more than you think you do.' And she was now going to the butcher's at the crossroads. Sausages, chops, maybe some calves' liver if they had it. She'd developed the habit of buying a week's supply of meat and keeping it in the fridge, to save her trailing down such a distance to the shops again. Especially now that she was in this condition. Especially during a heatwave. The butcher's was beside Madden's, the greengrocer's, where she'd get potatoes and a Savoy cabbage and some beetroot, which Gerry was very fond of. A taste of the earth, he said. And everything had gone according to plan and she'd had good crack with Old Trevor as he served the beetroot, stooping and bowing and scraping as if he was selling her golden apples. And she was joining in the fun as she received them, bowing and scraping back to him, like they were silver apples. The oul butcher kept up a banter with one of his young assistants, who was sharpening knives in the back by the sound of it, as he wrapped each item of meat separately in a membrane of grey tissue and parcelled them snugly together in brown paper. He was explaining how he was recovering from a bad shoulder – claimed he could tie the loops of his apron but damned if he could put on his bra in the mornings. And she laughed at the contortions of him trying to demonstrate his shortcomings – and failure. And then it was back into the crossroads and the blare of traffic and the heat shimmer of the asphalt when the eye could see the grey-green of the distant hills. The air shivering, it was so hot. And the Brit soldiers' vehicle approaching the lights that led to Andersonstown before they pulled in on her side of the road. And then something happened. She is crossing the road on a pedestrian crossing when she is hit. It feels like a car. But how could that have happened? The lights would have been red. Some drunk in the middle of the day. Careless driving. She felt she had to run. Something inside her, her very nature was saying *run*. And she was running, clutching her basket to her. She didn't know how long she ran for, how many steps, but for some reason the running became falling and she was down on the ground – had fallen her length, a slap forwards on the pavement – on her bump – and somehow she was unable to look around, to look down at her knees to see if she had skinned them or not. It was like 'holding in' as a child. Falling and the slap on the ground was such that her hands burned and her knees bled but she had not to cry whatever happened and she would run to the house, to her mother and hold in the crying and only when her mother put hands on her and held her face against her did the crying erupt. But her mother had died years ago and she, the daughter, was about forty miles from the home where she was raised and she couldn't understand why she was lying here. Sprawled. That was the word. She was sprawled on the ground on the dome that had grown within her. Unable to look down at her knees. And there was confusion. She thought there were some kids playing with cap guns. Utter confusion. But they should have been in school. In the classroom watching the board. Then she remembered it was the summer holidays. Pap, pap, pap, pappa. In front of her face was her basket and there was a hole in the raffia which had not been there before and something was seeping out of it, forming a trickle – which was moving towards her because of the slope of the terrain. Something must have burst when she fell – the beetroot or the liver – because the effluent was somewhere between maroon and purple. And she felt wet. Had her waters broken? She wondered if she could move her arm. To her amazement it moved when she willed it. She felt with her fingers all the way down to her waist. She definitely was soaking. They had done the breaking of the waters at her classes. Made it sound like a folk song. The Breaking of the Waters. She loved the Irish ballads and ballad singers. There was one – Molly Bawn – who gets shot by her lover when he mistakes her for a swan.

Because of her white apron. And the onset of darkness. A glimpse out of the corner of the eye. Like a warning signal, the scut of a rabbit. And he whirls and shoots. Her limbs they grew weak. Nevertheless she brought her hand up to her vision and it was blood. Jesus Mary, there was something very wrong down there. Maybe she'd been shot like Molly Bawn and was going to die. An Act of Contrition. Oh my God I am heartily sorry. You'd think you'd know a thing like that. Maybe she'd been shot through her basket. Her bloody breadbasket. She'd read in the paper about a Catholic boy who'd been shot in a drive-by on the Antrim Road and he'd run about half a mile, as far as Ponsonby Avenue, before dropping down dead. Pap, pap, pap. Somewhere a baby, a very young baby, a day-old-sounding baby was crying, yelling itself red in the face – mah mah mah – the squawks very quick, one after the other, in among the sounds of traffic, in among the roars of a motorbike – and she thought, is that my baby? – have I given birth lying here dying? Has it come out of me somehow without me knowing. Jesus have mercy. This was not how it was supposed to happen. She'd been to classes and nothing like this had been mentioned. The pavement was rough and pressed against her cheek. An inability to move. Except for shaking. Shaking was easy. Inside her stomach was being scoured with a metallic scrub – the kind of thing her mother did burned pots with. The kind of thing she quoted in English classes. Oxymoron – the hardness and the softness. Steel wool. She was by a low wall, a perimeter red-brick wall which would have been knee-high if she or anyone else had been standing up straight. It was at Safeways and there was a bunch of dandelions growing up out of a niche in the ground right by her face where her bag was sweltering in the summer heat. A couple of yellow ones, ones in flower, ones in bud. And another one – grey fluff – ready to be blown to the four winds. Was there any time left for her? For her baby? And God knows where her dress was. Could be up the back of her neck. There was a soldier on the other side of the wall – flat out. She didn't think he could see up her clothes from where he was. He was shouting at her but she couldn't make out what he was saying. What was the point of sending over people with such incomprehensible accents? What selfishness to be thinking of herself at a time like this when she should have been thinking of the child within her. That was what the papping was all about. She was utterly convinced it was a boy – said he was always tackling her with his studs on show. When she was in the bath she could actually see pale moving points on her stomach when he kicked her from within. Then she closed her eyes. A drawing down of blinds. She was aware of the red world behind her eyelids – the red world of her body. A man bent down and asked her if she was all right. He was gently shaking her arm but she could not be bothered to answer. The next thing she heard was the sound of an ambulance and for the first time in her life, which of late had been crisscrossed with such sirens, she realised this one was for her.

There was a clear plastic thing over her face for her to breathe into and she could hear faintly the nee-naw of the ambulance she was in. The ambulance man was busy doing things to her and occasionally he would break off to rub the back of her hand and say things to encourage her. Everything is going to be all right. Her head pounded with the realisation that if she'd been shot . . . her baby'd been shot. She began to pray, with an intensity summoned up from her penetrated innards, that if anyone was to die here it should be her, and not her baby. What she needed was a miracle. So she said a prayer until she trembled. And she made a vow. That if her baby was spared she would . . . someone was shaking her. Speaking to her. It was Gerry crouched in front of her. The place was still dark.

'What? What is it?'

'I thought you'd gone.' His voice was hoarse and hung-over. 'I've been looking for you. Everywhere.' He was almost on his hands and knees in an attempt to get down to her level. Stella straightened up in the seat, blinked and checked herself for drool by wiping the sides of her mouth. Her heart was still pounding.

'I wasn't asleep.' She shuddered and said, 'I haven't had one of those in years.'

He knew to look at her. He reached out and took her hand.

'It's the stress,' he said.

'Brought on by drunks.'

'You're shaking.'

'You think I don't know?'

Gerry rose from the ground at her knees and slid onto the empty seat beside her. He squeezed her hands hard. Encircled her shoulders with his arm, kept patting her. His breath smelled stale. Then he guided her head onto his shoulder. Laid his cheek against her hair and brow.

'You poor thing.'

'It's like it's happening all over again. Now. Still.'

'It may not be the best place in the world to be, but focus on here. Listen hard to the airport. Don't go back there. Concentrate. Stay with me, here.' He stroked the back of her hand with his fingers and held her tightly with his other arm. For what seemed like ages. Gradually her tremors began to lessen.

'What time is it?' she said.

'After seven.'

'Did you remember my bag?'

He pointed to it by his side. His own bag was at his feet. 'I'm parched,' he said.

When the tremors stopped Stella rummaged in her bag and produced the plastic bottle half full of water.

'It'll be tepid.' He put it to his mouth, tilted his head back and drank.

'At least it's wet.' He offered it to her. She drank but before she finished the last mouthful she paused and offered it to him. He nodded for her to finish it.

'Did you sleep at all?' he asked.

'Bits.' Stella looked over her shoulder towards the dark window. 'Still chucking it down.'

'It stopped a couple of times,' he said, nodding slowly. 'I thought you'd gone off and left me.'

'Where is there to go?'

All around them people were waking up. Airport chimes and announcements had begun. A child was crying nearby. As discreetly as she could Stella checked beneath her arms.

'And what about selling the flat?' said Gerry.

There was a long pause.

'You get me at a bad time, Gerry.'

'Sorry.'

'There would have to be compromises.'

'Like what?'

'The compromises a deluded alcoholic has to make.'

'I'm not a deluded alcoholic.'

'In saying that, you prove you're both. Deluded *and* alcoholic.'

'Nonsense.'

'Gerry, you can be such a pest. You think I don't know how much you drink? If I mention it, I become a nag. Do you not think I have a nose? Or a pair of eyes? You could go on doing it behind-backs until you've no liver left. And it's not just the drinking – it's all the deception that goes with it. There's nobody can fix this but yourself.'

'If you're serious, then so am I.'

'How many times have I heard this?'

'Once or twice.' He shrugged. 'So after last night I quit.'

'You're making a vow?'

'Yes.'

'A sacred vow?'

'I don't believe in such things. It's my vow. It's what I say I will do.'

'And if you fail?'

'I'll get help. Make it again.'

'You are the only one who can make the changes.'

'I gave up smoking – the hardest thing I ever did. Lying in the hearth puffing cheroots up the chimney when you'd gone to bed.'

'And you think I didn't notice? In the mornings when I went in to pull the curtains. When you did it eventually I was proud of you.'

He took her hand in his, stroked the back of it. The skin shone in the oblique light. He blinked a little then looked at her.

'I'm sorry,' he said.

'For what?'

'Everything.' He continued to stare at her. 'When I look at you I see all the ways you were.' There was a long silence between them. 'And are. You could have married anybody and made it work.'

'Except *you*, obviously.'

'Admiration is part of it too . . .'

'Of what?'

'Love.' He looked around to see if anyone could hear him. 'I love you,' he whispered. 'As well as admire you.' There was another silence between them. Stella withdrew her hand from his and raised her shoulders in a gesture.

'You would behave differently if you did. You used to be such a caring individual. Your drinking ruins everything – it leaves the other person lonely.'

'You planned this whole trip.'

'It was a notion I had,' Stella said quietly. 'I had to look into it.'

'I'm sorry about last night's performance . . .'

'I've heard all this before.'

'Last night was the end of my allocation.'

'Glad to hear it.' She folded her arms. Then turned to look straight at him. 'And what about the mockery?'

'I've never mocked you, Stella.'

'What about my faith?'

'That's a debate. We're talking about debating the greatest deception of our lives.'

'If that's not mockery then I don't know what is. People are looking for meaning and purpose.'

'But if the meaning and purpose they find is false,' said Gerry. 'What then?'

'Look again. Look harder. Look better, as Mister Beckett might say.'

'But if there's nothing there?'

'My religion is the *practice* of my religion. Mass is the most precious thing in my life. It's the storyboard of how to get through. It's what I am and you must respect me for it, not mock me.'

'But you must allow me *my* truth,' said Gerry. '*The* truth.'

237

'You're doing it again. Dismissing me,' she said. Stella stared at him. She lifted her washbag. 'Excuse me,' she said and got unsteadily to her feet. He looked up at her.

'I need to know.'

'It's okay, I'll be back.'

Overnight the level of detritus had everywhere crept up. The waste bins, which Gerry couldn't find the night before, were spilling onto the floor. Cardboard coffee cups with plastic lids, newspapers, pyramid sandwich wrappings, tissues, orange peelings and some things which looked suspiciously like tightly bound used nappies. But what could people do? They were trapped. Something glinted in the midst of the mess but it was only mica in the floor material. Like stardust. It flickered like frost as she moved along. Her hips were painful from whatever way she'd been sitting and her innards felt tight. They still seemed to be fibrillating from her flashback. And there was a great feeling of coldness as if she had swallowed too much ice. The female toilets were queued right out into the corridor so she continued past them. There was not a seat to be had anywhere nearby. She saw a gap – a space empty of people – by a wall. She set down her washbag and carefully lowered herself onto the floor, reversing herself in so's her back was supported. She was down but would she ever be able to get up again? Without a helping hand? From here she could keep an eye on the queue. Space to think. Sitting on the ground like a teenager with her knees pulled up in front of her. What was she to do? This arrangement she was proposing would have to be permanent. To beat a hasty retreat you first had to know where you were going. Her sanctuary had disappeared as of yesterday morning. She needed another place, another idea. And in a way she felt cheated. She had worked hard and endured much and felt that a companionable old age was something to look forward to, something owed to her. Like a pension. She deserved someone whose arm she could rely upon. What was love but a lifetime of conversations. And silences. Knowing *when* to be silent. Above all, knowing when to laugh. She closed her eyes and said a short prayer that she would make the right decision.

If Gerry stopped drinking then all things were possible. He was basically a kind and talented man who had a problem. She wondered if compromises could be made. Better for him to be in her life than not. If he was sober. If she was part of his life, the likelihood of him being sober would be greater. Although she was reluctant to become a scold. The change would come if she made him truly believe they were going to separate. In Glasgow one of the charity shops she went into had the slogan painted on the window, 'No one should have no one.' Was he wounded as well by what had happened to her in Belfast? She had healed but maybe he had not. Was his drinking *her* fault? Should she give him another chance because she was in the habit of giving him chances? The queue for the bathroom was beginning to shorten.

On the way back she felt much better. Her insides had calmed considerably. She stood on the travelator and enjoyed the pleasure of being borne along. Movement without effort, her hand resting but steadying her on the black handrail. Peppermint in the mouth, a fresh-washed glow to her skin. The queue for the toilet was nothing new. And the same again for a washbasin. All the paper hand towels had gone and most of them seemed underfoot, absorbing God knows what kind of wet from the floor – she'd dried her face against her sleeve.

Gerry was still sitting in the same seat. He looked stunned. She tried to tidy around him as best she could. Imposing her sense of order, making an encampment for them both, folding newspaper pages, pushing Gerry's bag further beneath the seat with her toe where it would not trip. She picked up and crushed a cardboard coffee cup but could find nowhere to dump it. So she just set it down where she'd found it. She shrugged and turned to Gerry, who was now on his hunkers vaguely trying to help.

'This is impossible,' she said. She sat down and indicated the empty seat beside her. Gerry half crawled, half sat into the chair. 'Now that an all-female religious collective is no longer an option . . .' She took in a long breath and exhaled an equally long sigh. 'If you are as good as your word – on giving up the drinking – the place may *not* have to be sold.' Gerry nodded his head and put his hand on her arm. There was silence between them for a while.

'All shall be well,' said Gerry.

'And again.'

'And all shall be well.' Stella made a pedalling gesture with both hands, as if there was more.

'And all manner of thing shall be well,' said Gerry. He paused. 'I hate myself when I'm drinking.'

'But sure you drink all the time.'

'So I hate myself all the time.'

'I'll help you fall in love with yourself again,' she said. His hand covered her hand which was holding on to the armrest. 'We haven't all that long so we should cherish each other.'

'Meaning?'

'A bunch of flowers would be nice now and again.'

He bent over and pulled his shoulder bag from beneath his seat. He unzipped it.

'For the gardener,' he said, pulling out the red onion bag.

'What are they?'

'Bulbs.'

'I'm not that stupid. I mean what kind of bulbs?'

'Mixed bulbs. That's what the guy said.' He handed them to her. She smiled and peered into the bag through the netting. 'You can plant them out front. Although we've missed the boat for this year.'

'Are they tulips?'

'I hope not. I'd never be able to live it down. *Tulips from Amsterdam.*'

'Thanks for . . . whatever they are.'

'There may well be some tulips among them. I've no idea what colour. Narcissi too. God knows what else. I thought for a minute they were going to confiscate them in security.'

'I'll plant them in the autumn,' she said. 'Next year we'll see.'

He produced the Werther's from his pocket and offered them to her.

'Bought in Glasgow.'

Stella thanked him, opened them and put one in her mouth.

'I think you should have one too.'

The snow was heaped mattress-thick on everything. Other places it had drifted even deeper. White undulations. Gentle slopes.

They sat together looking out, the dawn light steadily growing, beginning to appear as a pale bevel at the horizon. Nothing was said for a while. The air around them was filled with the smell of butterscotch. The airport was gradually becoming visible, taking on edges, outlining itself in the light of the fallen snow.

'Better or worse?'

'Much worse,' said Stella. 'What do you mean?'

241

'It's what the optician always says.'

'What?'

'Better or worse? When she's fitting you for lenses.'

'Better – now that I know the question. But worse last night.'

'Do you think we'll get away today?' said Gerry.

'We can only hope.' Stella put in her eye drops and blinked away the excess, then wiped her cheeks with a tissue. She smiled. 'Do not ignore the donkey braying from afar.'

Gerry nodded and said, 'And they returned under different skies than witnessed their commencement.'

They both looked out into the darkness. There was a bright light over the buildings at the end of the dock. It looked like a plane making an approach, coming in to land. Things must be beginning to move again. He nudged Stella with his elbow and nodded in the direction of the incoming plane. But the more they watched the less it looked like it was moving. It had a greenish tinge to it. After a while they agreed that it was not a plane but the morning star. Ablaze like a spotlight. Venus. Stella said that the Romans worshipped Venus as the goddess of love. Gerry claimed that he had read somewhere that sometimes it could be bright enough to cast shadows. If that was true surely the shadows would be there now on the unbroken snow. But no matter how they looked they could see no trace.

He tried to build a picture of this landscape before the snow. And when he succeeded in doing so, he subtracted the buildings. Dismantled them and imagined how it would have looked centuries ago, long before flight had been thought of, when transport would have been a family in a flat-bottomed boat or a hollowed tree fleeing danger, beating against the current. Thousands of years before

242

that – marshlands with sedge blowing and water reflecting the brightening sky. The sound of birds. Curlews flying from horizon to horizon in great circles. Flocks of waders rising simultaneously and explosively to meet the day. In such places people had been sacrificed, strangled, thrown into the fen and forgotten. Survivors' funerals. There they lay, victims of a religion without a name, until in our own time someone unearthed and drained them and marvelled at their preservation, their very stubble. Nothing, except their remains, would register their lives. Sitting beside Stella in this grey light seemed to Gerry such a privilege, such a wonderful thing to be doing, despite the nightmare of their surroundings. He believed that everything and everybody in the world was worthy of notice but this person beside him was something beyond that. To him her presence was as important as the world. And the stars around it. If she was an instance of the goodness in this world then passing through by her side was miracle enough.